UNDENIABLY THEIRS

UNDENIABLE SERIES BOOK THREE

RAMONA GRAY

EK PUBLISHING INC.

Edited by
L. Nunn Editing

Cover Art by
The Final Wrap

UNDENIABLY THEIRS

UNDENIABLE SERIES BOOK THREE

Two is always better than one...

Chloe Matthew's fresh start recipe:

Step one: new job at Dawson Clothing—check

Step two: stop worrying about sister—easier said than done.

Step three: find nice safe guy and fall in love—too bad Chloe can't one-click buy that.

Except tossing a complete stranger into the mix, banging him like a screen door, and having the best sex of her life could make her life's recipe fall flat. And that whole sneaking out before the hot stranger wakes up? Not her finest moment.

But new co-worker, Jackson Black, is just what she's looking for. Handsome. Reliable. Wicked sense of humour. Sleeping with a co-worker has never been so tempting.

Only, Jackson is more than a splash of vanilla. He shares everything with his best friend, Ian—including women.

Will Jackson's desires tear apart Chloe's vision of the perfect life? Or can they make something even better since

the sexy-as-sin, Ian Aldrin, is the stranger she spent one deliciously dirty night with?

CHAPTER 1

Chloe stared at the amber liquid. She normally avoided liquor of any kind, afraid she had the mutated gene or weakness or whatever the hell it was that ran in their family. Becoming like Lori or her mother was a low-grade fear in the pit of her stomach that never really went away.

But tonight?

Fuck tonight.

Tonight, she deserved a goddamn drink. One drink didn't make her a damn drunk. She had stopped at the first bar she came across. That this bar was attached to a hotel made no difference to her.

Her grandmother didn't live right in the Badlands. But she was close enough to its outskirts that a place like this, only ten minutes from her grandma's home, was on the seedier side. No doubt her sister frequented this place on a regular basis.

It was confirmed when a man slid onto the stool next to her and placed his hand on her leg. "Hey, Lori, you looking to make some extra cash tonight? I can get us a room upstairs and -"

She pushed his hand off her leg as he squinted at her. "Sorry, you ain't who I thought you was."

He hopped off the stool and nearly fell on his ass before catching himself on the edge of the bar. Straightening his ratty coat around him, he gave her an oddly dignified bow before staggering away.

She returned to her drink. Lifted the cheap glass. Studied the cheap bourbon in the dim light.

Drank.

It burned her throat and made her eyes water. She coughed, wiped her mouth and coughed again before setting the glass down.

There was movement to her right. The bartender – an overweight blonde with mileage on her face and a smoker's cough – appeared almost immediately. She purposely didn't look, purposely ignored the little shiver that went down her back at the surprisingly deep, surprisingly sober sounding voice of the man who sat beside her.

"I'll take a whiskey and another of whatever my friend is having."

"No." Chloe lifted her head and stared at the bartender. "I don't want another drink. You have me mistaken for someone else. I'm not Lori, and I'm not gonna blow you for a goddamn drink."

There was silence beside her. The bartender's overgrown eyebrows were raised in astonishment. She gave Chloe a girl-you-are-a-fucking-idiot look before smiling at the man.

"One whiskey, coming right up, sweetheart. I'll get you the good stuff."

"Thank you."

Another little shiver. God, his voice was insanely deep. She decided it wouldn't hurt to take one quick glance at the man who was probably one of many men in this bar who had fucked Lori for a handful of drinks and a carton of cigarettes.

She turned her head, peeked, and froze.

Holy shit. He was beautiful.

Adonis beautiful.

Dark hair, dark eyes, sexy stubble, beautiful.

She looked him up and down without a speck of shame. When one stumbled upon a god in broad daylight – well, dim bar light – one did not just simply look away. He was dressed in a leather jacket and jeans with dark boots. The jacket stretched across his broad shoulders and the jeans hugged his thick thighs. Her core tightened at the sizeable bulge at his crotch.

His clothing was too expensive for a place like this. He looked out of place. A glitch in the regularly scheduled programming. A pearl in a sea of pebbles.

His smile revealed perfect white teeth. "Hello, not Lori. My name is -"

"I'm not interested in your name."

"Fair enough," he said. "Is there anything about me you are interested in?"

She paused. "No."

His grin really should come attached with a warning sign of impending danger. "Did you... hesitate?"

"No."

"Huh. I could have sworn there was hesitation." His dark eyes studied her, made her feel like a bug trapped under glass.

She fidgeted on the bar stool, smoothed down her red hair, and told herself to just stand up and leave already.

"So, tell me, Red. What's a girl like you doing in a place like this?"

"Seriously? That's the pick-up line you're going to use?" She said.

"Not a pick-up line. I'm genuinely curious what a girl like you is doing in this bar. You don't exactly fit in with the rest of the clientele."

"Neither do you."

"True."

"Besides, you know nothing about me," she said. "Maybe I'm a drunk. Maybe I go to whatever bar I find."

"Maybe. But drunks don't normally turn down free drinks. Nor do they wear seven hundred dollar Dawson suits."

"Into fashion, are we?" She studied his hands. One rested on the bar and the other was curled around his drink. They were big hands. Rough hands. Hands that were meant for –

Tangling in your hair? Undressing you? Making you come?

Her traitorous skin flamed bright red.

She raised her gaze to his face. The look on it suggested that maybe he knew why she was blushing.

"I'm not particularly into fashion," he said, "but I have recently become more knowledgeable about that particular brand."

"Why?"

"Well, I -"

"Lori? Bitch, where you been?" A heavy hand fell on her shoulder and she cringed. "You wanna give me a handie in the bathroom? I'll buy you a fuckin' drink if you – ow! Jesus, fuck!"

The weight of his hand disappeared. The man sitting beside her was now standing. The man who had touched her was on his knees on the dirty floor. Her new friend was bending his thumb at an almost impossible angle.

"The lady isn't Lori," he said. "Apologize, please."

"Let me the fuck go, you fucking – OW! Motherfucker!"

4

Oh God. Chloe stared at the drunk's thumb as the man bent it back even further. The drunk was starting to cry, snot bubbling out of one nostril, as her new friend made a polite smile.

"Apologize to the lady."

"I'm sorry," the drunk moaned. "I'm sorry, lady. I thought you was someone else."

"That's fine," Chloe said.

He released the drunk immediately and the man climbed to his feet and staggered away. The bartender approached and leaned her sizeable rack against the bar. She'd unbuttoned three of the buttons, and Chloe stared at the spray-tanned flesh bulging out from the top of her bra.

"You need another drink, sweetheart?"

"No, thank you," the man said.

"My name is Gina. You need anything, you just holler. Okay?" She traced one pink-painted talon down his forearm. "Anything."

"Thank you, Gina."

He waited until she left before turning to Chloe. "You okay?"

"Yes, thank you. That was um, very nice and also terrifying to watch."

"I didn't mean to frighten you."

"No, I didn't mean that you – I should go."

He rested his hand on her forearm. "Stay and tell me why you're here."

She couldn't tell this complete stranger her sob story. The smart thing to do was to leave. Instead of leaving, she said, "Lori is my sister. She's a drunk. I was visiting her tonight and it didn't go well. I stopped in at a bar because – honestly, I don't really know why, I hate drinking. But here I am, at the first bar I found. Apparently, she spends a lot of time here trading sexual favours for alcohol. The worst part is – I'm not even surprised by that. She's ruining my life. I don't know how to stop allowing her to take all the good things from me. I'm not strong enough to kick her out of my life."

She glanced at him, saw pity in his eyes, and slid off the barstool. She rarely spoke about her sister outside of Al-Anon meetings. She didn't want anyone's pity, let alone this sexy stranger's.

"Wait," he said.

"I have to go." She hurried across the bar and pushed open the door to the hotel lobby. The lobby was empty and the clerk standing behind the desk didn't look up from his cell phone. There was a narrow hallway to her right. She walked a few steps into it and leaned against the wall. Her heart pounding and sick to her stomach, she fought back the hot tears. What was wrong with her? Why did she -

"Red?"

Her eyes flew open and she stared at the stranger from the bar. He stood in front of her and she had to crane her neck to look at him. He was well over six feet and – holy god – how was it possible he looked even better in the fluorescent light of the hallway?

"Are you okay?" He asked.

"I don't want your pity," she said. "I don't – that isn't what I want."

"What do you want?" His big hand smoothed a strand of hair away from her cheek.

"I want to forget about her for one night," she whispered. "I want to do something to get her out of my goddamn head for just one night. Can you help me with that?"

"Yes." He stepped closer and slipped his arm around her waist. His hand cupped her hip and he bent until his mouth was hovering over hers.

She waited.

He didn't move, and she realized that she needed to make the first step. He was willing to help her forget, but not until she showed him that it was what she really wanted. They stood in the hallway, his warm breath washing over her mouth.

Chloe, a night of sex with a stranger isn't going to help you forget.

It might.

It won't. Don't be an idiot, Chloe. You know nothing about this guy. He could be a serial killer for all you know.

She pressed her mouth against his. He immediately took control of the kiss, teasing her lips apart with small licks and nips. He sucked on her bottom lip and then ran the tip of his tongue across her upper one. She moaned into his mouth and he deepened the kiss, sliding his tongue into her mouth to taste and tease.

When he released her, the voice in her head was quiet. She bit her bottom lip. "I want to have sex with you."

"I want to have sex with you too," he said. "I don't live around here. Do you?"

"No. I'll get us a room here."

He frowned. "I'll get the room."

She pulled back and ran a hand over her swollen mouth. It was suddenly important that she pay for the room. She supposed it made her feel less like a whore. "I pay for the room or this doesn't happen."

He studied her and then nodded. "All right."

She took his hand and he followed her out of the narrow hallway and toward the front desk.

THE ROOM WAS NOTHING SPECIAL, JUST A DOUBLE BED, AN ancient-looking television on top of a dresser, a closet, and a door leading to the bathroom. Chloe hung the 'do not disturb' sign on the door and closed it tight before locking it.

The room had cost her eighty-nine dollars. She'd paid for it with the emergency cash she kept in her wallet and made sure to keep her back toward the stranger when she gave the clerk her driver's license. Not that it mattered, her soon-to-be one-night stand had stood a respectful distance from the front desk while she was getting the room. Surprisingly, she hadn't even felt like a whore as she booked a room for the sole purpose of fucking a stranger.

She walked across the room and turned on the lamp next to the bed before drawing the curtains over the dirty and chipped window.

"My name is -"

"No." She hugged her torso and stared at the emerald coloured drapes. "No names. No, this is what I do for a living, this is my favourite food, this is my damn life story. Agreed?"

"Sure."

She took a deep breath and turned around. He was standing in front of the door, his big body blocking her only exit, and his face hidden in shadows. Unease trickled down her spine. Was she really going to do this?

Well, you kind of have to now, don't you? You asked him for this. You invited him up to the room and if you think he's going to let you leave without giving him sex, you're a naïve idiot.

Her mouth was bone dry and there suddenly didn't seem to be enough air. Her heartbeat tripled, her ears began to ring, and she was more than certain she was about to faint.

"Are you all right?" He was standing in front of her now. Jesus, he was quick. Quick and eerily quiet.

"I…fine, I…" her voice was wheezing out of her like she was an eighty-year-old smoker with emphysema.

She clutched at his forearm. She shouldn't be touching him, shouldn't be showing him how weak she was, but she had no choice. She was about to crumple in a heap.

One thick arm slipped around her waist. "Don't faint on me, Red."

He helped her to the bed and made her sit down before pushing her upper body down until her head was between her knees. "Take slow, deep breaths."

She concentrated on her breathing, ignoring how his warm hand felt kind of nice rubbing her lower back, until the lightheaded feeling was gone. She sat up and turned her head back and forth experimentally.

"Better?"

"Yes. Sorry."

"It's fine."

There was an awkward silence. He had stopped rubbing her back and was sitting next to her with his hands clasped loosely in his lap.

She twitched a little when he said, "If you've changed your mind, tell me. I'll walk out of this room right now, no hard feelings. You don't have to be afraid to tell me you don't want this anymore."

She stared up at him, one hand smoothing the skirt of her suit compulsively. "How-how did you know I was thinking of changing my mind?"

He shrugged and gave her a slow smile that obliterated the unease. "Let's just say that it comes in handy in my job to be good at reading body language."

"Oh." She chewed on her bottom lip and stared at his hands again. "I'm sorry."

"Don't be sorry. If you've changed your mind, I'll leave. If you change your mind after we start, tell me and I'll stop immediately and leave. You have my word."

She didn't know him from a hole in the ground, so why did she believe him? She searched his face, her gaze landing on those chocolate-coloured eyes. God, he had long lashes. Had she ever met a man with such long lashes?

Chloe, focus!

She took another deep breath. She believed him. Right or wrong, she believed him. If she wanted to stop, he'd stop. Simple.

"Okay, thanks."

"Should I go?"

She shook her head. "No."

He didn't ask her if she was sure, and she was grateful for it. She might say 'no' if he did, and she wasn't entirely certain that was what she wanted. What she wanted was for him to kiss her again, to make her forget that her life was a mess and she was about to fuck a stranger.

"I've never done this before, have you?" She asked.

"I've gone home with a woman the same night I've met her," he said. "It's not normally this quick, but -"

"I'm not a whore," she said.

"I know. What I meant is that I usually have to work hard to charm them first, especially if I'm alone." He gave her an easy grin that sent tingles of awareness up and down her spine.

"I doubt that."

"It's true," he said.

"You have the face and body of a god, and you're trying

to tell me you have to charm your way into a lady's pants? I call bullshit."

He laughed. "You're great for my ego, but you should know that you don't need to charm your way into *my* pants."

A thought struck her. "What do you mean, if you're alone?"

He hesitated briefly. "I meant, if I don't have a wingman with me."

He gave her a wink and crinkled his nose at her in a way that shouldn't have been cute but was. "I don't normally hit on woman when I don't have a wingman waiting to tell you how great I am, but I wanted you from the moment I saw you."

She blushed, and another slow smile crossed his face. "Do you have any idea how gorgeous you are, Red?"

"I – I'm pretty, not gorgeous."

He touched a strand of her hair, rubbing it between his fingers as he studied her face. "Gorgeous. Beautiful green eyes, pale skin and sweet freckles." His gaze lowered to her mouth. "Perfect, pink mouth."

He lowered his head toward hers. She parted her lips in anticipation, before her eyes widened. "Oh, shit."

He stopped immediately. "What's wrong?"

"I don't have a condom. Do you?"

He reached into his back pocket and pulled out his wallet. She looked away when he flipped it open. She didn't want to see his driver's license, didn't want to know his name. This was about a release and nothing more.

Besides, the god sitting next to her might be acting like she was his equal, but they both knew it wasn't true. Women like her didn't date men like him. He was way out of her league. He'd chosen her because it was a dive bar, and she was the only woman in the place with all of her teeth. He'd never date her, even if she gave him the chance.

Only you would be sitting next to a total stranger you're about to have a one-night stand with and be thinking about dating him.

Her face flushed at the derision in her inner voice. Yeah, only her.

He held up the condom as he stuffed his wallet back into his pocket. She stared at the package before raising her eyebrows at him. "Magnum sized?"

His grin widened when her gaze dropped to his crotch. She cleared her throat. "Just wishful thinking on your part or…"

"Not wishful thinking, Red."

Well, shit. Now she definitely needed to see it. Her ex-fiancé, John, was a good size, at least she thought he was. The only other dicks she'd seen were from the porn videos John asked her to watch with him and comparing his dick to porn star dick seemed unfair.

The stranger's big hand rested on her leg and she stared up at him. He gave her another grin. "Does it make you more inclined to stop or start?"

"Start. Definitely start."

"Good." His other hand cupped her face and he kissed her. Like before, he took control of the kiss. She returned his kiss, leaning forward and touching his chest tentatively. One big hand was still rubbing her thigh and she traced her fingers across his broad chest. He shrugged out of his jacket and she ran her hands over the wide span of his shoulders.

Still kissing her, he slid his arm around her waist and lifted her into his lap. She squeaked in surprise and he said, "Okay?"

"Yeah, good." Her voice was husky and low with need.

His size, his brute strength and the ease with which he could move her around, was an unexpected turn-on. She supposed it should have made her nervous, but the sudden wetness in her damn panties made it more than obvious that it wasn't nerves she was feeling in her belly.

His hand gripped her hip and he kissed her again. Slow, deep kisses that left her feeling drugged with pleasure. She explored his mouth, he tasted like the whiskey he'd been drinking, and he made a low groan when she nipped at his bottom lip.

He shifted her on his lap and, just like that, she could feel him.

Feel it.

The magnum-sized dick.

She pressed her ass against the hardness and was rewarded with another low groan. He cupped the back of her neck and lifted his head when she kissed the rough stubble on his throat. His other hand slipped under her skirt and rubbed her nylon-clad thigh as she nipped at his throat before licking and kissing her way to his ear. She kissed below his earlobe and this time he moaned, an honest-to-god moan that made her suit feel too tight and her skin too hot.

She moved restlessly on his lap and his hand tightened on her thigh before he reached for the buttons on her suit jacket. He unbuttoned them and pushed her jacket off her body. She smiled a little when he caught it before it could fall to the ground.

He draped it across the end of the bed before turning back to her. "Still good?"

She nodded, and when he didn't unbutton her shirt, she did it for him. She took it off and he placed it with her jacket. She sat on his lap, telling herself to just take her bra off for

13

fuck's sake, her hands clenching and unclenching in nervous fists.

He stared at her tits – god, why did they have to be so small – before leaning forward and pressing a kiss against her collarbone. She shivered all over and arched her back a little. He didn't take the hint and, instead of cupping her breast, he kissed his way up to her ear. He sucked on her earlobe before breathing, "You're so damn sexy, Red."

"Thank you," she whispered. She tugged on his shirt. He leaned away and stripped it off, dropping it carelessly on the floor.

"Holy moly," she said.

He laughed, and she flushed a little. "I mean, you look like you know your way around the gym."

He laughed again, and she muttered a curse. "Oh my God, I am so bad at this."

"You're not," he said.

She licked her lips and studied his chest. His upper chest was covered in a light layer of dark hair that narrowed down into a line below his belly button. After years of being with John who was blond and waxed his chest bare, the sight of the stranger's dark chest hair was unexpected. She touched the coarse hair, traced her fingers across it and realized that she liked it. Liked it a lot, actually.

She ran the ball of her thumb over one flat nipple. He groaned, and his pelvis jerked beneath her. She smiled at him before leaning down and sucking on his flat nipple.

"Christ." His hand tangled in her hair, tangled and held fast before he pulled her head back. She stared up at him and when he tugged on her hair again and made her straighten, she was surprised at the wave of lust that rolled over her.

"Take off your bra, Red."

With his hand still in her hair, she reached behind her and

unfastened her bra. She slipped it down her arms and dropped it on the bed. His gaze immediately dropped to her tits. She raised her arms to cover her chest, stopping when he shook his head.

Feeling weird and self-conscious, she said, "They're small."

"They're perfect." He cupped her breast in his hand and tugged her head back until she was staring at the ceiling. His hand was warm and rough, and when his thumb rubbed over her nipple, it hardened immediately.

He made a low sound of approval before kissing and licking her neck. She arched her back when he squeezed her breast gently before plucking at her nipple. His warm wet mouth kissed down her chest and he pressed a kiss between her breasts before he licked around her nipple.

She cried out, her hands clutching at his head. She tried to guide his mouth to her sensitive tip, groaning in frustration when he ignored her and kissed the soft fullness of her breast. He pinched her nipple and she gasped from the sharp bite of pain, but he immediately sucked it into his mouth. His tongue licked away the sting, and when he sucked hard, it sent pleasure straight to her throbbing core.

"Please," she whispered.

"Stand up, Red."

He slid her off his lap, steadying her on her feet before he stood up. She reached out and palmed the bulge in his jeans. He hissed out a breath and quickly unzipped her skirt and pulled it down her legs. She stepped out of it and he laid it on the bed with her suit jacket and blouse as she peeled off her nylons and left them on the floor.

He pulled her against him, his hands cupping her ass and kneading her flesh through her panties. She pressed a kiss against his sternum and unbuckled his belt.

He caught her hand before she could unbutton his jeans. He brought her hand to his mouth and kissed the knuckles. "You still sure about this?"

"Hell, yes," she said. "Let me see this monster dick of yours."

He burst into laughter, and she grinned at him and unbuttoned his jeans. He took a step back and unzipped before motioning to her panties. "Lose those."

Feeling a little nervous again, she skimmed her panties down her legs as he dropped his jeans and briefs. He stepped out of them as she stepped out of her panties, very thankful she'd kept up her damn grooming routine even after John dumped her.

She kicked her panties to the side and, trying not to look too eager, finally looked at the stranger's crotch. Her mouth dropped open and she couldn't even hide her gasp of surprise. Holy crap, he had a porn star dick.

Double crap.

She took a step back as she raised her gaze to his. He had a smug little grin on his face as he said, "Let me guess...holy moly."

"Nope, that deserves a holy fucking hell," she said.

He laughed and she took another step back. "Hey, keep your giant dick under control. It almost slapped me in the face when you laughed."

"It's not that big," he said with another laugh.

"Oh yeah? How big is it?"

"I don't know, I've never measured," he said.

"Like hell you haven't." She stared down at her crotch. "I'm not sure you'll...fit."

"I will."

"You might not. I've only slept with one guy before you and he didn't have a porn dick."

"I promise you that I'll fit, Red."

"How do you know?" She finally looked up and made a startled sound when she saw how close he was standing to her. "Jesus, you're so damn quiet."

He cupped her face and rubbed his thumb over her bottom lip. "It'll fit, Red. I won't hurt you."

"Right," she said. "But I'm on top."

"Whatever you want."

She licked her lips and it was his turn to make a startled noise when she wrapped her hand around his hard length. She stroked him tentatively and he closed his eyes and groaned, pumping his hips back and forth as she rubbed harder. She ran her thumb over the wide head, staring at the smear of moisture across her thumb.

His hips slowed to a stop, and he studied her before cupping her hip. "Okay?"

"Yes." She picked up the condom from the bed and handed it to him. "Here, put this on and lie on your back."

He took it from her but didn't move.

"What's wrong? Oh God, have you changed your mind?" She asked uncertainly.

"No, but you're first."

She gave him a bewildered look. "Me first, what?"

"You're coming first before we have sex."

Her face turned bright red. "Uh, I can, um, climax from sex, so..."

He grinned at her. "I guess that means you're coming twice tonight."

He lifted her and dropped her on her back onto the bed before lying on his side next to her. He cupped one breast, toying with her nipple as she gave him an uncertain look. "You don't have to make me come before sex. I don't need to have an orgasm first."

17

He nuzzled her neck before kissing the tip of her right nipple. His hand wandered over her ribs and down to her navel. He circled it with his finger as he stared at her. "No one *needs* to have two orgasms, Red, but I'm guessing your pussy will be the tightest little pussy I've ever had the pleasure of fucking." His finger dipped lower and traced the patch of red curls at the top of her sex. "Which means I want you nice and wet when you take my cock. I promised I wouldn't hurt you. and if I'm going to keep that promise, you need to let me make you come all over my fingers before you come all over my cock. Are you good with that?"

The tip of his finger slid over her wet pussy lips and she moaned and parted her legs. "Yeah, I'm good with that."

He kissed her until she was breathless, until she was clinging to him and kissing him back with a sort of recklessness she hadn't even believed existed in her. His finger was still tracing her pussy lips and she moaned into his mouth. Her clit was throbbing and if he didn't touch her, she'd lose her damn mind.

As if he'd read her mind, his finger brushed across her swollen clit. She squealed into his mouth, her short nails digging into his biceps. He nipped her bottom lip. "Spread your legs wider, Red."

She did as he asked. and he rubbed her clit with short firm strokes that sent her careening out of control to the very edge of her climax. He stopped just before she could find that bliss, and she smacked him on the back in frustration.

"No, don't stop!"

"Shh," he said. "I want to find out how tight you are."

"I want to come," she said.

"No, not yet."

She reached between her legs. If he wasn't going to make her come, she'd damn well take care of it herself.

She gasped when his hard hand wrapped around both of her wrists and he pulled her arms above her head. He held them down firmly and pushed one heavy thigh between hers. She tried to pull free and his grip tightened. She squirmed helplessly in his grip as he stared down at her with a look of amusement. When she finally gave up and glared at him, he smiled.

"I said no, Red."

Her belly tightened with pleasure and liquid gushed from her pussy. Holy shit, she was not getting turned on by this. She couldn't be. Being told what to do, being held down in bed, was *not* her thing.

"This isn't my thing," she told him. "I don't like being told what to do."

"No?" He reached down with his free hand and swiped his fingers across her pussy before showing them to her. "This would suggest otherwise."

She groaned in embarrassment. Liquid was dripping down his fingers, a shameful amount of liquid, actually.

"I – that was from before."

He grinned. "I don't think so."

"I don't like being held down, I don't like being told…oh my God."

His finger had pushed into her and her hips suddenly developed a mind of their own and bucked upward. She took him deep, and he made a low noise of satisfaction before adding a second finger. She widened her thighs, relaxing in his grip as he thrust his fingers back and forth.

"So damn tight, "he muttered.

She didn't pay any attention to him. Her hips were rolling and flexing and she was working hard toward her orgasm. His fingers were thick enough to rub against her inner walls in all the right ways and she bit down on her bottom lip as she thrust harder. God, it felt so good, felt so…

"No, goddammit!" The shout spilled from her lips when he slipped his fingers out of her pussy. "I hate you!"

He laughed and nuzzled her breast before licking her nipple. "Baby, I love your hot little temper."

She glared at him before trying to kick him with her foot. "I don't have a temper."

"No?" His fingers traced her inner thigh as she struggled against his strong grip.

"You'd be pissed too if you kept getting your orgasm denied," she snapped.

"It's called edging, baby."

"I don't care what it's called, make me come right now or I'll…"

"You'll what?" His lazy, sardonic grin both infuriated her and made her hot as fucking fire.

"Please?" She decided switching her approach was needed. She made her voice low and conciliatory before giving him a pleading look. "Please make me come. I need it."

The grin never left his face. "Let's see, anger, fake sweetness… what's next, Red?"

"My foot in your butt!" She threatened.

He laughed so hard, the bed shook. "I'm not into ass play, but I appreciate your willingness to go there."

"I swear to God, if you don't make me come right now, I'll… oh, oh, ohhhh…"

His fingers were back on her clit, rubbing in firm circles. She closed her eyes, her hips rising and falling, feeling nothing but the sensation of his hand around her wrists, his thigh heavy against hers and his fingers…his delightfully rough, warm fingers… touching her with exactly the right strokes she needed.

"Please don't stop, please don't stop," she begged repeatedly.

"Shh, baby, I won't. Not this time." He tugged on her clit and then rubbed it again when she squealed with pleasure. "Come all over my fingers. Let me see how pretty you are when you're coming."

She gasped in air, her pelvis pressing upward against him. He rubbed harder and that was all it took. Her body stiffened and she bit her bottom lip as her orgasm washed over her. It was the strongest, hardest climax of her life, and she moaned and shivered and rocked against his hard body as he sucked on her nipple.

She collapsed against the bed and he licked her nipple before raising his head. His hand was still on her pussy, and he rubbed gently but avoided her sensitive clit. She panted and stared at the ceiling as he sat up. He ripped open the package and slid the condom down over his dick before lying next to her in the middle of the bed. He stroked his own dick a bit lazily as she tried to catch her breath.

"Holy shit," she finally whispered. "That was, I mean… there might be something to this edging thing."

He laughed. "Baby, that was barely edging."

She sat up and he shifted over so she could straddle his hips. "It was really good, thank you."

"You're welcome. Ready for your second one?"

She didn't reply. She could have an orgasm from sex, but she wouldn't come again. Not after an intense climax like that one. Besides, she'd never been a multiple orgasm type of girl. One and done seemed to be her body's motto, and she had accepted that a long time ago.

She was trying to figure out how to sexily crouch over him, when his big hands cupped her hips. "Ready?"

She nodded, bracing one hand on his chest and holding the base of his dick with the other when he lifted her. Christ, he was strong. She pressed the head of his dick against her opening and gave him an anxious look. "Slow, okay?"

"Yes."

She was more nervous than she needed to be. Despite his size, her wetness made it easy for her to take him. She slid him into her slowly, surprising herself when she took all of him without any pain. She stared at where their bodies were connected. She had never felt completely and utterly filled before, and she could feel her inner walls stretching around his thick shaft.

"Good?" His voice was only a little strained sounding.

"Yeah, really good." She rested her other hand on his chest as well and made a few experimental thrusts. Her eyes widened as pleasure speared through her. "Holy God."

"What?"

"I – that feels – I think I'm going to come again."

"That's the idea, Red."

"No, I don't normally – I mean, I'm not a come-more-than-once kind of girl."

He arched one thick eyebrow at her. "Maybe you are and just didn't know it."

"I, yeah, maybe." She didn't want to talk anymore. She wanted to ride that lovely, incredibly thick cock that was giving her more pleasure than she could imagine.

She moved up and down, her head falling back and her eyes closing as she took what she wanted from him. His hands rested on her hips, but other than occasionally giving her a little extra lift when she rose up, he didn't move at all.

"You okay?" She moaned.

"I'm good, baby."

"Don't come, okay?" She moved a little harder and faster. Her ex had always come quickly, a lot of times before she could get herself off, and normally she accepted it as a part of sex. But not tonight. Not when she knew what kind of orgasm she could have. If the stranger below her came before she could have that second one...

She moved even faster, gasping out, "Don't come yet. Oh God, don't, just hold on, okay? I'm almost there."

"Red." His hands gripped her hips tight, forcing her to a stop. She made a mewl of disappointment and tried not to dig her nails into his chest.

"I'll be quick, just don't come. For the love of God, don't come," she said.

He rubbed her hipbones with his thumbs. "Look at me, baby."

She opened her eyes and stared down at him. He smiled and reached up to cup her breast. "You can go quick or you can go slow, whatever feels good to you, but I won't come before you do. So, stop worrying about that."

"Do you promise?" She sounded pathetic, even to herself, but she couldn't help it.

"I promise." He teased her nipple with his thumb. "Take your time, if that's what you want."

He gave her breast a final squeeze before tucking his hands under his head and grinning at her. "Have at it, Red. It's all yours for as long as you want it."

She giggled and leaned down to give him a slow and thorough kiss. "Thank you."

He cupped her ass and squeezed it. "You're welcome. Now, let me see your sweet tits and that pretty little pussy while you ride me."

She straightened and when he raised his legs, planting his

23

feet on the bed, she rested her hands on the top of his knees. Her back arched as she rode him with long slow strokes. He could see everything, but she didn't feel a lick of self-consciousness. He found her beautiful, the look on his face as he watched her body, the rock hardness of his dick as she rode him, made her more than sure of it.

Each stroke of his thick cock felt incredible. She squeezed around him, gasping when it sent a bolt of pleasure from her pussy straight down to her thighs. She'd been moving slowly, enjoying the slow glide of his cock in and out of her, but now, she wanted more. She leaned over him again, bracing her hands on his chest and fucking him harder. He kneaded her breasts, teasing and playing with her nipples before cupping her ass. He was moving now, meeting each of her thrusts with a hard stroke of his own, but she was no longer worried that he would come before she could.

He'd promised her he wouldn't.

"Oh God," she panted. Her hair was sticking to her face and she shook it back with an impatient noise. He reached up with one hand and smoothed it back from her face, holding it in a loose ponytail at the nape of her neck as she bounced on the most amazing goddamn cock she'd ever felt in her life.

He drove in and out of her, their bodies slapping together in a rough and almost punishing rhythm. She cried out and then ground herself down on him, her inner muscles squeezing around him as she climaxed for a second time.

He groaned, his hips thrusting up and down, one big hand gripping her ass so tight, she was sure she would have bruises, the other holding the nape of her neck. He groaned again when her pussy squeezed around him with the last of her orgasm.

"Fuck, Red, you feel so good. So tight, so wet, so…"

His voice trailed off and he made two more hard pumps

before he shouted hoarsely and his body stiffened under her. He froze for a few seconds and then thrust back and forth, the cords in his neck standing out as he climaxed.

When he collapsed on the bed, she rested her head on his chest. Her heart was thudding heavily beneath her cheek and he drew lazy circles with the tips of his fingers on her upper back as he caught his breath.

"That was really good," she mumbled.

"Yeah." He yawned, and she smiled a little before slipping off of him.

He disposed of the condom and before she could ask him if they were supposed to leave now, he was crawling under the covers and holding them open for her. "Get in."

She absolutely could not go to sleep with a stranger. Nope, it was a very, very bad idea.

"Red, climb in."

She climbed in beside him, curling on her side and tucking her hand under the pillow. He spooned her and cupped her breast, kissing the back of her shoulder before yawning again. He didn't speak and she listened to his breathing slow and deepen as she stared at the wall.

She waited for the regret and the shame to fill her up and fell asleep still waiting.

CHAPTER 2

"Chloe?"

She swung around in her office chair, smiling at the head designer of Dawson Clothing. "Hi, Amy. How are you?"

"Good." Amy studied her office. "I don't think I've been to your office before."

Chloe glanced around. Her office was large, but it was a bit cramped with the two desks and a small loveseat in the far corner. Amy sat down at the empty desk and ran her fingers across the smooth top of it. "I hear your new team mate starts on Monday."

"He does."

"Cool. Did you get a chance to meet him during the interview?"

Chloe shook her head. "No, I was, uh, out sick that day."

She hadn't been sick. She'd been dealing with her sister again, but she couldn't tell Amy that. Not only had she only been at this job for a month, Amy Dawson was her professional idol. Chloe might have been hired at Dawson Clothing to help design and market a new digital storefront, but her first love was clothes design and always would be. Amy Dawson was one of the hottest clothing designers in the country right now, and Chloe still couldn't get over the idea that she not only worked for Amy's company, but that they were friends.

Friends? You've had lunch a few times and gone shopping with her once. That's hardly friends.

She ignored her inner voice. She didn't have many friends – okay, scratch that, she didn't have *any* friends, and there was no harm in pretending that Amy was her friend. As long as Chloe didn't get weird and go all *Single White Female* on her, it was fine to pretend.

"Have you met him?" She asked.

Amy shook her head. "Nah, I stay out of the business side as much as possible. I just want to design, and both Luke and Mark know that."

Her face softened when she said Mark's name and Chloe smiled a little. Mark Stanford was the CFO of Dawson Clothing, and he and Amy had recently started dating. Despite knowing Mark from the weekly Al-Anon meetings they both attended, Chloe didn't know much of the details of their relationship, but she did know that both of them had been in love with each other for years.

"Luke met with him and really liked him. Which, between you and me, means he's probably a stick in the mud," Amy said with a laugh. "I love my brother, but Luke is kind of a hardass about the business. Of course, I guess that's what makes him such an effective CEO, right?"

"Right," Chloe said. Luke was her boss and while he was blunt and to the point, she liked him as a boss. She didn't like wasting time deciphering what her superior wanted, and Luke's directness and his communication skills meshed with her working style.

28

"Anyway, how are you doing?" Amy asked

"I'm good." She was lying. She'd been dumped by her fiancé six months ago, her sister was ruining her life, and she'd fucked a complete stranger last night.

Her cheeks flushed and she resisted the urge to fan her face as Amy studied her. "You sure?"

"Yeah, I'm good," she said. "What can I help you with?"

"Jane is coming to my place tonight for dinner and I'm inviting you to join us."

"Seriously?"

Amy laughed. "Yes, seriously. Luke and Mark are doing some guys' night out thing, so I figured I'd do a girls' night. If you're available? I know it's a Friday night and short notice."

She should say no. She'd slept terribly last night, probably because she was in bed with a goddamn stranger, and she'd snuck out of the motel room as soon as the sun rose. She should go home and have a hot bath, contemplate what exactly was broken inside of her to allow her to just recklessly sleep with a man she didn't know, and then go to bed.

"Chloe? What do you say?"

"Yes," she said. "I'd love to. Should I bring anything?"

"Nope. Jane's bringing some wine and I've got the food covered. Around seven, okay? I'll email you my address."

"All right. Thanks, Amy."

"You bet. See you, Chloe." The curvy blonde left her office, the bracelets around her wrists jingling with every step.

Chloe sat back in her chair and stared blankly at her computer screen. She was having dinner at Amy Dawson's house. Holy shit.

Jackson watched his best friend grunt his way through another set of reps before he dropped the weights to the floor. He winced, even though the new hardwood they'd installed was protected by a thick layer of mats.

"Careful, Ian."

Ian grabbed a towel and wiped the sweat from his face before grabbing a set of hand weights. He lifted them rhythmically, the veins in his upper arms standing out in harsh relief.

Jackson leaned against the wall. "You ever gonna tell me what's got you so pissed?"

"I'm not pissed," Ian panted.

"Something's got you in a lather." Jackson glanced at his watch. "Are we going out tonight or not?"

"No," Ian grunted.

"Seriously? Dude, it's Friday night and for once you're not working. What happened to our plan to go out and find a lovely lady to charm into getting naked with us."

Ian set the hand weights down and wiped his face again before chucking the towel into the laundry basket. "Changed my mind."

Jackson followed him out of the spare room they'd turned into a gym and down to the kitchen. Ian guzzled a bottle of water before glaring at him. "What?"

"Don't what me. What the fuck is up your ass tonight?"

"I told you – nothing. Jesus, when are you gonna get a job and stay out of my business?"

"You know damn well I start my new job on Monday. If we're not going out, pass me a beer."

Ian grabbed two beers from the fridge and passed one to Jackson. He sat down at the island and Jackson joined him. They drank in silence for a few minutes before Jackson said, "Tell me, Ian."

"Christ, you're a pain in my ass. I can't believe I haven't just fucking shot you yet."

Jackson laughed. "At the very least, I'm surprised you haven't tased me."

"Don't give me any ideas."

"Where were you last night?"

"Now you're my dad?" Ian said.

"Christ, you're a grumpy motherfucker tonight," Jackson said.

He studied his best friend for a moment. Ian wasn't what you would call a fun-loving guy, never had been even when they were kids, and he could get in what Jackson liked to call his "moods", but this surliness and attitude was a bit excessive even for him.

Ian sighed. "Sorry."

"What's going on with you?"

Ian studied the beer bottle in front of him. "I slept with a woman without you last night."

Jackson shrugged. "So what? It's not like we're joined at the hip when it comes to fucking women. There's no rule that says we always share a woman, you know that, Ian."

"Yeah, I know. It's just been a long time since I've fucked a woman without you."

"Aww, did you miss me, big guy?"

"Shut up, dickhead."

Jackson laughed and took a swig of beer. "So, who was the woman?"

"I don't know. She wouldn't tell me her name."

"Interesting. Where did you meet her?"

"At Rusty's."

"Shit, a bar in the Badlands? One, what the hell were you even doing in the Badlands, and two – the women at the bars

31

in the Badlands aren't known for their… class. Not that I'm judging," he grinned at Ian, "you do you, buddy."

Ian rolled his eyes. "One – I was supposed to be meeting Tony for drinks and he picked the place, and two – she didn't exactly fit in with the rest of the crowd."

"No?"

"No. She was wearing a Dawson suit, one of the expensive ones."

"Do you know what I love?" Jackson gave Ian a shit-eating grin. "I love that you now know how to recognize a Dawson suit."

"Yeah, well, when every time I turn the fucking computer on, there's a picture of a Dawson suit, what do you expect?"

"Hey, I needed to do research for the best job of my life, didn't I? And it worked, I got the job. Besides, you have to admit it's better than the porn that's usually on the computer."

That got him a rare smile from Ian and he grinned at him. "So, I'll admit that I'm a little surprised you snagged a woman without me. You're not known for your pickup techniques. I usually have to do all the work."

"I can be charming when I want to be."

"Can you, though?" Jackson said.

Another rare smile from Ian before he shrugged. "Yeah, you're right. It was just a case of right time, right place."

"I doubt that," Jackson said. "I mean, yeah, I'm way more charming than you, but ladies love the mysterious, quiet type. Now, tell me about this Dawson suit wearing woman."

"Not much to tell. She was hot as hell, in the middle of a crisis, and wanted a night of meaningless sex to forget about it."

"And lucky you just happened to be there. Did Tony get pissed you dumped him for some meaningless sex?"

"He never showed." Ian picked at the label on his beer

bottle. "It was good, Jackson. Really fucking good. She was so damn responsive in bed. Her little pussy was hot as hell and tight. Fuck, was it tight. She got nervous about my size and wanted to be on top. At first, she acted like she had to hurry, kept begging me not to come and saying that she was almost done."

"Sounds like her last dude was a 'minute man'," Jackson said. "Poor girl."

"Yeah, well, truthfully her pussy was so fucking tight, it was a real goddamn chore not to come right away. Anyway, I told her she could slow down, that I wouldn't come before she did. After that, she was... the way she moved when she was riding me... fuck. The only thing that would have made it better, is if you'd been there fucking her ass while she rode me." He reached down and adjusted the crotch of his jeans. "Christ, I'm getting hard just thinking about it."

"Hell, I'm getting hard just hearing you talk about it," Jackson said. "Did you get her number?"

Ian shook his head. "No, I didn't even get her name. She wouldn't tell me, and she didn't want to know mine. When I woke up in the morning, she was gone."

"She snuck out of the room without you waking up? Christ, man, you're a cop. Aren't you supposed to be trained to be aware of your environment?"

Ian flipped him the bird before standing and staring out the window.

"So, what, you're pissed because you're never going to see her again? Just go back to the bar, she'll probably show up again at some point. Hell, I'll go with you. If she's as hot as you say she is, maybe we can convince her to have a go at both of us."

Ian shook his head. "She doesn't normally go to that bar, she told me that herself. Plus, she was...sweet, Jackson. She

33

wouldn't sleep with two men at once. Hell, I was only the second guy she's slept with."

"How do you know that?"

"She mentioned it." Ian was still staring out the window and Jackson stood and joined him.

"Shit, you were really into this woman, weren't you?"

He shrugged. "I don't know. She was different from our usual women. Maybe it was just the novelty."

"Maybe." Jackson leaned against the counter.

"It doesn't matter anyway. I'll never see her again. This is a big fucking city and, like I said, I don't even know her name."

"Sorry, man." Jackson clapped Ian on the back.

"No big deal. Listen, if you still wanna go out, we can. Give me ten minutes to shower."

Jackson studied him before shaking his head. "Nah, let's stay in tonight. We'll order a pizza and watch *Die Hard* or some shit like that. Sound good?"

"You sure?"

"Yep. I should probably take it easy this weekend anyway. I wouldn't want to start my new job in a haze because of all the boning I did over the weekend."

Ian laughed and Jackson clapped him on the back. "C'mon, you order the pizza. I'll even let you get those moth-erfucking anchovies on it."

"OKAY, BE HONEST WITH ME...CAN I PULL OFF PALE yellow?" Jane smoothed down her t-shirt.

"Nope." Amy popped another shrimp into her mouth.

"Amy!"

Chloe laughed as Amy shrugged and said, "You told me to be honest."

"I know, but still… I really like yellow."

"Your complexion doesn't like it. Chloe, have some more to eat." Amy passed her the bowl of pasta and shrimp.

"I'm good, thanks." She set the bowl on the table and took a sip of wine. Drinking two nights in a row, damn it was a record for her.

She smiled at Jane when the petite brunette sighed and grabbed her own glass of wine. Jane worked at Dawson Clothing in the finance department. She used to be Luke's personal assistant, but had switched to finance. Chloe had a feeling it was so that she and Luke could start dating.

"Your brother told me I looked pretty," Jane said to Amy.

"You're frackin' gorgeous but that doesn't mean you can wear yellow and, also, my brother doesn't make the big bucks at the company because of his fashion sense," Amy said.

Jane laughed. "Okay, fine. I won't wear yellow again."

"Burn that shirt when you get home," Amy said.

"Now you're just being mean."

"Maybe a little," Amy said with a grin. She touched the pretty purple choker necklace around her neck, her fingers toying with the heart locket that dangled from it. "Now that we've discussed your inability to wear yellow, let's team up and figure out what's wrong with Chloe tonight."

Chloe gave her a startled look. "There's nothing wrong with me."

"Do you believe her, Jane?" Amy asked.

"Nope," Jane said.

"I get that we don't know you that well, but you're being pretty quiet tonight, even for you, and you seem sad. Tell us what's wrong. We're excellent problem solvers," Amy said.

"You're also kind of my boss, and," Chloe glanced at Jane, "you're dating my actual boss."

Amy made a zipping motion across her lips. "Hey, what you tell us during girls' night stays between us, and when we're working, we magically forget all the personal shit about each other."

Chloe shook her head. "You wouldn't be able to forget this."

"Oh, this is juicy," Amy leaned forward and gave her a look of glee. "Now you have to spill it, Chloe."

She fidgeted with the stem of her wine glass. She was surprised to realize she did want to tell Amy and Jane what had happened last night. Her lack of any real friends was starting to wear on her, and she realized she missed having girlfriends to confide in."

"Chloe, I'm serious." Amy's lighthearted tone had disappeared. "Obviously you don't have to tell us what's going on, but know that if you do, we won't judge or think differently of you. Don't take this the wrong way, but I get the feeling that you could use a friend or two, right now."

Chloe swallowed hard. Amy had the sensitive, intuitive artist thing down to a science and she could feel her resolve weakening. "Okay, fine. But you have to swear not to say anything to anyone at work. Especially Luke"

"We won't," Amy said. "Right, Jane?"

"Yes," Jane said. "I love Luke, but that doesn't mean I share every personal thing someone tells me with him."

"She means it," Amy said. "Hell, she didn't say a word to Luke about how I like it when Mark spanks me."

Chloe's mouth dropped open as Amy said, "Shit. I think I'm a little drunk. Goddammit, wine!" She glared at the glass in her hand. "Why would you betray me this way?"

Jane burst into laughter and Amy gave Chloe an apologetic look. "Sorry, Chloe. That was really personal information and I probably shouldn't have -"

"I slept with a stranger last night," Chloe blurted.

Amy blinked at her before holding out her fist. "Nice work."

Chloe blushed and bumped her fist. "Thanks."

"Were you safe?" Jane asked.

Amy snorted laughter and Jane shrugged. "What? I can't help it. You try working at a strip club for years, and not immediately worry about STDs."

"You worked at a strip club?" Chloe said.

"As a waitress," Jane said. "Part time thing. I don't work there now. Anyway, this is about you. Go on."

"We were safe," Chloe said, "and normally I don't do this type of thing, like ever, but I just…"

Amy and Jane gave her encouraging looks. She took a sip of wine to buy some time. She never talked about her sister if she could help it. She supposed it was partially because of embarrassment and partially because Lori already took up so much of her time and energy, if she didn't have to think about her, she didn't.

But, if she didn't give Jane and Amy something of an explanation for why she slept with a total stranger, they'd think she was a slut and she didn't want that. She wanted their friendship, wanted it desperately, in fact. They both knew her sister had trouble with alcohol. She would give them the basics, she didn't need to go into detail about how Lori had ruined both their lives.

"So, you guys remember that I have a sister who is an alcoholic?"

Jane and Amy both nodded.

Chloe sighed. "She's…difficult to deal with. She's been on a real bender since she left rehab, and last night my grandmother called me to come talk to her. Lori is living with her again and my grandma, she, she does this weird thing where she enables her, but she also freaks out when Lori gets too drunk. Then she calls me to come over and calm her down. I went over after work and it didn't go well. Lori was so drunk, and she said horrible things to me and our grandma. It's not the first time she's done that, but it was…"

Amy reached out and squeezed her hand. "I'm so sorry."

"Yeah. Anyway, Lori passed out after a few hours of screaming at us, and then I left. I rarely drink, but I went to a hotel near my grandmother's house. I needed something to do. I couldn't stand the thought of going back to my apartment and sitting alone. I knew the hotel would have a bar, so I stopped and ordered a drink."

She laughed bitterly. "Lori goes there often, apparently. Trades sexual favours for drinks."

"Oh God," Jane said.

"Yeah. Lori and I look alike. She's older than me, but only by eighteen months. The alcohol has done some damage to her skin, but we have the same colour of hair, and our body shapes are similar. A few guys mistook me for her and they-they were asking me for handjobs and blowjobs …"

"Oh gross," Amy said. "That's really awful. I'm sorry, Chloe."

"Thanks. Anyway, this guy sat down next to me and I figured he was another drunk who had mistaken me for Lori. But he wasn't. He didn't know who Lori was and he was hitting on me because…well, I don't know why."

"Uh, because you're frackin' gorgeous?" Amy added more wine to her glass and Jane's before looking at Chloe. She shook her head and Amy set the bottle back on the table.

"*He* was gorgeous," Chloe said. "Way out of my league, you know? He was tall with dark hair and looked like some kind of Greek god. I wasn't planning on sleeping with him. In fact, I left the bar, but then he...and I... I got us a room at a hotel and we had sex."

She fell silent and Amy said, "Uh, I'm gonna need more information on the sex part."

Jane poked her, and Amy grinned. "Oh please, you were thinking the same thing, Jane. Spill it, Chloe. Give us all the juicy details."

Chloe turned bright red and Jane said, "You don't have to tell us anything."

"Says you," Amy replied. "I, for one, would like to know if this tall handsome stranger was amazing or a dud in the sack."

"Amazing," Chloe said. "Definitely amazing."

She took another sip of wine. She didn't want to admit it, but she was actually dying to tell someone about last night. Apparently when a person had the best sex of their life, they wanted to share the happiness.

"On a scale of one to ten?" Amy said.

"Twelve."

"Damn. Nice work."

"I don't have a lot of experience," Chloe said. "I've only slept with my ex-fiancé before last night, but I'm pretty certain this guy has skills. I had multiple orgasms. I've never done that before. He made me come before we had sex, and he lasted long enough that I could come again during sex. How crazy is that?"

Jane and Amy glanced at each other and Chloe frowned. "What? That's crazy, right? My ex never lasted very long once we were having sex. He said it was normal, said that no guy lasted more than a few minutes."

"Girl, that ain't normal," Amy said solemnly.

"Oh." Chloe sat back in her chair. "Maybe he doesn't

have skills then. Maybe he's typical and I only thought he was incredible because apparently my ex sucks in bed."

"Maybe," Jane said. "I mean, I don't have that much experience either, but I think if you found it amazing, then that's all that matters. Right?"

"Yep," Amy said.

They were silent for a few minutes before Amy said, "So, are you going to see him again?"

"No. I woke up before he did and I kind of, maybe, snuck out of there," Chloe said. "I was feeling weird and self-conscious, and... I don't normally do stuff like this. Only, I'm regretting it now. Isn't that stupid? I wanted a one-night stand to help me forget about my messed-up life, I got what I wanted, and now I'm wishing I could have another night with him."

"Not that surprising," Jane said. "If all you've ever known is bad sex and suddenly you find out how awesome it can be, it's addicting. Your sexual experience and mine are pretty similar, and trust me, trying to resist Luke after finding out how good he was in bed, was impossible."

"Gross and also, good for you, honey," Amy said.

Jane laughed and clinked her wine glass against Amy's. "Maybe you could look him up. He's gotta have a Facebook account at least, everyone does."

"I don't even know his name," Chloe said.

"Not even a first name?" Amy asked.

Chloe flushed. "No. I told him I didn't want to exchange names or any personal details, and he agreed."

"Well, that might make it more difficult," Amy said. "Any distinguishing marks or scars that could help identify?"

Jane laughed again. "How is that going to help her find him, Ames?"

"I don't know, I'm throwing out ideas here. When my

friend wants to find the mystery man who gave her the best sex of her life, I'm here to help."

Chloe felt a surge of warmth. God, it was stupid to be so happy that Amy called her a friend, but she couldn't help it. The woman she had admired for years, thought they were friends.

"I appreciate that," she said to Amy, "but I don't think there's any way that I can find him again."

"You could go back to the bar."

Chloe shook her head. "My grandmother lives on the outskirts of the Badlands and that hotel/bar probably isn't all that safe. Besides, he didn't look like the kind of guy who goes to a bar like that on a regular basis."

"Was he, like, a business guy or more of a blue-collar type of guy?" Jane asked.

"He wasn't dressed in a suit, just jeans and a t-shirt, but his leather jacket looked expensive. Oh, and," Chloe paused, "he knew that I was wearing a Dawson suit. Even knew it was one of the ones from our more expensive line."

"Seriously?" Amy said.

"Yes."

"He must be in the fashion business then," Jane said. "The average guy wouldn't recognize a Dawson suit."

"Oh my God." Amy leaned forward, her eyes wide and her cheeks a little flushed from the wine. "Do you think...no, it can't be."

"Do I think what?"

"Maybe he's your new co-worker."

"What?" Chloe said.

"Maybe the guy is your new co-worker, what's his name...oh shit, Jane, what's his name again?"

"Jackson something," Jane said.

"Right! Jackson Black." Amy gave Chloe an excited look.

"Oh my God, maybe you banged your new co-worker!"

"I didn't," Chloe said.

"You don't know that," Amy said.

"The odds of her unknowingly banging the guy she's going to be working with are astronomically low," Jane said.

"It happens all the time in romance books," Amy replied.

"This is real life, not a romance book," Chloe said. "It wasn't him."

"Could have been." Amy refused to give up. "He knew what a Dawson suit was. What guy knows that unless he works for Dawson Clothing?"

"No, he – I mean, you're a popular designer. He could have dated someone who only wore Dawson suits," Chloe said. "There are a ton of reasons for why he knew what brand my suit was, and none of them involve him being my new co-worker."

Amy shrugged and sipped her wine. "I guess you'll find out on Monday."

Chloe stared at Jane. "It wasn't him. Tell me it wasn't him."

"It probably wasn't him," Jane said.

"Probably?"

Amy laughed. "Oh God, if it was, you two are totally gonna start banging in your office. Am I right, Jane?"

"We won't be banging in the office!" Chloe said. "I don't date co-workers."

"There's no office rule against it." Amy snickered and nudged Jane. "Obviously."

"Yeah, well I am not getting fired because of my libido. Anyway, it doesn't matter. The guy I slept with isn't this Jackson Black. Stuff like that doesn't happen in real life."

"Like I said," Amy gave her another grin, "I guess we'll find out on Monday."

CHAPTER 3

C hloe smiled at the blonde woman sitting outside of Luke's office. "Hi, Mary. How are you?"

"Good, thank you. How are you?"

"I'm good. Enjoying the new job?"

Mary nodded before picking up her phone. "I am. It's only been a couple of weeks, but I think I'm getting a handle on the day-to-day stuff."

"Glad to hear it. Mr. Dawson emailed me to come to his office."

Mary punched in the four-digit number to Luke's office. "Mr. Dawson? Ms. Matthews is here."

She hung up the phone. "Go right in, Chloe."

"Thank you." She knocked briefly on the doors to Luke's office before opening one and stepping inside.

He was sitting at his desk. A large, dark-haired man was sitting in the leather chair across from Luke's desk and he didn't turn around when Chloe shut the door. She stared at the back of his head, her heart beginning to pound. Oh shit. He was the right size, the right broadness across his shoulders, and his hair was same dark shade of brown.

Oh shit. Oh shit. Oh fucking shit.

Amy was right. She had fucked her new co-worker. She was living in a goddamn romance novel.

"Chloe, thanks for stopping by," Luke said. "I wanted to personally introduce you to Jackson."

She walked forward on feet that felt like wooden blocks as both Luke and Jackson stood. Her stomach was in knots, sweat was sliding down her back and she knew her skin was currently the same colour as her hair. She thought she might pass out as Jackson turned to face her with his hand held out.

So sure was her certainty that Jackson was the stranger from Thursday night that, for a moment, she actually did see his face. As his big hand surrounded hers, she swallowed compulsively.

"Chloe, are you all right?"

She swung her gaze to Luke. He was hurrying forward. "Are you going to faint?"

The hand holding hers tightened and a deep voice said, "Maybe she should sit down."

Her breath rushed out of her and she stared mutely at Jackson. It wasn't him. It wasn't the stranger. Her mind had been playing tricks on her, that's all. Cursing herself in her head, she said, "I – no, I'm all right."

"Sit down, Chloe," Luke said.

Jackson was still holding her hand and she had no choice but to follow him when he tugged her toward the empty chair next to his. She sat down, smoothing her skirt and trying to smile normally at him.

"Are you feeling all right?" Luke sat on the edge of his desk next to her chair.

"Yes, I'm perfectly fine. Sorry." Chloe brushed her hair back from her face and tried to sit straighter. "I, uh, I skipped breakfast this morning and was a little lightheaded for a second."

"I can get Mary to grab you something from the café downstairs." Luke reached for his phone and Chloe shook her head.

"No, no, I'm fine. I have an apple at my desk. I'll eat as soon as I'm back in my office. Sorry, really." She gave Jackson an apologetic smile.

"It's fine. It's nice to meet you." He smiled at her and her damn pussy actually fluttered.

Stop it! She snapped inwardly to her crotch. *Are you kidding me right now? What is wrong with you?*

She supposed there was nothing wrong with her. Now that she'd gotten over her mini heart-attack, she could focus a little better on Jackson, and holy hell, he was delicious. She had no idea why she'd seen him as her mystery man for even a second. Sure, they had the same big build and dark hair, but the similarities ended there. Instead of chocolate coloured eyes, Jackson's eyes were a brilliant blue, and he projected an easy-going and relaxed nature that her mystery man definitely didn't have.

Her sexy stranger had been sweet and he'd been kind to her, but she couldn't fool herself into believing there wasn't a hardness inside of him. Not after what she witnessed him do to the drunk in the bar who had touched her.

Jackson though, he practically radiated goodness and light. She had to stop herself from giggling inappropriately. What was wrong with her? Guys didn't just radiate goodness.

"Chloe?" Luke's voice startled her a little. "Do you need a glass of water?"

She was still staring intently at Jackson's face and she blushed again and tore her gaze away. God, this was embarrassing. But what were the odds that she would meet not just one, but two Greek gods in her lifetime?

She forced herself not to look at Jackson again, not to study those high cheekbones and the smooth jaw that she suddenly wanted to lick. She studied his hands instead. They were big hands, big and weirdly rough and callused looking for a guy who worked with computers.

What did he do that made them so rough? How would that roughness feel against her skin? Would it feel as good as her mystery man's hands had? Would they do just as well at touching her, making her come? Would he hold her down while he rubbed her clit and -

Chloe! Stop it! Have you gone insane?

She clenched her hands into fists. Her pussy was throbbing and her nipples were hard against her bra. She thanked God she was wearing a suit jacket as she shifted in her chair. No, not insane. Just suddenly and incredibly sexually frustrated. One night of mind-blowing sex with a stranger and she was suddenly a nympho. At least, that's what she told herself over the weekend as she'd repeatedly masturbated to the memory of the stranger's low voice, his hard body and his incredible dick. Of course, tonight she might substitute Jackson for the stranger and –

Chloe! For fuck's sake! Get it together!

Luke had moved to his credenza and when he returned with a glass of water, she took it with a nod of thanks. She sipped at it and it eased the dryness in her throat as Luke returned to his chair and sat down.

She could feel both Jackson and Luke staring at her and she cleared her throat. "Sorry again. Jackson, it's nice to meet you."

"You as well, Chloe. Luke's told me good things about you."

"Well, that's very kind of him." She stared straight ahead, afraid if she looked at Jackson again, she might ask him something highly inappropriate… like whether he could give a woman multiple orgasms.

A spat of nervous giggles erupted from her chest. She turned it into a coughing fit and then took another drink of water.

"So," Luke was giving her an odd look, but it was obvious he had decided it was best to just move on, "I wanted you to meet Jackson one-on-one before Maria introduces him at the staff meeting in an hour. Jackson comes highly recommended from Herrod's Clothing Downtown. He developed the software for their inventory database and was instrumental in helping turn the company around."

Chloe glanced at Jackson and he gave her another easy grin. "A slight exaggeration."

"That isn't what Ron says," Luke replied. He turned to Chloe. "Ron owns Herrod's and recommended Jackson after his contract was finished."

"So, you're only contracting with Dawson's?" Chloe asked.

"That's what I've been doing the last ten years or so," Jackson said. "I work with a company to update or create a new software program and then once the software is up and running, I train existing staff on how to use it and move on when they're proficient at it."

"But, luckily for us, Jackson decided he'd like something more permanent," Luke said. "So, he'll not only be creating the software for our new digital storefront, but he'll also be updating and improving other existing software within the company and sticking around to maintain it."

"Which means you're stuck with me," Jackson said.

His gaze dropped to her mouth for the briefest of

moments, but it was enough to make her nipples stand to attention again.

"Anyway, Jackson will be with Maria in HR for most of the morning, but you and he can meet in the afternoon and get better acquainted," Luke said.

She'd love nothing more than to get better acquainted with Jackson. In fact, her brain was coming up with all sorts of delicious ways to get to know him better, and not one of them included her or Jackson wearing clothing. Was his dick as big as her mystery man's? God, what she wouldn't do to find out.

"Chloe?"

She pulled her mind out the gutter with a hard jerk and smiled at Luke. "Yes?"

He was giving her another odd look. "I said, that's it for now. You can head back to your office."

"Right, okay. Thanks." She stood up, Jackson and Luke both stood up with her, and she discreetly wiped her sweaty palms on her suit jacket before holding out her hand to Jackson. "Good to meet you."

"You too. I'll see you this afternoon."

"Of course." She walked out of Luke's office, managing not to fall flat on her face despite the way her legs were shaking. The moment the doors were closed behind her, she leaned against them and fanned her face.

"I know how you feel. He's something else, isn't he?" Mary said from her desk.

Chloe straightened. "Uh, what do you mean?"

"Please, that Mr. Black is straight out of *GQ*. He's super hot and unbelievably charming. We chatted for a few minutes before he met with Mr. Dawson and wow... I mean, I'm a lesbian and I still wondered what he looked like naked."

Chloe gaped at her before slapping her hand over mouth

to muffle her laughter. Mary grinned at her. "Good luck working with him."

JACKSON PAUSED IN THE DOORWAY OF HIS NEW OFFICE. HE'D just finished having lunch with Luke, Mark and Amy, and he thought it went well. He'd been a little apprehensive about lunching with all three bosses at once, but they had made him feel welcome and at ease. It was obvious that Luke and Amy were close for siblings, and while neither Mark nor Amy had made any indication, he was almost certain that they were a couple. They hadn't held hands or even touched one another, but the occasional look between them, the way Mark stiffened whenever another guy even glanced at Amy – they were banging.

He grinned a little as he thought about the pretty purple necklace Amy wore around her neck. He recognized a slave collar when he saw one. He and Ian had gone to various BDSM clubs around the city over the last few years, and while he wasn't into the real kinky stuff that went on, he had seen and learned a lot.

For a while, he'd thought Ian might go full on Dom with the women they fucked – his best friend was a control freak through and through – but it eventually became obvious that it wasn't Ian's thing either.

Ian liked being the one in control during the fucking, but apparently that control didn't extend to putting collars on women or spanking them beyond the occasional butt smack here and there. And hell, who didn't occasionally love smacking a woman's smooth, firm ass when he was fucking her? The way her pussy or ass clenched around his dick at the sharp bite of pain, the way their pale skin would turn red... fuck, you didn't need to be full on kinky to enjoy that.

Speaking of pale skin turning red... he could see the back of Chloe's head as she worked at her desk. Their desks were side by side, both facing the row of windows that dominated the far wall. It was a nice office, bigger than he was used to, with a small leather loveseat pushed into one corner, and a bookshelf at the other. Truthfully, he'd been a little annoyed at the thought of having to share an office, but that was before he met Chloe.

He studied her long red hair and squeezed the doorframe when immediately an image of that red hair wrapped in his fist, flooded through him. Christ, what he wouldn't do to see her on her knees in front of him, her full lips stretched around his dick as she sucked him off.

He shook his head and tried to curtail his thoughts. It wasn't easy. He'd wanted Chloe from the moment he'd turned and saw her. Her slender body, that pale skin with the surprisingly small number of freckles for a redhead, her gorgeous green eyes and that mouth...

His cock twitched and he cursed inwardly. Shit, resisting her was going to be very difficult. He was already picturing how she would look between him and Ian, her pale body sandwiched between their tanned ones as he took her ass and Ian took her pussy.

He was starting to get a fucking hard-on and he immediately looked away from Chloe. What the hell was he doing? He had been at his new job for half-a-day and already he was trying to get himself fired. Fucking a co-worker was a bad idea.

But not against the rules.

His inner voice did have a point. He'd read through the employee handbook that Maria had emailed after he'd signed the paperwork. There'd been no mention of sexual relationships with coworkers. A bit odd for a company this size, but not his problem. In fact, it made things that much easier if he decided to go ahead and seduce Chloe.

Stop thinking with your fucking dick for once.

Hell, his inner voice was hitting all the right notes today. He did have a habit of letting his dick lead the way, although he'd never actually gotten fired over it. But if he was honest, the reason he and Ian got laid so much was because of him. Ian wasn't a monk, by any means, but it was Jackson who always suggested they go out. Jackson who normally chose the woman to seduce. Jackson who refused to let anything get serious.

Yeah, and why is that exactly? You and Ian aren't getting any fucking younger. You want kids and you know Ian does too, so why are you still acting like you're horny twenty-two-year old's who want to fuck which ever woman catches your eye?

He knew the reason, but hell if he wanted to think about it.

Of course you don't want to think about it. Settling down, finding a woman to marry and have babies with, means never getting to fuck a woman with Ian again. That terrifies you, doesn't it? For whatever goddamn reason, you can't even get it up with a woman anymore if Ian isn't there. As soon as Ian decides he's done with this little tag-teaming effort you've been doing for the last five years, you'll never fuck a woman again. You know it, and that scares the hell out of you. So, you keep pushing him not to get into a relationship, and what kind of fucking best friend does that? Huh?

"Jackson?"

Her soft voice made him jerk. What the hell was he doing? Was now really the time to start wondering what the fuck was wrong with him? To wonder what kind of mental instability he had that made it impossible for him to sleep with a woman unless she was being fucked by his best friend at the same time? No, it goddamn wasn't.

"Are you all right?" Chloe had stood up from her desk and moved closer to him. Unlike their initial meeting in the office, she was poised and confident sounding. She had a soft look of worry on her face, and he made himself smile at her.

"I'm good. Sorry, didn't mean to be standing in the office like a creeper. I was just, uh, thinking."

Christ, now he sounded like a moron.

"Oh, that's okay." She gave him another hesitant smile – shit, she had a beautiful smile – and returned to her desk. "How was lunch?"

"Good. I met Amy Dawson, she seemed...cool."

Cool? She seemed cool?

He wanted to smack himself in the head. Normally, he was excellent at flirting, at disarming women with nothing more than a smile and his words, but he couldn't seem to get it together with Chloe. Not that it mattered, he absolutely could not and would not flirt with his damn co-worker.

Just before lunch, he had grabbed his box of stuff from his car and dropped it in the office. Chloe hadn't been in their office and he'd been weirdly disappointed. Now, he crossed the room and sat down in the chair at his desk. He took the picture frame out of the top and set it on his desk. Chloe was staring at her laptop, but she gave the picture a quick look.

"That's a nice picture."

"Thanks. It's me and my mom at the Grand Canyon. She's always wanted to go there so I took her last year."

"How nice."

"Yeah." He cleared his throat. "She raised me on her own and we're pretty close. I mean, I'm not like a mama's boy or anything like that, but she's pretty great, and I spend a lot of time with her. She's really…uh, great."

Fucking hell, he sounded like a complete dork.

"Are you close to your parents?" He could feel sweat dripping down his back.

"No," she said. "They moved to Iowa when I was nine-teen. We don't talk much."

She turned back to her computer and while his ability to charm women might have taken an abrupt nose dive, his ability to sense when he was being told to mind his own busi-ness hadn't. He silently emptied out the rest of the box, setting some of the items on the desk and putting others in the drawers. He opened his laptop and logged in with the user-name and password Maria had given him, before changing the password and setting up his email.

He had a few emails, most of them company-wide announcements, and he read through them before opening up Dawson Clothing's website and studying it. He'd already looked at it a few times, but the thick silence coming from Chloe's side of the room was making him tense. He didn't think she hated him or anything, but it was obvious that he'd said something to upset her.

He was about to apologize when she said, "I'm sorry. I – I'm being rude and that's not like me. I've had a strange day and…well, I shouldn't be taking it out on you."

He gave her an easy smile. "That's fine."

"It isn't," she said. "There's a Starbucks down the street. I was going to grab a coffee. Can I buy you one to say sorry?"

"Sure. But only if you let me go with you. We can talk about your thoughts on how the current digital storefront looks and what you have in mind for marketing strategy."

"All right," she said. "Let me grab my coat and we'll leave."

Ian read the text from Jackson. He'd left the office twenty minutes ago and was almost home. He turned the broiler on. The steaks were prepped and ready to go. He'd start them in about five minutes and then make the salad when Jackson got home.

He sat down at the table and took a swallow of beer, staring out the window at the falling snow. Work was uneventful today. A few traffic stops, a domestic, and a couple of stupid kids making a drug deal right on the street corner in broad daylight. After the hellish week he'd had last week, he should have been happy. Except, it had given him way too much time to sit in his damn car and think about the hot-as-fire redhead who'd given him the best ride of his life.

He muttered a curse and propped his feet up on the chair beside him. Why the fuck didn't he wake up when she left? He was a light sleeper, always had been, but he hadn't heard a damn thing. Sure, it was an insane week at work and he'd hadn't gotten much sleep before that night, but still…

He took another drink of beer. He'd fully planned on convincing the woman to give him her name and her number. One night with her wasn't enough. He'd known it the minute she slid her tight little pussy down over his cock. The way she moved, the way she looked and sounded when she was coming. He wanted more. He needed more.

Only he'd fucked up and now he'd never see her again.

He stood and put the steaks in the oven before setting the timer. Maybe it was for the best. It was ridiculous, considering he didn't even know her name, but he could see himself wanting more with her. Wanting to build a life, settle down and make sweet redheaded babies with her.

He shook his head. Christ, what was wrong with him?

Imagining a life with a woman he'd had a one-night stand with was ridiculous. He was losing his mind. Besides, he might be ready to start looking for the one, but Jackson wasn't. He'd never specifically said that, but it was more than obvious. He wasn't ready for the white picket fence lifestyle and was perfectly happy to continue with things the way they were. The two of them banging women in a casual, no strings attached way.

Are you sure you're really ready to settle down? Once you start down this path, there's no going back. You won't be with Jackson and a woman together ever again. Is that what you want?

The hell of it was, he didn't know. He wanted to be married, he wanted to have kids, but he also wanted Jackson there with him. But it's not like they would find a woman who would want the both of them for the rest of her life. For most women, sleeping with two men at once was a chance at making a fantasy come true, nothing more.

Being fucked by two men was great. But actually living with two men for the rest of her life? Finding a woman who wanted that would be close to impossible. Even if they did – what would they tell their friends and family? They already thought it strange that he and Jackson lived together. Hell, most of them believed they were secretly gay.

A smile crept across his face. If only they knew the real truth. He wasn't sexually attracted to Jackson nor was Jackson attracted to him, but they both got off on watching each other fuck a woman or fucking a woman together. Hell, even with his mystery woman, there'd been more than once as he was fucking her, that he'd wished Jackson was there with them.

He drank half of his beer in three big swallows. He really needed to stop thinking about her. He'd never see her again and he needed to accept it. The idea of going back to the bar had crossed his mind more than once over the weekend, but he was one hundred percent certain she wouldn't be there. She'd only been there because it was the closest place to her mother's – he stopped and thought for a minute – no, grandmother's place. She'd said grandmother. He had a good memory for details, it was partly what made him good at his job, but the redhead had him so mixed up, he didn't know if he was coming or going. She'd been at the bar because it was close to her grandmother's house and she'd had a fight with her alcoholic sister.

He sighed. The woman was hot and gorgeous but a little broken, and he'd be fooling himself if he didn't admit that was partially his attraction to her. He liked helping people, liked finding a solution to the problem, and liked protecting those who couldn't protect themselves. It was his driving force for becoming a cop.

The front door opened, bringing a draft of cold air into the kitchen. He opened the fridge and pulled out the bagged salad as Jackson walked in and dropped into a chair.

"Christ, is it cold out tonight."

"Yeah. How was the first day?" He opened the bag of salad mix and poured it into a bowl.

"It was good." Jackson loosened his tie. "How was your day?"

"Slow." He opened the oven door and checked the steaks.

"Smells good," Jackson said.

"It'll be ready in about five."

"Yeah, okay. Ian, you all right, man?"

He turned to face his best friend. "Yeah, just tired. Tell me about your first day."

"Not much to tell. Meetings with HR in the morning, I also met Chloe, she's the one I'll be working closest with. I had lunch with Amy, Mark and Luke – they own the company– and in the afternoon Chloe and I went over her marketing strategy for the new digital storefront. She's got some good ideas."

Ian placed the bowl of salad on the table and grabbed plates and cutlery. "So, she's hot, huh?"

"Why do you say that?"

He grinned at Jackson. "You've got that look on your face."

"What look?"

"That look you get when you wanna fuck a woman. Fucking your co-worker is a stupid idea."

"Yeah, don't I know it. But, Jesus, Ian, she's hot. In a sweet, kind of naïve sort of way. You'd like her too."

The timer went off and Ian pulled out the steaks before setting them on the stove to rest. "If she's sweet and naïve then she's not the one for us. You know that."

Jackson shrugged. "Sometimes the sweet ones have a hidden naughty side. Besides, she's a redhead, they're always slightly naughty, right? Ian, what's wrong?"

Ian shook his head. "Nothing."

Jackson studied him for a moment before standing. "I'm gonna get changed. Be back in five."

He left the kitchen and Ian stared at the steaks. So Jackson's new co-worker had red hair, it didn't mean it was his one-night stand. Christ, the city was way too fucking big for those types of coincidences.

She was wearing a Dawson suit.

He transferred the steaks to plates and set them on the table. So fucking what. Half the women in the city wore Dawson suits. This Chloe wasn't his mystery woman.

CHAPTER 4

"Hey, Chloe? Take a look at this, would you?" Jackson pointed to his screen.

Chloe stood and walked to his desk. She rested her hand on his desk and bent a little to stare at the screen. "Hey, that looks good."

She tried to ignore the amazing scent of Jackson's aftershave. It was bad enough trying to ignore how damn hot he looked every day for the last week, the fact that he smelled delicious as well, was making it pure torture.

She'd masturbated every single night this past week, a new record for her. Sometimes it was her mystery man, sometimes it was Jackson, but regardless, both fantasies never failed to get her off. Unfortunately, her need seemed to increase rather than decrease with every orgasm she gave herself. She was at the point where she was seriously considering ordering a vibrator online. She needed something, anything, to help with the ache in her pussy that never really seemed to go away.

She drew in a shaky breath, yanking her hand back when Jackson grazed it as he reached for the mouse.

"Sorry," he said.

"That's okay." She chewed on her bottom lip and tried to focus on what Jackson was showing her. He'd been working on creating the new digital storefront all week, and he'd already created a template for how the front page would look.

"So, here right across the page, we can showcase the latest designs in a changing banner." Jackson pointed to the screen. "Customers will see immediately what's new in the Dawson Clothing world."

"I like it," she said. "What about the sales stuff?"

"That will go here, right below it and a bit to the right. So, still where the customer can see it, but the new stuff will catch their eye first."

"That's great. You're really fast at this." She smiled at him, her gaze dropping to his mouth when he returned her grin.

God, he had great lips. That lower one was really suckable, wasn't it? She wondered what he'd do if she leaned forward a little and kissed him. Would that be so bad? Coworkers kissed occasionally, right?

"Chloe." His voice was low and husky.

She moved her gaze to his, her eyes widening. Shit, was he… turned on? Did he want her like she wanted him?

"Yeah?" She whispered.

Before he could answer, there was a knock on their door. Chloe stumbled back, her cheeks flaming red, and stared guiltily at Amy standing in their doorway.

"Oh, uh, hi, Amy. Jackson and I were …" Shit, what were they doing?

"Going over a prototype of the front page of the online store," Jackson said smoothly. "How are you, Ms. Dawson?"

"I told you to call me Amy." Amy smiled at him. "How's your first week?"

"Going well."

"Good."

Amy turned to Chloe and Chloe tried to look innocent. "What can I help you with?"

"Can I see your sketches, please?"

She gave Jackson a quick glance. "My sketches?"

Amy nodded and glanced at her watch. "I know you have them with you. Do you mind if I look at them again?"

"How do you know I have them with me?" Chloe said.

Amy laughed. "If you're anything like me, you always have sketches with you."

She stared expectantly at Chloe who shrugged and reached under her desk. She brought out the oversized leather bag she used as a purse and grabbed her sketch book out of it. Amy was standing beside her desk now and she took the book and set it on the desk before flipping through it. Chloe watched each of her drawings flip by, that weird excitement and nervousness crowding into her belly that always appeared when she showed someone her work.

She knew she wasn't a great designer, but she loved doing it and to have Amy Dawson looking at her work... shit, it felt good.

"This is new from the last time I looked at your work, right?" Amy pointed to a sketch of a pair of capri pants and a crop top.

"Yes."

Amy had been gracious enough to look at Chloe's work about a week or two after she'd started at the company. She'd even been kind and said nice things. Chloe suspected she wasn't being exactly truthful, but it had still given her a high that had lasted for more than two days.

"These are really good." Jackson had rolled his chair over and was staring at the designs as Amy flipped through them.

Chloe ignored her urge to slam the sketchbook shut and stuff it back into her bag. Somehow, Jackson looking at her designs was more nerve wracking than Amy looking at them.

"Oh, um, thank you."

"I know I'm not an expert or anything, but these look great to me," Jackson said. "I didn't know you were a designer as well, Chloe."

"Oh, well technically I'm not. I do it for fun. It's more of a hobby," she said.

"You seem pretty damn good for it to be just a hobby," Jackson said.

"She is." Amy's voice was distracted. She flipped back through the sketchbook again. "Where is that...ah, here it is."

Chloe peered at her sketchbook. Amy had stopped at a sketch of a summer dress. It was a knee-length, sleeveless, A-line with a beaded lace bodice. It was one of Chloe's personal favourites.

Amy tapped the dress with the tip of one blue-painted nail. "I want this."

"I'm sorry?"

"I want this dress for my new casual line."

Chloe stared up at her in stunned silence. She had to have heard Amy wrong. "You want...this dress for your...casual line?"

Amy nodded. "Yes, and maybe," she flipped back to the capri pants and crop top, "these too."

"You're joking, right?" Chloe said.

"No." Amy stepped back and smiled at her. "Now, most of my designers work directly for Dawson Clothing, but since you're already an employee, I think we should set you up as subcontractor with the company for your design work. Keep it separate, if you're all right with that?"

"If I'm all right with that..."

"Yes." Amy laughed before squeezing her arm. "Take a deep breath, Chloe."

She took a deep breath and released it. "You seriously want that design."

"I seriously do. I'll have a contract drawn up and you can take a look at it. If it works for you, we'll go from there. Sound good?"

"Uh, it sounds really good."

"Excellent. I'll have the contract for you to look at by Monday afternoon. Have a good weekend."

"Th-thanks, Amy. You too."

Amy left and Chloe, her heart skipping in weird erratic beats like a stone skipping across the surface of water, stood and paced back and forth in the office. She was a designer. She was officially a designer.

"Chloe? You okay?"

Jackson had stood up and she stopped in front of him. "I-I'm a designer. Amy Dawson wants one of my designs for her new casual line."

"I heard." Jackson gave her a small grin. "Congratulations."

"I'm a designer!" Joy flooded through her and without thinking, she flung her arms around Jackson and hugged him. He returned her hug, his big hands warm on her lower back.

She grinned up at him. "This is the best day of my life."

"Well, I'm glad I could be here for it." His gaze dropped to her mouth again. "We should celebrate."

She realized she was still pressed up against him. She took a step back, breaking his hold around her, and crossed her arms over her torso. "What do you mean?"

"Let me take you for dinner to celebrate," he said. "Unless, you want to celebrate with your boyfriend?"

"I don't – I don't have a boyfriend."

"Then let me take you to dinner," he said.

She chewed on her bottom lip. "Um, I'm not trying to be rude, but dating a co-worker isn't, I mean, I don't think…"

"It's not a date," Jackson said so quickly that she immediately felt stupid. "It's just two co-workers celebrating a success. We can invite some of your other friends if you want?"

"I don't have -"

Shit, she almost told him she didn't have any friends. She might be a loser, but she didn't need the tall, impossibly gorgeous man standing in front of her to know that.

"You don't have what?"

"Nothing. I…"

She should say no. She should say no and go home and have a hot bath and… sit alone with absolutely no one to share her exciting news with. Some of the joy leaked out and she blinked rapidly to stop the hot tears that were threatening. Her parents didn't even know she designed clothes and her grandmother…well, she could call her, and her grandmother would be genuinely happy for her. For about five minutes. Then the call would become about Lori, it always did.

"Hey, you okay?"

She stared up at Jackson. She'd only known him for a few days, but already concern was etched across his face for her. It sent a tingle of warmth through her.

God, girl, you really are pathetically lonely, aren't you?

"Yeah, I'm okay. I would love to have a celebration dinner with you."

"Great!" Jackson's face broke out in a delighted smile. "I know the perfect place."

"To Chloe," Jackson held up his glass and Chloe followed suit, "for achieving her dreams."

They clinked glasses and drank before Chloe smiled at him. "Well, I'm not sure if I've achieved them yet, but it's a start, right?"

"It is. Have you always wanted to be a designer?"

"Yeah, pretty much. I was designing clothes for my Barbie dolls when I was a kid."

"That's cute." Jackson smiled at her as the server approached.

"Ready to order?" The server was young and perky and not shy about giving Jackson an appreciative once-over.

"Ready, Chloe?" Jackson asked.

She nodded and they ordered their meals. Chloe bit back her smile and a weird tingle of jealousy when the server lingered for a bit, smiling at Jackson and making meaningless small talk. When she finally left, Jackson said, "So, why did you go into marketing instead of design?"

"Honestly? Because I couldn't get into design school. I was rejected from every school I applied for." She took a sip of her drink. "I needed a career, so I went to business school instead and sort of fell into the marketing thing."

"Do you like it?"

She thought for a moment. "I don't dislike it, and I'm good at it. But it's not my passion, you know?"

"I get it."

"What about you? Do you do what you love?"

He laughed. "Well, when I was a kid, I wanted to be a professional skateboarder and also be a Hollywood stuntman with my best friend, so, no, I guess I'm not."

"A career in computers is probably about as far from skateboarder/stuntman as you can get."

"True," he said, "but I do like my work and I get a great deal of satisfaction from helping clients achieve their goals."

"What about your best friend? Did he become a stunt-man?" Chloe asked with a small smile.

"Nope, Ian's a cop."

"Are you still best friends?"

"We are. We live together actually."

"Oh. So, uh, your girlfriend doesn't mind that you have a roommate?"

He grinned at her. "No girlfriend."

"Right." She could feel herself blushing and took a quick sip of her wine.

Smooth, Chloe. Real smooth.

She glanced around the restaurant. "So, how are you liking the new job so far?"

"I'm really enjoying it," Jackson said. "I know I have a tendency to talk to myself, I hope it's not too distracting for you."

"It isn't," she said. He did talk to himself a bit, but after working in cubicles for most of her career, she was a pro at blocking out any noise. His tendency to shed his suit jacket halfway through the day so she could see the way his shirt stretched across those broad shoulders, and the way his ass looked in a pair of dress pants…now those were much harder to ignore.

More heat rose to her face. "So, uh, have you always lived here?"

He nodded. "Yes. My mom moved here shortly before I was born. She's a doctor, and she works at Mercy Hospital on the west side. My mom and Ian's mom are best friends. Ian and I basically grew up together."

"It's nice that you're still best friends," she said. "Sometimes friends drift apart as they get older or, you know, life happens, and people get busy…"

It was Kandace she was thinking of. They'd been best friends from elementary school all the way through college and into their first jobs. She'd been there for Chloe through thick and thin, until Lori had ruined their friendship in one single night.

Her stomach clenched, and her appetite dropped away. Lori had taken away or ruined every good thing in her life, yet she still came running whenever Lori or her grandmother called. Lori's demons weren't hers, but she couldn't stop the guilt, couldn't stop from trying to fix her sister's life.

"Chloe?"

She shook her head to clear the bad memories. She wouldn't think about Lori tonight. Tonight, she would celebrate the fact that Amy Dawson wanted her designs, and enjoy dinner with a very sexy man who she wanted to do very bad things with. The fact that she absolutely could not do those very bad things with him was worth remembering, but a little fantasy didn't hurt.

"Sorry. You were talking about your best friend?"

"He's a good guy. He'll probably drop by the office at some point and you'll get to meet him. Anyway, this night is about you and your new career as a designer."

The server returned with their food and Chloe put her napkin in her lap as Jackson did the same. The server left, and Chloe ate a forkful of pasta. "I don't know if it's a new career, but it sure feels good. This is delicious, by the way."

"I'm glad you like it. Do you want more wine?" Jackson had ordered a bottle and she put her hand over the top of her glass.

"No thanks. I don't – I'm not much of a drinker."

"All right." He poured himself half a glass before taking a bite of food. "So, what do you like to do for fun?"

"Oh, um, I don't know. I like to design, obviously. I'm a big fan of the food network."

Jackson laughed. "Oh man, you really do need to meet Ian. He does all of the cooking and I swear to God, the food network plays 24/7 at our house."

"I'm not great at cooking, but I like to watch the food shows and pretend," Chloe said with a grin.

"Nothing wrong with that. You said your parents lived in Iowa, right? Do you have any other family here in the city?"

She fidgeted with her fork. "Uh, my grandmother and older sister live here."

"Are you close with them?"

"Yes." She decided he didn't need to know that she didn't want to be close to them.

"That's nice. I'm an only child and I always wanted a sibling. Ian is like a brother to me but it's not the same, you know?"

"Siblings aren't always what they're cracked up to be."

Shit, even she could hear the bitterness in her voice.

She gave Jackson an awkward smile as he studied her thoughtfully. "No, I suppose not."

Anxious to steer the conversation away from her family, she said, "So, does anyone ever call you Jack?"

He burst out laughing. "Only Ian when he's trying to bust my balls or get under my mother's skin. She loathes it when someone calls me Jack. So, it makes perfect sense that she called me Jackson, right?"

She laughed. "Perfect sense. What do you like to do for fun?"

"I'm pretty low key. I like to work out, go to movies, and I'm in a chess club."

"You're in a chess club?"

"Yep. Why are you so surprised?"

"I'm not," she said. "But you don't look like the chess playing type. I mean, I can tell you work out, but…" Her gaze drifted over his upper body.

She blushed when Jackson leaned forward and gave her a flirty grin. "I need to keep my body in shape for the…"

He paused, and her heartbeat thundered in her ears. He was going to say sex, he was going to say for the sex he had, and lord have mercy, she was down with that. In fact, suddenly the idea of banging her co-worker didn't seem all that crazy. She could be discreet, she could keep it under wraps that she was riding Jackson like a crazy cowgirl. As long as they didn't bang at the office, no one would –

"Basketball league."

"I'm sorry?" She gave Jackson a bewildered look.

"I have to keep my body in shape for the basketball league I belong to."

"Oh right, of course."

He gave her another flirty grin. "What did you think I was going to say, Chloe?"

"Uh…" Dammit, why did she have to blush so much? "I figured you to be more of a football guy, not basketball."

"Is that right?" Was it her imagination or did Jackson keep stealing little glances at her breasts?

"Yes. So, um, tell me more about this chess club."

He leaned back, the flirty smile faded to his usual light-hearted one, and while her body was immediately disap-pointed, she knew it was for the best. She couldn't sleep with Jackson. He was her damn co-worker.

"I know you're mocking me," he said, "but since I love chess and will use any excuse to talk about it, I don't care.

69

Hell, by the end of it, you'll be so impressed by my love of chess, that you'll probably want to join the club too."

She laughed and ate another forkful of pasta. "Dazzle me with your chess talk. I'm ready."

"HEY, CHLOE?" JANE POPPED HER HEAD INTO THE OFFICE. "You got a sec?"

"I do. I was about to take a break." Chloe smiled at the petite brunette. "Is that coffee for me?"

"It sure is." Jane handed her the coffee and sank into Jackson's empty chair. "Where's your office mate?"

"Uh, I'm not sure. Meeting with Luke, maybe? Thank you so much for the coffee, Jane. You didn't have to do that."

Jane sipped at her own coffee. "I wanted to. Luke told me last night that you got a contract to do design work for the company. Congratulations."

Chloe flushed with happiness. "Thank you. Amy had the contract ready yesterday. I read through it last night and then chatted with Amy this morning before signing it. She's using one of my dress designs as well as a pair of pants and top for her new casual line, and she wants me to come up with another couple dress sketches for her to look at."

"That's exciting," Jane said.

"It is. You have no idea." Chloe could hear the giddiness in her voice, but she couldn't reign it in. She couldn't wait to get home and work on a few of the ideas already brewing in her head.

Jane smiled at her. "I'm so glad for you. Hey, did you know Amy's birthday is coming up?"

Chloe shook her head. "I didn't."

"I'm thinking of doing a surprise party for her not this weekend, but next, so keep your Saturday free, okay?"

"Sure. Do you want some help planning it?"

"Maybe. I'm going to talk to Mark about it, but I know he's pretty busy right now, so I could probably use your help."

"All right," Chloe said.

"Hello."

Chloe's stomach made a happy flutter when she heard Jackson's voice.

Stomach? Girl, it's your pussy that's fluttering and don't try to deny it. Hell, at this point, you get wet just hearing his voice.

She shoved her inner voice out of her head and smiled at Jackson as he walked into the office. Jane stood up and smoothed down her skirt before holding out her hand. "Hi there. I'm Jane, I work in finance. I don't think we've met yet."

"Jackson Black. Nice to meet you, Jane."

"You as well. Anyway, I'll let you get back to work, Chloe. I'll text you later."

"Okay."

Jackson sat down at his desk and Chloe suppressed a grin when, the moment his back was turned to her, Jane fanned her face and gave Chloe a wide-eyed look of delight.

"So hot," she mouthed before fanning herself again.

Chloe made a shooing motion with her hand and Jane grinned at her before walking out of the office.

"So, is that the woman that Luke is dating?" Jackson asked.

She gave him a look of surprise. "How did you know that?"

He grinned at her. "What can I say? I've been sitting in

the office staff room at lunch the past couple of days and the admin staff love to chat."

She rolled her eyes. "Office gossip is the worst."

"Yep," Jackson agreed. "So, is she?"

"Yeah. Jane and Luke have been dating a while. She lives with him, actually."

"So the boss dating an employee is why this office doesn't have a 'no dating the co-worker' rule?"

"I don't know, I've never asked," Chloe said. "I'm not interested in dating a co-worker so it's not important to me."

"Ouch," Jackson said with a small grin. "I'll try not to take that personally."

"You shouldn't. Besides, even if I did want to date a co-worker, I'm not sure the chess nerd is the guy for me. Rumour has it that Robert in inventory is involved in a secret underground fight club kind of deal. That's...kind of hot."

"Robert in inventory is fifty-eight and wears a fanny pack. Nice try."

"You've worked here a week. How can you possibly know Robert from inventory already?"

Jackson wiggled his eyebrows at her. "I'm incredibly charming. People love me."

She crinkled her nose at him and his grin widened. Ever since their date – *dinner, Chloe, it was dinner, not a date* – on Friday night, he'd been progressively flirtier with her. She should be telling him to stop. Instead she was encouraging it and maybe, in her own awkward way, flirting back a little.

She really needed to stop, but it was fun to flirt with him. Fun to feel like maybe she would have a chance with someone who looked like Jackson.

Why wouldn't you? You snagged one Greek god, remember? Why couldn't you snag another?

Yeah, she remembered. Even a week and a half later,

she could easily remember her mystery man. She had a feeling her brain and her pussy would never let her forget him.

Her cell phone rang and she pulled it out of the drawer of her desk, her stomach curling when she saw the number. She took a nervous glance at Jackson. He had turned away to his computer and was reading his emails.

She didn't want to answer the call. Her finger hovered over the decline button before she hit answer. If she didn't take the call, her nana would call the office and make the receptionist find Chloe.

"Hi there. What's up?"

"Chloe?" Her grandmother's voice was on the edge of tears and full of panic. "Chloe, it's your sister, she's in trouble."

Of course she was, Lori was always in trouble.

"Can I call you back later?" She asked. "I'm at work and -"

"No, it can't wait!' Her grandmother's voice rose two octaves. "She's been arrested, Chloe! She was arrested for-for prostitution yesterday."

Chloe sighed and rubbed at her temples. Her grandmother might be acting like this was a crisis, but it wasn't the first time Lori had been arrested and it wouldn't be the last. "Okay. I'll go after work and take care of it."

"After work?" Her grandmother cried. "My precious baby cannot stay in that-that cell all day, Chloe. She said she's been through the arraignment and just needs the bail money. You need to go right now."

"I can't. I have a busy day and she'll be fine where she is, until tonight," Chloe said.

"Fine? She'll be fine? Do you know the filthy type of criminals in those places?" Her grandmother's voice was full of horror. "What kind of sister are you to leave her in that awful place all day?"

"She did this to herself," Chloe's voice was sharp, and she tried to rein in her impatience. "I can't drop everything and -"

"I can't believe this. You – you're not the girl I thought you were, Chloe. It's fine though, if you don't want to help your sister, I'll go down to the station and do it myself."

"Nana, no!" Chloe stood up, only vaguely aware of Jackson turning in his chair to stare at her. "Do not go down there. Do you hear me? I will take care of it. Do not go there. Nana? Nana, are you there?"

There was nothing but silence and she stared at the screen of her phone before stuffing it into her bag. "Shit, shit, shit."

"Chloe, what's wrong?"

She stared blankly at Jackson. "Uh, it's a family thing. I have to go. I won't be long, but can you let Luke know that I'll be back in a couple of hours?"

"Sure. Is there something I can do?"

"No, but thank you." She grabbed her purse and ran out of the office.

CHAPTER 5

"Excuse me, officer? Excuse me?"

Ian turned around. An older woman, her short silver hair sticking up, and her too-thin body wrapped in a fur coat that had seen better days, was standing behind him.

"How can I help you, ma'am?"

"My granddaughter's been arrested. She didn't do anything, and they have her locked up somewhere in this building." She clutched at his arm and gave him a panicked look. "She's a good girl. She wouldn't do what they said, officer. But I still have to pay her bail."

He patted her liver-spotted hand. "You'll need to go to the front desk, ma'am. They'll direct you to holding."

"Oh, thank you, officer. My granddaughter is innocent. She's-she's not a prostitute." The old woman's mouth was trembling, and he patted her hand again before opening the door to the station.

He walked the woman to the front desk before heading to the back. Five minutes later he was at his desk, tuning out the sounds of his fellow officers and trying to get through his never-ending pile of paperwork.

"Ian? Hey, Ian?"

"Hey, Tony." He nodded to the short and stocky man leaning against his desk.

"Sorry I bailed on you the other night, my ma called and needed me to fix her washing machine again."

"A text would have been nice." He leaned back in his chair as Tony gave him a sheepish grin.

"Yeah, I know. Sorry, man. Let me make it up to you. Drinks tonight?"

He shook his head. "Not tonight."

"C'mon, let me buy you one. I've had a fuck of a day and -"

"I can't. Jackson's car is in the shop and I'm picking him up from work," Ian said.

"So, pick him up and bring him along," Tony said. "I haven't seen old Jackie boy in forever."

"Not tonight," Ian repeated.

"All right, another night then. Have a good one." He walked away. "Rick? Hey, Rick? You wanna catch a drink tonight?"

Ian tapped his pen on the stack of papers before leaning forward and staring blankly at the top page. Fuck, he needed to get his head in the goddamn game or he wouldn't finish before he had to leave to pick up Jackson. Too bad he still couldn't stop thinking about his mystery woman. He'd masturbated every night to thoughts of her, and he was still horny as hell.

He sighed and tried to focus on the paperwork. Maybe what he needed to do was go out this weekend with Jackson and find a warm and willing woman to help him forget all about the redheaded spitfire.

CHLOE RAN UP THE STEPS OF THE POLICE STATION. IT HAD taken her forever to get there. The roads were slick from the afternoon snowstorm, traffic was a tangled snarl of a nightmare, and then she'd had to drive around for almost fifteen minutes before she found a parking spot.

She slipped on a step and grabbed the ice-cold railing to save herself from falling on her ass. The door to the station opened, and her heart sunk when her grandmother, wearing her favourite fur coat, stepped out into the bitter wind. She was followed by Lori, and Chloe tried not to wince. Her sister was wearing a leather jacket with a thin tank top under it, a skirt that barely covered her ass and thigh-high boots. Her long red hair was a dirty and knotted mess. Her sister may not have been an actual prostitute, but she was doing a bang-up job of dressing like one.

"Nice of you to show up," Lori said.

Chloe held her tongue as they walked down the steps past her. She followed them to the sidewalk, grabbing Lori's arm when they didn't stop. "Next time, call me, not Nana."

"Why?" Lori turned to face her, and Chloe grimaced when the scent of stale beer and cigarettes washed over her. "So you could leave me in jail to rot?"

"I would have bailed you out, Lori. I always do, don't I?"

"You act like I'm always getting arrested. One time and -"

"This is the second time since you left rehab and the fourth time this year."

Lori glared at her. "You're such a bitch, Chloe. You think you're better than me, you think -"

Chloe sighed wearily. "Keep your voice down. You're upsetting Nana."

"No, you upset her when you refused to come get me."

Chloe glanced at her grandmother as Lori gave her a triumphant grin. "That's right. Nana told me how you refused to come bail me out. I'm sitting in jail for nothing, and you won't even -"

"It wasn't for nothing. It was for prostitution, Lori. Again. What are you thinking? You can't -"

"Oh, of course you believe the cops," Lori sneered. "I couldn't have been falsely arrested, right? Not your fuck up of a sister. You think you're so perfect, Chloe, you think that your shit don't stink, but you know what? You're as bad as I am. At least I'm not a self-righteous, stuck-up bitch who doesn't give a shit about her family."

"Girls, stop it." Her grandmother's voice was full of tears. "You know I hate it when you fight."

"She started it," Lori said sullenly. 'She thinks she's better than me."

"I don't," Chloe said. "But you have a drinking problem and if you would go back to rehab and -"

"Shut the fuck up about rehab," Lori said. "Jesus, it didn't work, okay? I tried it and it didn't fucking work. I'm not going back."

"Instead you'll keep using Nana and her money to buy you booze and bail you out of jail? She's on a fixed income, Lori. You're taking the money she needs for her meds and for food."

Lori slapped her hard across the face. Her head rocked back and she made a startled cry. Her grandmother moaned, and tears slipped down her wrinkled cheeks. Lori bared her teeth at her. "Stop talking to me like you're my mother. Nana's doing fine and having me there is helpful to her. Isn't that right, Nana?"

"Yes," her grandmother whispered.

Chloe pressed her hand against her cheek. It was hot to the touch and pain was radiating down into her neck.

"C'mon, Nana, let's go. It's fucking freezing out. We need

to stop at the store and pick up some beer." Lori took her grandmother's arm in a firm grip.

"Nana, don't," Chloe whispered.

Her grandmother hesitated, and Lori made an impatient noise. "She wanted to leave me here. Remember, Nana?"

Her grandmother straightened and gave Chloe a sad look. "You should be nicer to your sister, sweetie. She needs your support."

She and Lori walked away before Chloe could reply. Chloe rubbed her cheek and watched them walk down the sidewalk before turning and trudging back to her car. Her cheek was throbbing, and she wanted to burst into tears. Instead, she rubbed delicately at the skin beneath her eyes and stared at herself in the rear-view mirror. Her face was pale except for the bright red mark on her cheek, and her eyes were watery with the unshed tears.

She turned the car on, blasting the heater on full, and checked the time. She wanted to go home, have a hot shower, climb into bed, and pretend the day had never happened. Instead, she pulled out onto the street and headed back to the office.

———

JACKSON STEPPED INTO HIS OFFICE. THE OFFICES AROUND HIS were dark and he hadn't seen anyone on his way back from Luke's office. The receptionist for their floor seemed to be the only one left. His meeting with Luke had gone a little long, but Ian had texted him to say he was stuck in traffic and would be late. He'd have enough time to –

"Chloe?" He stared in surprise at the back of her head. "What are you doing here?"

"What's it look like? I'm working." She didn't turn around and he hesitated before walking toward her.

"I thought you had a family thing."

"I did. I took care of it and came back to work."

He touched her shoulder. "Chloe, what's wrong?"

"Nothing." She pulled away from his touch. "I'm fine."

"You're not fine," he said. "Please look at me."

"I don't want to," she whispered.

"Please, Chloe."

She sighed and turned around. His eyes widened, and he touched the bright red mark on her cheek before he could stop himself. "Who did this to you?"

"It doesn't matter."

Anger was filling him up. "Yes, it fucking does matter. Who did this, Chloe?"

She pressed her lips together and shook her head. "Just leave me alone, okay? I've had a long day and I -"

"Tell me who hurt you, honey."

He hadn't meant to call her that, the endearment had just slipped out. But the moment it did, her face crumpled and she burst into tears.

"Shh, it's okay." He pulled her to her feet and put his arms around her. She buried her face in his neck and sobbed.

"It's okay, honey. It's okay. Come here." He grabbed the box of tissue from her desk and led her to the small loveseat. He sat down, drawing her into his lap. She curled into him like a scared kitten, and he rubbed her back as she cried.

After about five minutes, her sobs turned into the occasional sniffle. He handed her some tissue and she wiped her face and blew her nose. She tried to sit up and he tightened his hold around her, pressing her head against his chest.

"I'm so sorry," she whispered.

"It's fine." He kissed the top of her head. "Tell me what happened, honey."

"Lori is what happened," she said.

"Who's Lori?"

"My sister. She's a drunk and she got herself arrested again. My grandmother went to bail her out, I told her not to, but she was upset and scared."

She took a deep breath. "Traffic was horrible and by the time I got there, Nana had already paid her bail and they were leaving. We-we got into a fight and Lori slapped me across the face."

"I'm so sorry, honey."

She shrugged. "It isn't the first time." She pushed up the sleeve of her blouse and showed him the thin scar that ran down the outside of her arm from her elbow to the middle of her forearm. "This was from last year. She sliced me open with a box cutter when I poured her alcohol down the sink."

"Jesus," he said. "Maybe you should -"

"Maybe I should what?" She sat up, her slender body stiff and fire in her eyes. "Maybe I should give up on her? Maybe I should let her drink herself to death? Is that it?"

"Shh," he said. He pulled her back into his embrace and rubbed her back again until her stiff body relaxed. "I'm sorry. It's none of my business."

She shook her head. "No, I'm sorry. I shouldn't have snapped at you. You're being very kind and I'm being awful."

"You aren't."

"I'm just," she let her breath out in a shuddering sigh, "so tired of dealing with it, you know? She's ruining my life and I'm letting her, and I don't know how to stop."

She sat up and stared at him. "I don't know what to do."

Tears were starting to slide down her cheeks again and he

wiped them away with his thumbs, being careful not to press too hard on her injured cheek. "Don't cry, honey."

"I'm so tired of crying, so tired of worrying and – and…"

Her gaze dropped to his mouth and he made a muffled sound of surprise when she pressed her mouth against his. She kissed him hard and he made another shocked sound when she slipped her tongue into his mouth. Jesus, she tasted sweet.

He gripped the back of her neck and pulled her back before he could do something incredibly stupid like kiss her back. "Chloe, wait."

"Oh my God," she whispered. "Oh my God, what am I doing? I'm so sorry. I shouldn't have done that, and I don't know why I did."

"It's fine," he said.

She stared at him with wide eyes. "I'm going to be fired for sexually harassing my co-worker."

He tried not to grin. Chloe was obviously panicking, but her thinking that kissing him was sexual harassment, when he couldn't stop fucking masturbating every night to thoughts of her, was laughable.

"I have to tell Luke what I did," she said. "I have to tell him and hand in my resignation before -"

"Chloe, it's fine. Really."

"It isn't. I'm a-a sexual predator."

This time he did grin, he couldn't help it, and her panic disappeared to be replaced with a flash of temper. "You think this is funny?"

"No, it's -"

"It's not funny, okay? I finally got the chance to live my dream of being a designer – maybe – and I've ruined it by kissing you. I forced my goddamn tongue into your mouth like some, some kind of…well, I don't know what…but it wasn't appropriate and now I'm going to be fired. I'm going to be fired and lose my chance of being a real honest-to-god designer all because I couldn't keep my tongue out of the mouth of a co-worker who doesn't even like me. Who doesn't even want me, or -"

He stopped her talking with a kiss. She squeaked into his mouth and he traced her upper lip with his tongue before nipping at her bottom lip. She parted her lips and he slid his tongue into her mouth to taste her again. She sat passively in his lap, but a soft moan escaped when he sucked on her bottom lip and her ass pressed against his growing erection.

He released her mouth but kept his hand on the nape of her neck. "I want you, Chloe. I want you very much."

"Why?" She whispered.

"Because you're beautiful," he kissed her again, "sexy, sweet, and," he kissed her a third time, "have a great fucking ass."

She smiled a little and he pulled her closer. "Kiss me."

She pressed her lips against his and he relished the feel of her soft mouth before sliding his other arm around her and pulling her tight against his body. She rocked her ass rhythmically against his erection as they kissed. He nuzzled her neck before sucking on her earlobe and sliding his hand under her to squeeze that delectable ass.

She moaned into his ear and he squeezed her ass again. "Come back to my place, Chloe. Come back to my place and -"

"Jackson? Sorry I'm late. The receptionist was leaving, but she told me it was fine to come back to your office. Are you ready to...shit, sorry."

He cursed inwardly at the sound of Ian's voice. Chloe had stiffened on his lap and the look on her face was one of complete and utter shock.

He peered around Chloe's body. "Sorry, Ian. Uh, give me a minute, okay?"

"Yeah, sure, sorry again, I'll…"

Ian's big body froze as Chloe slowly turned her head to stare at him.

"It's you," his best friend breathed as Chloe made a low moan of dismay.

"What's happening?" Jackson said.

Chloe scrambled off of his lap and backed toward her desk, never taking her eyes off of Ian.

"Chloe, what's wrong?" Jackson stood and stared first at Chloe before turning to Ian. "Ian, tell me what the fuck is happening."

"It's her," Ian said. "The girl from the bar."

"Chloe?" Jackson felt like he'd been hit by a truck. "Chloe is the woman you slept with?"

"Oh my God," Chloe moaned. "You-you told him."

"He's my best friend," Ian said.

Jackson had never seen Ian look so disarmed before.

"I have to go," Chloe whispered. Tears were sliding down her cheeks. She grabbed her purse and her jacket, shaking off Jackson's hand when he reached for her arm.

"Chloe, wait."

"No, I can't… oh my God, I have to go." She stopped in front of Ian who was blocking the doorway. She whispered pleadingly, "Please move."

He gave her a weirdly tender look. "Baby, it's okay. Don't cry."

"Please let me go," she whispered.

He stepped aside and she ran past him. Jackson stared at Ian. "What the fuck just happened?"

CHLOE PULLED HER FLANNEL PAJAMAS ON BEFORE SLIPPING into her robe and belting it securely around her waist. A towel was wrapped turban style around her wet hair, and she wiped away the fog on the bathroom mirror before staring at herself. The spot where Lori had slapped her wasn't as red, but the rest of her skin was so pale she looked like a ghost.

"I slept with Ian," she said to her reflection. "I slept with my co-worker's best friend who also happens to be a cop."

She barked out a laugh. Jagged and sharp as broken glass.

"I'm lucky *I* didn't get arrested for prostitution."

Another jagged laugh. She didn't like the hysteria that was in it, and she gripped the bathroom sink with white knuckles. "Deep breaths, Chloe. Deep breaths. You're okay. Tomorrow morning, you'll hand in your resignation to Luke, and you'll never see Jackson or Ian again. Everything's fine."

Yeah, everything was fine. She was about to lose her one and only shot at being a designer, but everything was fine.

She staggered out of the bathroom and made her way to the kitchen to make herself a cup of tea. She would have a nice hot cup of tea while she composed her resignation letter. Her dad always said that tea made everything better.

She swiped at the tears before cursing under her breath. She didn't want to cry anymore. She was an adult who had made a mistake and now she had to face the consequences of that mistake.

She turned the teakettle on and leaned against the counter. It was bitterly ironic that instead of it being her sister who ruined her career, she'd done it to herself. She'd always blamed Lori for the bad stuff that happened to her, but maybe, just maybe, it was her own damn fault. Maybe she projected all the bad shit onto Lori because she didn't want to face the fact that she was a fuck-up too.

There was a knock on her door and she made a startled

jerk. Who the hell was knocking on the door of her apartment? She clutched the neck of her robe closed and walked to the front door. Before she could look, Jackson's voice drifted through the door.

"Chloe, honey, let us in."

Us? *Us?*

She checked the peephole. Shit, both Jackson and Ian were standing in the hallway, their cheeks red with cold.

"Go away," she said.

"We just want to talk to you for a minute," Jackson said.

She chewed on her bottom lip. "I – I don't want to talk to you."

"Let us in, Red." Ian's voice held a certain amount of demand to it that had her automatically reaching for the lock. She snatched her hand back.

"No. Go away."

"We're not leaving until you talk to us. We'll discuss the whole thing here in the hallway through the door if you prefer."

Her eyes widened. Shit, she did not want her neighbours hearing all about her night of sex with Ian. She opened the door and yanked it open, glaring at the two of them. "Don't say another word in the hallway. Get in here, both of you."

Jackson smiled at her as he stepped past her and took his boots off. Ian brushed past her and removed his boots as well as she slammed the door shut. "How did you guys even get in the building? There's a buzzer to open the front door."

Jackson shrugged. "One of your neighbours was coming out, Ian showed him his badge and he let us in."

"That's a misuse of your power," she said to Ian.

He didn't reply, but he didn't look ashamed in the least. The teakettle started to whistle and, her mind spinning, she trailed after Jackson and Ian when they followed the sound to the kitchen.

"I like your place." Jackson shut off the burner and poured hot water into her mug. He grabbed two more mugs that were hanging from hooks beneath the cupboards and opened up the canister that was marked 'tea'. "Ian, do you want a cup?"

Ian nodded, and she watched in silent disbelief as Ian draped his coat over the chair and sat down. Jackson poured water into the two mugs and smiled at her. "Sit down, Chloe."

"How do you even know where I live?" She sat down as Jackson set the mug in front of her. He found spoons and sugar in the cupboard and opened the fridge to get the milk before sitting down beside her.

She gave Ian a suspicious look. "Did you look me up in some police database or something?"

Jackson laughed. "We Googled your address, Chloe."

She stared into her tea before squeezing the tea bag with her spoon and lifting it out of the mug. She set it on the table, added a generous splash of milk, and took a sip. "Why are you here?"

"We were worried about you." Jackson took his own sip of tea.

"Why? You don't even know me."

"We were still worried. Plus, we wanted to talk to you about what happened."

"What happened?" She gave that weird, ragged laugh she couldn't seem to get rid of. "What happened was I slept with a-a damn cop who could have arrested me for prostitution, and then I tried to sleep with my co-worker who just happens to be the cop's best goddamn friend!"

Her voice was rising and she took a deep breath, resisting the urge to jump up and run to her bedroom.

"I wouldn't have arrested you for prostitution." Ian's deep voice washed over her, and a small shiver went down her spine. She wanted to stare at him, wanted to see if he was as beautiful and god-like as she remembered, but she kept her gaze on her mug of tea.

"What happened between us wasn't prostitution, Red."

"Yeah, okay," she mumbled.

"Chloe, please don't be upset," Jackson said. "I'm not going to say anything at work and -"

"It doesn't matter. I'm giving my resignation to Luke first thing in the morning."

"Like hell you are," Jackson said.

She flinched at the anger in his voice and Ian made a low growl. "Watch your tone, Jackson."

She could hear Jackson take a deep breath and then he said, "Honey, you're not resigning."

"I can't work with you. Not after I slept with your best friend and then sexually harassed you in our office. I'm a goddamn whore and now both of you know it."

"You are *not* a whore, don't let either of us hear you say that again, Chloe. And I told you before, you didn't sexually harass me." There was a thin thread of impatience in Jackson's usual affable tone. "I want you as much as you want me."

She peeked at Ian. She couldn't help it. He was staring at her gravely, but he didn't seem upset by Jackson's statement.

Disappointment crawled into her belly. Maybe he didn't want her anymore. Maybe he'd had his fill, or maybe it hadn't been as good between them as she remembered.

Chloe! What does it matter? Have you lost your damn mind? You can't go near him or Jackson ever again!

"You should go," she whispered. "I-I'm very tired."

"Honey, will you give us five minutes?" Jackson said. "Please?"

She hesitated. "Yeah, okay."

Jackson glanced at Ian who nodded. She didn't object when Jackson peeled one of her hands away from her mug and held it in his big hand. He squeezed her hand until she looked at him. "We don't think you're a whore for sleeping with Ian and then being attracted to me. Do you understand? You are free to sleep with whomever and however many men you want. Got it?"

She didn't answer, and he squeezed her hand. "Chloe?"

"Yes," she whispered.

"Good. Both Ian and I want you. Very much."

"What?" She gave him a surprised look. "You – you're kidding me."

"He isn't," Ian said.

She spared a glance at him, blushing at the look on his face. "Why?"

"Because, like I said before, you're beautiful and sexy and smart and neither of us can stop thinking about you," Jackson said.

She swallowed and stared into Jackson's eyes as he smiled at her. "You want both of us, don't you?"

She chewed at her bottom lip, not sure if she could admit what they wanted to hear.

"Don't you?" Jackson prompted.

"Yes," she sighed. "I'm sorry, but, yes, I do want both of you."

"You don't need to apologize for that." Jackson glanced at Ian again. "Both of us are very good at…sharing."

Her mouth dropped open as the implication of what he was saying sunk in. "Sharing? I –you can't be serious."

"We are. We both want you, you want both of us. It's perfect, Chloe."

Her mind wanted to skip over the delicious and intoxicating thought of having sex with both men, of getting to have her cake and eat it too, and so she pounced on another problem. "We work together, Jackson."

"So, what?" He shrugged. "I can keep it professional at the office, if you can."

"I – what if we got into a fight or…"

"What if we did? I won't let it affect our working relationship."

"Have you ever slept with someone you worked with before?" She asked.

"No, but I know me. I don't hold a grudge, and I can keep my personal and professional life separate."

She didn't reply and he squeezed her hand again. "Look, Chloe, we're going to be completely honest with you. Neither Ian nor I are looking for anything permanent."

She peeked again at Ian. His jaw had tightened, but he gave her short nod of agreement.

"Nothing permanent," she repeated.

"That's right," Jackson said. "We want you, and we want to have…fun with you, but we want you to know what this would be. A mutual good time for three consenting adults. We're not looking to date or for a relationship."

She wondered if she should be upset that she was good enough to sleep with, but not good enough to date. She felt like she should be, but truthfully, what Jackson was saying was incredibly appealing.

She'd been in a relationship before and it had ended badly because of her fucked-up life. The thought of growing attached to Jackson or Ian, of maybe falling in love with one of them only to watch that love be destroyed by the toxicity of her sister made her feel sick to her stomach.

She couldn't – wouldn't – go through that again. A no-strings-attached relationship worked fine for her.

"So, it would just be a mutual itch scratching then?" She said.

There was no bitterness in her tone but Jackson winced a little. Still, she was impressed when he didn't try and gloss over it. "A bit of a crude description, but accurate enough."

Chloe, you can't do this. You work with Jackson! And you can't have sex with two men ....nice girls don't do that!

She shoved her inner voice down to the bottom of her brain. She was tired of being a nice girl, dammit.

"So," she was impressed at how steady her voice was, "if I agree to this, how does it work? Do we do like an every other weekend thing? Just switch off or…"

"What do you mean?" Jackson gave her a puzzled look.

Her cheeks flushed a little. "I mean, do I spend one weekend with Ian and then the next weekend with you? Or does this itch scratching work during the week too? And if so, is it one week on and one week off with each of you?"

"No, Chloe, we, "Jackson glanced at Ian, "we'd all be together. At once."

She cocked her head. "Together. All of us."

"Yes. The three of us together."

Her mouth dropped open and she knew she looked like an idiot, but she couldn't help herself. "Do you mean like a…a threesome?"

Jackson grinned and Ian gave him a sharp look. "Don't tease her, Jackson."

"I'm not going to," he said defensively. "Yes, we mean a threesome, Chloe."

She stared silently at them for a moment. "Are you and Ian, I mean, do you and Ian like to…"

Ian shook his head. "No, Jackson and I are only into women."

"It's fine if you, um, like each other," she said quickly. "I don't – I mean, I'm cool with it. Love is love, right?" She finished lamely.

Jackson laughed. "Yes, but Ian and I aren't bisexual. We do, however, enjoy fucking a woman together."

She blushed at his crude language before glancing at Ian again. "But you slept with me, uh, alone."

"We occasionally sleep with women individually," Ian said.

"But our preference is together," Jackson said.

"Right." She stared into her tea again, trying to wrap her mind about what they were asking her to do. Anxiety and worry were creeping into her stomach. She hardly knew how to please one man, let alone two. What if she did or said something stupid? What if she couldn't keep up with them? She'd watched threesomes in porn from time to time, and it occasionally looked…painful. The men were sometimes rough and they…

They wouldn't be rough with you, Chloe. You know they wouldn't.

No, maybe not. But if she tried to sleep with both of them at once, she'd end up disappointing them both. She didn't have enough experience for a goddamn threesome. She'd be humiliated and they'd wonder what the hell they ever saw in her in the first place.

You can learn. Ask them to teach you how to –

Nope. She couldn't. Besides, thinking that she was the type of girl to sleep with two men was ridiculous. She was a one-guy woman, a one-orgasm girl, a one -"

"Chloe? You okay?"

"I can't," she said abruptly. "I'm sorry. I – I appreciate the, um, the offer, but I can't do that. It doesn't have anything to do with either of you, it's all me. I'm not that type of…girl."

"Chloe, don't say no right away. Think about it and -"

"Jackson," Ian said, "she said no."

Jackson took a deep breath. "Yeah, okay."

"I'm sorry," Chloe whispered.

"Nothing to be sorry about," Jackson said. "But if you change your mind, you know where to find us, right?"

"Right," she whispered.

He was still holding her hand and he squeezed it again. "Promise me you won't quit, Chloe."

She didn't reply, and he said, "If I find out you handed your resignation in, I'll quit on the spot and leave before you can. Do you hear me?"

She frowned at him. "No, you can't."

"I can, and I will. Don't quit, Chloe. I won't make this awkward at work, I promise."

"Okay," she said.

Ian visibly relaxed and she gave him a tentative smile. He smiled back but it was strained, and she bit back the disappointment when he stood up. "We should go, Jackson."

"Yeah. I'll see you tomorrow at work, okay, Chloe?"

"Okay." She followed them to the door and waited as they slipped into their boots.

"Bye, Chloe."

"Bye," she said.

They left, and she shut and locked the door behind them. She reached up to run her hands though her hair and groaned when she remembered the towel. Shit. She stared at her flannel pajamas and her terry-cloth robe. Could she be wearing anything less sexy?

What does it matter. You rejected them. Two Greek gods wanted to fuck you and you said no. You asshole.

She banged her fist on the wall and then grunted a curse before rubbing her aching hand. It was for the best. She couldn't sleep with two men at once. She couldn't.

CHAPTER 6

"Okay, so if you're sure you don't mind picking up the cake, I'll grab the rest of the decorations." Jane studied the piece of paper in front of her before taking a bite of her sandwich. "Oh crap, I forgot about the booze."

"I can pick that up as well," Chloe said.

Jane shook her head. "Nah, that's fine. I'll get Luke to pick it up Saturday morning."

Chloe sat back in her chair and poked at her salad. It was Thursday at lunch and, afraid Amy would walk into the staff lunchroom and catch them, Jane had brought her to Luke's empty office to eat lunch and finish the plans for Amy's birthday party.

She poked again at her salad. She'd had very little appetite since Ian and Jackson had left her place Tuesday night. She knew she needed to eat, but it was hard to eat when you were consumed by the thought that you had made the biggest mistake of your life. Why couldn't she have at least considered sleeping with them both? Why did she have to say no so damn quickly?

Because you'd make a fool of yourself, that's why. You

can't sleep with two men at once, especially two men who have the experience that they do. Until Ian, you'd slept with one man and you weren't known for your adventurous nature in bed, were you?

"Mark's telling her he's taking her for dinner, but that he has to stop by our place first, so as long as all the party guests are there by seven, we should be fine."

Jane was still talking, and Chloe forced herself to concentrate on the small brunette. She set her container of salad on Luke's desk. "If you need me to come early and help decorate, I can."

"Yeah?" Jane gave her a look of gratitude. "If you're sure you don't mind, that would be so helpful. Amy's mom was going to come early and help, but she got roped in to some volunteer thing, so she can't."

"I don't mind at all," Chloe said.

They both turned when the door opened and Amy strolled in. "Hey, Luke? I know it's lunch, but do you have time to... hey, what are you guys doing in here?"

"Oh, uh, hi," Jane said. She scrambled to turn the paper over when Amy joined them at the desk. "Luke is, uh, having lunch with Mark, and Chloe and I are, we're, um... hanging out in here for lunch because, uh... the lunch room was really full."

Oh lord, Jane was a terrible liar.

"Oh yeah? Because I was just downstairs in the lunch room and there were only three people in it." Amy grinned at Jane who gave Chloe a desperate look.

"Oh, actually I had a terrible headache and Jane suggested we sit here in Luke's office because it was busier and noisier in the lunch room earlier," Chloe said.

Crap. She was a terrible liar too.

Amy hesitated. "Is this about my birthday party?"

Jane's mouth dropped open. "Son of a bitch! Who told you?"

"I'm sorry." Amy sat down in the chair next to Chloe. "On Tuesday night, I'd grabbed Mark's phone to look up something just as you texted him about the party. It was really bad timing, that's all."

"Shit," Jane said.

"I'm so sorry," Amy repeated. "I didn't tell Mark that I knew. In fact, I was going to keep it a secret. Don't be mad, Janie."

"I'm not," Jane said. "I feel bad that the surprise is ruined for you."

"It was a lovely surprise on Tuesday night," Amy said.

Jane burst into laughter. "Oh good, I'm glad."

"You're the sweetest woman ever, and I adore you." Amy reached across the desk and squeezed her hand. "Thank you, Jane."

"You're welcome."

"Okay," Amy stood up, "well, I'll leave so -"

"Stay," Jane said. "We're done the party talk, and you can help me find out what's wrong with Chloe."

"There's nothing wrong," Chloe said.

"I know that isn't true. Tell us why you're sad, honey," Jane said.

"I'm not sad, I'm…"

She stared at Amy who gave her an encouraging look.

God, she really shouldn't be telling either of them this, but she needed to tell someone. She couldn't eat or sleep, even the clothing sketches she was trying to do for Amy were turning out terrible. She was consumed by thoughts of Ian and Jackson, and if she wanted to get back to normal, wanted to have a shot at becoming a full-time designer, she needed to get them out of her head.

She took a deep breath. "The guy I slept with? The one-night stand? He's Jackson's best friend, Ian."

"Holy shitballs." Amy stared wide-eyed at her. "How do you know? When did you find that out? Does Jackson know? Okay, you know what… start from the beginning."

Her cheeks red and her pulse skittering like a jack rabbit, Chloe told them everything. It took almost fifteen minutes, even with glossing over the confrontation with her sister. When she was finished, she stared at her lap, a little afraid to see the look on their faces. What kind of woman even entertained the idea of sleeping with two men at once?

"You seriously turned them down?"

Chloe's head snapped up and she stared at Amy. "Of course, I did."

"Why?" Amy grinned at her. "Jackson is super hot, and from what you told us before, so is Ian."

"Be-because I work with Jackson and because…nice girls don't do threesomes."

"We nice girls do all sorts of bad things," Amy said with a laugh. "It's what makes us so awesome."

Jane grinned at her. "It really is."

"Oh, so both of you have slept with multiple men at once?"

"Is two really considered multiple?" Amy asked.

"Yes, it is."

"Is it, though?" Amy said. "I mean I hear multiple, I think three or more. What about you, Janie?"

"Definitely three or more," Jane said.

"Fine," Chloe said. "Have either of your ever slept with two men at once?"

Jane shook her head as Amy said, "No, but Mark ties me up and spanks me on a regular basis, and in the bedroom, I call him Master or Sir and he calls me his slave."

Chloe sat back in her chair, staring dumbfounded at Amy. Amy grinned at her and stole one of Jane's crackers from the container on the desk. "I think I've completely shocked her."

"Yep." Jane ate another bite of her sandwich.

"Really?" Chloe said.

"Really, really," Amy said.

"Mark seems so…nice," Chloe said.

Amy laughed. "Mark *is* nice. The nicest, sweetest man I know. He also happens to be a Dom who's into impact play in the bedroom."

"Which you like?" Chloe said.

"Very much so. I'm a submissive who's also into impact play. It's one of the things that makes us perfect for each other." Amy stole another cracker. "My point is, don't let society or what other people think, dictate what you should and shouldn't do in the bedroom. If you want to sleep with two men at once, sleep with two men at once. There's no shame in a woman taking what she wants."

"I work with Jackson, remember?"

Jane grinned at her. "I work with Luke and Amy works with Mark. You're talking to the wrong women about whether you should have a relationship with a co-worker."

"It wouldn't be a relationship, just sex," Chloe said quickly.

"Right, you mentioned that," Amy replied. "And you're good with that? Because honestly, that's the part I'm worried about for you. You don't seem to be the type of girl to have sex without a relationship. No judgment for that – I'm the same way."

"I didn't think so either, but that was before…"

"Before what?" Jane asked.

"Before I realized I was terrible at relationships."

"Are you?" Jane said.

Chloe nodded. "Yes. After John broke up with me, I really thought what I wanted was to find another nice guy and fall in love again. Only, I keep putting my sister and her problems first, and I've realized in the last few weeks that I'm not meant to be in a relationship. I can't stop trying to save my sister no matter what she does and says, and it takes up a great deal of my time and energy."

She stared at the smooth surface of Luke's desk. "I was with John since college and he tried to be supportive, he did, but I don't blame him for finally dumping me. The amount of times I had to cancel plans on him to take care of my sister... I don't want to get into it, but trust me, it was all my fault that our engagement ended."

"Eh, not sure if I believe that," Amy said.

"Anyway, I'm not interested in getting into a relationship again after all, so the no-strings-attached part is actually perfect. But, again, there's the fact that I work with Jackson and -"

"Has he made it weird since you turned them down?" Amy asked.

Chloe shook her head. "No. I – actually, I'm pretty impressed by how normal he's acting. He's been the perfect gentleman and he's made no mention of...you know."

"Well, that's good," Jane said.

"Yeah." Chloe wondered if they could see the disappointment on her face. Jackson really had been a perfect gentleman the last two days. In fact, she'd have no idea he was even attracted to her if they hadn't made out in their damn office. Gone was the flirting and the occasional lingering glance. He was his usual friendly and funny self, but also completely and utterly professional at all times.

She was happy about that. She didn't miss his flirting. Nope, not one bit.

"Is it good?" Amy asked. "No offence, Chloe, but I'm wondering if you're upset because he's being a perfect gentleman."

"Oh God." Chloe buried her face in her hands. "I'm such an idiot. I have stupid amounts of regret over turning them down. I know it's for the best, but I want to sleep with both of them. I really do."

"Then you should," Jane said.

Chloe didn't reply, and Amy touched her shoulder. "Chloe? Is working with Jackson the only reason why you don't want to sleep with both of them?"

Chloe lowered her hands but continued to stare at them as they twisted in her lap. "I'm afraid I'll disappoint them. I could barely satisfy one man in bed. My ex and I didn't have sex a lot and when we did... I mean, it was good, but it wasn't..."

"Blow your hair back, good?" Jane said.

"Yeah, and I think it was partially his fault and partially my fault, but still – having sex with two men is very different than having sex with one man. Ian was really amazing in bed and I have a feeling Jackson is too, and I don't... I don't want to disappoint them."

"Well, everyone has to learn," Amy said, "and I bet those two will be amazing teachers. You'd be surprised how far enthusiasm and a willingness to learn will go when it comes to sex."

Chloe sighed. "Yeah, maybe."

"I think you should at least think about it," Amy said. "I'm sure if you decide this is something you want, both Jackson and Ian would be more than happy to hear you changed your mind. Now, I'm gonna grab something from the café downstairs for lunch before I eat all of Jane's lunch."

Jane laughed and Amy grinned at her. "Thank you again

for the party, honey. I promise to act surprised on Saturday night."

Jane shook her head. "I don't think we need to keep up the ruse. Just be there for seven-thirty like planned."

"All right. I'll talk to you ladies, later. Oh, and Chloe, if you can, I'd like at least two sketches from you by Monday. Okay?"

"Uh, yes, that's no problem," Chloe said. "Sorry, it's taking me so long."

"It isn't," Amy said. "But I'd like to include scans of them in the digital package I'll be sending to Pierre and Julien. I'm emailing it on Wednesday, but that'll give us time to look them over and make any tweaks if necessary."

"I'll have it to you on Monday," Chloe said.

"Good. See you later." Amy left the office and Jane gave Chloe an encouraging smile.

"I'm so happy that you're doing some design work, Chloe. Amy told me you've always wanted to design."

"Thanks. But if I don't get my shit together, it'll be over before it's even started. I can't even seem to get anything on paper, lately. I'm just so…"

"Horny?" Jane gave her an innocent grin and Chloe burst into laughter.

"I'd like to say no, but I'm not a very good liar."

Jane popped the last bite of her sandwich into her mouth. "Maybe what you need is a little help from two really hot men."

"Maybe," Chloe sighed. "Maybe."

"THANKS FOR MEETING ME FOR LUNCH." JACKSON STUDIED Ian as the big man stirred his soup. He was wearing his uniform and that, combined with his size, meant more than one person in the café was staring at him.

"How's work?" Ian ignored the stares, like he always did.

"How's Chloe, you mean."

"Is her cheek bruised?"

Jackson shook his head. "No. It looks fine. You have to stop obsessing over her, man."

"I'm not."

"You think I can't hear you jerking off every night through the goddamn wall?"

Ian stirred his soup again. "You're one to talk."

Jackson set down his chicken wrap. "We're both idiots."

"Yeah."

"She's not going to change her mind."

"Nope," Ian said.

"We need to go out this weekend and find someone else to fuck. It's the only way to get her out of our heads."

Ian ate a spoonful of soup. "Are you actually interested in sleeping with someone else?"

Jackson sighed. He wanted to say yes, but he couldn't lie to Ian. "No."

"Me neither."

"Christ, we're really screwed."

"No, we're not screwed. That's the problem." Ian drank some water and wiped his mouth. "I've been thinking about it and maybe if we told her we were open to the idea of sharing her, just not at the same time, she'd be more willing to give us a chance."

Dread filled Jackson's stomach, but he forced himself to nod. "Maybe. But is that what you really want?"

"You know it isn't," Ian said. "I want both of us with her at the same time, but if she doesn't want that, then the alternative is sharing her separately. If you're okay with it, I think we should talk to her about it."

Jackson stared at his half-eaten wrap. His appetite was gone, and he yanked at the knot on his tie. He was suddenly too hot and the air in the café had turned to soup."

"Jackson? You okay?" Ian was always too goddamn perceptive.

"Yeah, I'm ... I would prefer us to be with her together."

He tried to stop the bitter laugh from bubbling out. That was the understatement of the century. He wanted Chloe, wanted her desperately, but he wasn't sure he could sleep with her if Ian wasn't there.

He swallowed down the anxiety brewing in his belly. It had only been in the last six months or so that he'd started to realize what was happening. Hell, it was only in the last two months that he could admit to himself that the reason he no longer slept with women without Ian there, was because one - it held zero appeal to him and two – he stayed as limp as a motherfucking noodle.

"I would prefer that too," Ian said in a low voice. "But, Christ, Jackson, I can't stop thinking about her. I'm rubbing myself fucking raw every damn night."

"I know, me too."

Ian had been with Chloe. He knew how she looked naked, how tight her pussy was, and for the first time in his life, Jackson was jealous of his best friend. He didn't think Chloe would ever change her mind about a threesome, which meant he'd never get to be with her. Even if they did what Ian was suggesting and tried sleeping with her separately, he'd just end up humiliating himself. He couldn't even risk trying to sleep with her without Ian around, which meant that Chloe would be with Ian and only Ian.

They'd end up dating and then they'd get married and

have babies and he'd be alone, exiled to the occasional dinner with them, and only ever being Uncle Jackson to their kids. The anxiety was turning to panic, and he gripped the edge of the table as Ian said, "Jackson? What's wrong?"

"Nothing." He cleared his throat.

"You don't look so hot."

"Just feeling a little sick to my stomach."

"Shit," Ian glanced at Jackson's half-eaten wrap, "I hope you didn't get food poisoning."

"I don't think so." Jackson drank some water. "I'm all right."

"You sure?" Ian said.

"Yeah." He wished the café wasn't so damn crowded. It really did feel hard to breathe. "Do you want me to talk to Chloe this afternoon?"

Ian shook his head. "No, I think we should both be there. I have to work tonight and tomorrow night, but I'm off Saturday and Sunday. Ask her to meet with us for coffee this weekend."

"Yeah, okay."

"Are you sure you're good with this?" Ian asked.

Jackson nodded. He wasn't, not by a long shot, but he couldn't tell Ian that. He wasn't about to fuck up Ian's chance with Chloe, just because he suddenly couldn't get his shit together.

"Okay, good." The relief in Ian's voice was palpable.

"Jackson? Hey there."

Jackson stood as Ian did the same, and smiled at Amy. "Hi, Amy. How are you?"

"Good. Just grabbing a sandwich. The café is busy today, huh?"

Jackson nodded. "Would you like to share our table? We've got an empty chair."

"Yes, thanks." She held her free hand to Ian. "Hi, I'm Amy."

"Oh sorry," Jackson said. "Amy Dawson, this is Ian Aldrin, my best friend and roommate. Ian, this is my boss Amy Dawson."

"It's nice to meet you," Ian said.

"You as well." The three of them sat down and Amy opened her bottle of water. "How long have you been a police officer, Ian?"

"Almost a decade now."

"I bet you have some interesting stories to share." Amy smiled at him.

"Probably a few more than most people." Ian studied the purple choker around her necklace. "That's an interesting necklace."

Ian knew as well as he did that it was a slave collar. Despite the anxiety still coursing through him, Jackson had to bite back his small smile when Amy touched the heart that dangled from her collar and blushed softly. "Thank you. It was a gift."

Ian studied her, and Jackson watched as Amy returned his look for only a few seconds before she lowered her gaze to the table. He hadn't known her very long, but she was assertive at the office and obviously knew what she wanted and how to get it.

She'd never had any trouble meeting his gaze or anyone else's from what he could tell, but only a few minutes after meeting Ian, her submissive tendencies were emerging. He wondered again why Ian hadn't gone full Dominant. He had a damn knack for knowing when women were naturally submissive.

Thanks to the slave collar, Jackson knew Amy was submissive, but he was certain that Ian would have known even if she hadn't been wearing a collar. Amy was still studying the table, that soft blush covering her pale skin.

"Jackson tells me you're an incredible designer," Ian said.

Amy took another drink of water. "I enjoy what I do."

She stared at Jackson – she had no problem meeting *his* gaze – and said, "We're very happy Jackson has joined the company. He's been doing amazing work on the new digital storefront in such a short time."

"Thanks, Amy," Jackson said. "I'm really enjoying working for you and your brother."

There was a moment of silence before Amy cleared her throat. "Actually, I'm glad I ran into you, Jackson. It's my birthday this Saturday, and Jane and Luke are throwing me a party at their place. I'd love it if you, and," she paused, her gaze landing on Ian for the briefest of seconds, "Ian came to the party."

"Oh, uh…" Jackson hesitated. He didn't know Amy that well, and he knew for certain that Ian would definitely not go. His best friend wasn't a hermit, but he was an introvert and Jackson would never get him to agree to go to a party full of people he didn't know."

"There's going to be other work people there," Amy said. "Quite a few actually. I know you don't know a lot of people in the company yet, but Chloe will be there, so you can stick with her."

"Chloe's going?" Could Amy hear the eagerness in his voice? Jesus, he hoped not.

"She is," Amy said. "She's been helping Jane plan the party. The party starts at seven-thirty, you can come by any time after that. So, what do you say? Will you and Ian be there?"

Before Jackson could reply, Ian said. "We will. What should we bring?"

Amy smiled at him. "Just yourselves. I am way too old for presents, and Luke is providing all the alcohol and food."

She stood and picked up her water bottle and unopened sandwich. "I'll email you Luke's home address, Jackson."

"Uh, okay. Sure."

"Great. Ian, it was nice to meet you."

"Nice to meet you too, Amy."

Jackson waited until Amy had left the café before staring at Ian.

"What?" Ian said.

"What? You're going to a party full of people you don't know. What do you mean, what? Are you having a stroke?"

Ian ate more soup and Jackson poked him in the shoulder. "Dude, seriously?"

"I'm fine," Ian said.

"It's because Chloe will be there, isn't it?"

"Yes," Ian said bluntly. "We'll talk to her about our new…idea at the party, okay?"

"Is that really the best time?" Jackson said.

Ian shrugged. "If she doesn't want to talk about it, we can at least ask her to go for coffee with us on Sunday."

Jackson leaned back in his chair and stared at Ian. "Yeah, okay."

Ian studied him. "You're sure you're okay with this? If you're not, we don't have to -"

"It's fine," Jackson said. "It's a good idea."

He stared down at his wrap as Ian finished his soup. It was a good idea. It was a fine idea, and he could sleep with Chloe without Ian around. Everything would be fine. Just fine.

CHAPTER 7

"Holy shit." Jane was suddenly standing behind her and Chloe gave her a curious look.

"What's wrong?" She studied the living room of Jane and Luke's home. It was filled to the brim with people, and she smiled when she saw Amy, giggling and her cheeks flushed, walking toward them. Amy's birthday party had only been going for about an hour, but it seemed to be a success.

"Look who just walked in." Jane was staring at the entrance to the living room. Chloe followed her gaze, her mouth dropping open when she was who was standing with Luke.

"What the hell are they doing here?" She said.

"I invited them." Amy joined them and threw her arm around Chloe's shoulder before kissing her cheek. "You're welcome."

"I – you don't even know Ian. Do you?" Chloe gave her a confused look.

Amy grinned at her. "I met him Thursday. Remember when I went to the café to grab lunch? Jackson was having lunch with Ian and I sat with them for a bit."

Amy glanced behind her before leaning closer and saying, "That Ian...whew, he's something else. I mean, Jackson is gorgeous and reminds me a little of Mark with his sweetness, but Ian's got the dark and mysterious vibe in spades. Why didn't you tell me he's a Dom, Chloe?"

"He – what? He's a Dom?" Chloe said.

Amy nodded. "Pretty damn sure he is."

"How do you know?" Chloe asked.

"I don't know," Amy shrugged. "It was more of a feeling, really." Her slender fingers touched the necklace around her neck. "I'm almost positive he knew my necklace is actually a slave collar, and Jesus, at one point when he looked at me, I couldn't stop from going all submissive. Like, bowed head and two seconds away from calling him 'Sir', submissive."

"No," Jane said. "Are you serious?"

Amy nodded. "Yeah. I've had that happen before at the club. Although it's usually with a specific Dom there named Wallace. I don't know why. Other Dominants I'm like whatever, dude, but sometimes..."

She shrugged again. "Mark says it's not uncommon, but I've never had it happen outside of the club."

"What club?" Chloe asked. She glanced at Amy's necklace, her face going a little red. "Slave collar?"

"Oh, sorry, it's a BDSM club that Mark and I go to. Mark's part owner actually. And the collar is...well, it's locked around my throat with a key and Mark carries the key."

"He owns a BDSM club and you wear a collar?" Chloe's mind was overloaded with information.

Amy laughed. "Okay, so not the time to talk about this, but we'll go for coffee later next week and I'll explain it all then. Just be prepared that at some point Ian might want to tie you up when you're banging him."

"One, I'm not going to bang him again, and two, he did kind of pin me down and not, uh, let me climax until he said I could."

Her face was bright red now, but Amy gave her a look of triumph. "Told you. He's a Dom."

"I still don't know why you invited them to your party," Chloe said.

"You said you thought you'd made a mistake. This gives you the chance to talk to them, tell them you've changed your mind."

"I, I don't think I have, I mean, I can't -"

"Amy?"

"Hey, honey."

"Hi." Mark kissed Amy's neck above her necklace.

No, her collar, Chloe thought bewilderedly. She was wearing a collar.

"Are you having fun?" Mark asked.

"I am."

"Good. Can I steal you away from Jane and Chloe for a minute? Valerie wants to do a birthday shot with you."

"Oh hell, yes," Amy giggled. She waved at a pretty brunette across the room. "On my way, you sexy girl!"

Amy took Mark's hand and they walked toward Valerie. Chloe's stomach tensed when both Jackson and Ian looked over at her. Jackson waved and Ian nodded, and she plastered a smile on her face before giving them a limp wave in return. They followed Luke to the bar set up in the corner.

"You okay?" Jane asked.

"Yes, I'm fine," she replied.

"You don't look fine."

"I'm a little nervous," Chloe said. "I'm not sure what I'll say when they come over or…"

She watched in astonishment as both Jackson and Ian

grabbed drinks but stayed with Luke. They were engrossed in conversation with Luke in less than a minute and neither of them even looked her way.

She swallowed down her disappointment. Why did she even think they would come chat with her anyway? She'd turned down their offer and they'd been clear what they wanted from her.

"Chloe?" Jane touched her arm.

Chloe smiled at her. "I'm fine. I – excuse me, I need to use the ladies' room."

Forcing herself not to glance at Jackson and Ian, she walked out of the living room.

He hesitated only a moment before sliding open the door and stepping out onto the patio. He should have been waiting for Jackson, but it'd been almost two hours since they'd arrived at the party and he couldn't stay away from her a minute longer.

It was cold outside, and he frowned. She wasn't wearing her jacket and she was shivering. He wasn't wearing a jacket either and he stepped closer to her, touching her arm through her sleeve. She made a soft sound of surprise, her entire body jerking before she stared up at him.

"Hi," he said.

"Hi, Ian. How-how are you?"

"Good. You?"

"Good. Enjoying the party?"

"I am. It's too cold for you out here." He wanted to pull her shivering body into his arms.

"I needed some fresh air." She wouldn't look at him and,

unable to resist, he stepped behind her and put his arms around her.

To his surprise, instead of pulling away, she leaned back against him. He held her a little closer, his big hands rubbing her upper arms. She was wearing a thin sweater that hugged her breasts, and a pair of tight jeans that showed off the curve of her ass.

He willed himself not to get an erection as he inhaled the sweet scent of her hair. She had it in a simple braid and he wanted to unbraid it and thread his hands through the fire coloured softness.

"I'm sorry," she said.

"For what?"

"For, uh, kind of freaking out on Tuesday night. I made a fool of myself."

"You didn't." He squeezed her a little tighter. "It was a shock for all of us."

"Yeah." She sighed and stared up at the faint light of the stars. "Valerie seems nice."

"Who?" He asked.

"Valerie. Pretty brunette. You and Jackson have been talking to her almost all night."

He could hear the slightest hint of jealousy in her voice and a slow grin crossed his face. If she was jealous, he and Jackson might have a chance with her after all. It would have to be separate, but separate was better than not at all.

Is it? Jackson said it was fine, but he looked miserable about it.

He sighed and rested his chin on the top of Chloe's head. He was almost positive that Jackson didn't want to sleep with Chloe separately, but what choice did they have?

"Ian? Are you and Jackson going to, uh... date Valerie?"

"We don't date and no, we're not. She's nice, but I didn't even remember her name."

He could feel some of the tension leave her body before she glanced up at him. "Sorry, it isn't any of my business."

"You're the only one we want, Chloe."

Shit, he shouldn't have led with that, he sounded like a deranged stalker, but it had just popped out.

"Why?" She whispered. She didn't seem too freaked out by his admission, and hope made an unexpected appearance inside of him.

"Because you're beautiful and sexy, and fucking you was amazing. I can't stop thinking about you, Red."

Even in the pale glow of the moon and the stars, he could see her soft skin turn red. "Fucking you was amazing for me too."

He glanced behind him. The patio opened up off of the dining room and the room was dark and empty. He wished that Jackson was with them, before deciding to go for it. "Chloe, what would you say if Jackson and I agreed to sleep with you separately?"

She craned her neck to stare up at him, shock covering her delicate features. "I – what? You said you didn't want that."

"No, we said our preference was together, but we talked about it and we're willing to share you in a different way. Whatever makes you comfortable."

"Really?"

"Yes." He stared down at her sweet face, his gaze dropping to her mouth. God, he wanted to kiss her.

When her lips parted, he couldn't resist any longer. He bent his head and kissed her, softly at first but with growing need when she pressed her ass against him and opened her mouth wide. He tasted her, his tongue stroking against hers as he cupped one firm breast.

"I've missed you," he breathed against her mouth.

"I-I missed you too," she whispered.

He kissed her again, kneading her breast through her sweater and her bra. She arched into his touch, her cold hands clutching at his forearm. The door slid open behind them and he knew instinctively it was Jackson.

He stopped kissing Chloe but when she tugged at his hand still cupping her breast, he shook his head.

"Ian, it's not -"

"Jackson doesn't mind," he replied.

Chloe stared up at Jackson who gave her a slow grin. "Hello, beautiful."

He dropped his gaze to her breasts and Chloe made a low moan. "I-I'm sorry."

"You have nothing to be sorry about," Jackson said.

Chloe's nipple was hard against Ian's palm, and he plucked at it through her sweater and bra. Jackson's nostrils flared, and Chloe made another low moan.

"Does it feel good, honey?" Jackson asked.

Chloe nodded. "Yes."

"I talked to her about us sharing her separately," Ian said. He rubbed his thumb over Chloe's nipple as his other hand rubbed her hip.

"Ian, stop for a second," Chloe said. "I can't think straight when you do that."

He let go of her breast reluctantly, but kept his arm around her waist. Jackson had moved closer until she was completely sheltered from the cold wind by their big bodies. She stared up at him and then at Jackson.

"Are you really willing to do that?" She asked.

"Yes," Ian said.

Jackson hesitated, and Ian wanted to kick him in the ass.

"Jackson?" Chloe said.

"Yes, it's fine," Jackson replied.

Chloe studied him silently for a moment, and Ian decided he really would kick Jackson's ass when they were alone. He loved the guy, but he was fucking this up.

"Is it?" Chloe asked. "You don't look like you believe that, Jackson."

"He does," Ian said quickly. "It's just not our usual thing, so the idea is taking a bit to get used to."

"I'm not sure that asking you to do this is a good idea," Chloe said quietly.

"It is." Shit, any minute now he was going to outright beg. What the fuck was wrong with him? He glared at Jackson. "Tell her, Jackson."

Jackson shoved his hands into the pockets of his jeans. "Can I ask you something, Chloe?"

"Yes."

"Why don't you want to do a threesome? Is it because of what people will say? Because I promise that Ian and I are very discreet. Neither of us will say a word to anyone. What happens between the three of us is private and we'll keep it that way."

"Jackson," Ian said, "we talked about this and we agreed that we would -"

"It's just a question, Ian," Jackson said.

"It's none of our business. If Chloe doesn't want us together, then we need to respect that and stop badgering her."

"It's okay." Chloe squeezed his arm. "Really."

He relaxed a little but glared again at Jackson. Jackson ignored him, staring intently at Chloe as she studied the snow-covered ground.

"I'll embarrass myself," she finally said.

Jackson frowned. "What do you mean?"

"I don't have a lot of experience in the bedroom. Until Ian, I'd only slept with one guy, and I'm not – that is, I don't…"

"You don't what?" Jackson asked gently.

"If the three of us are together, I'll have to-to please both of you and I can barely please one guy in bed. The thought of trying to make both of you feel good and failing at it, makes me feel stupid and ashamed. I guarantee you that you guys will lose all interest in me, and then I'll… I'll be a failure."

Jackson glanced at him before leaning down and pressing a kiss against Chloe's mouth. Her ass pressed against Ian's dick and he couldn't resist cupping her breast and rubbing her still-hard nipple again as Jackson kissed her deeply.

Jackson broke the kiss and smiled at her. "Sweetheart, you misunderstand. The three of us together isn't about you pleasing us. It's about *us* pleasing *you*."

"I – what?" Chloe gave him a dazed look of incomprehension. Her mouth was slightly swollen from his and Jackson's kisses, and Ian wanted very badly to just pick her up and carry her to the car. They'd take her back to their place and show her exactly what she'd been missing out on.

Jackson glanced into the empty dining room behind them before his fingers traced the button on Chloe's jeans. "The only thing we want is to watch you coming on our cocks and our fingers and our mouths."

Chloe's soft little moan set Ian's nerve endings on fire. "You don't want to come?"

He bent his head and nipped her earlobe. "Of course we do, and we will. But you don't have to worry about pleasing us, baby. Trust me – just thinking about being in your hot little pussy makes me want to come."

"Oh God," Chloe's hips arched when Jackson rubbed her pussy through her jeans. "I – I don't want to disappoint you."

"You won't, honey." Jackson glanced at him. "Spread your legs for me, Chloe."

"We can't. There are people here and…"

"No one can see us." Jackson nipped at her bottom lip before unbuttoning her jeans. "Open your legs so we can show you what we want to do to you."

Ian turned her until her hip was pressed up against him. He pulled on one thigh and she spread her legs as Jackson moved in front of them. Chloe's slender body was blocked from the patio door, and Ian took another quick glance into the dining room. It was still empty, and he slid his hand into the back of her jeans and inside her panties as Jackson slipped his hand into the front of her panties.

Ian gave her ass a quick squeeze before sliding his hand between her legs. Her pussy was soaking wet and he made a low sound of approval. "Just as wet as I remembered, baby."

Chloe was already panting, and he pressed his mouth against hers, swallowing her squeak of surprise when he pushed two fingers inside of her.

"Cold," she moaned when he released her mouth.

"I know, Red." He sucked on her bottom lip before making two gentle thrusts with his fingers. "But you're so hot and tight, you'll warm me right up."

Chloe's eyes widened, and he knew the exact moment that Jackson touched her clit. Her sweet mouth dropped open and with one hand, she clutched at his arm that was wrapped around her, and at Jackson's arm with the other.

"Jackson, I…oh God."

"Does that feel good, honey?" Jackson kissed her as Ian licked and sucked at her neck.

"Yes," she moaned.

Ian kissed the side of her neck again and fucked her tight pussy with his fingers as Jackson rubbed her clit in firm circles. Her moans were getting louder, her soft body squirming and writhing between them. His cock was hard and throbbing, and he could see the bulge in Jackson's jeans even in the faint light.

"Come home with us tonight, Chloe," Jackson said. "Let us show you how it can be with both of us. If you don't like it, we can share you separately after that. But try being with us both tonight. Will you do that?"

When Chloe didn't reply, Ian stopped moving his fingers as Jackson did the same. She made a little whine of disappointment and Ian nipped her neck. "Answer him."

"Yes," she said immediately. "Yes, I want to try at least once. Please."

"That's our good girl," Jackson said. He started to rub Chloe's clit again and Ian shook his head. Disappointment crossed his face, but he pulled his hand out of Chloe's pants as Ian did the same. Jackson buttoned her jeans and straightened her sweater.

She stared up at Ian, her hip still pressing against his throbbing erection. "Ian? What? Why did you stop? I don't want you to stop."

"Shh, Red," he said.

"No!" She gave him a fierce look of anger and he wouldn't have been surprised if she stomped her foot. "I want to come."

"I know you do."

She glared at him before turning to Jackson. "Keep going."

"Not here, honey."

"Goddammit," she snapped.

"It's called edging, remember?" Ian said with a grin.

"I hate you, and your stupid edging," she said.

Jackson laughed, and Ian grinned at him. "She has a bit of a temper when she doesn't get what she wants."

"I do not," Chloe said. "But it's very rude to leave a woman on the edge of her…"

"Edge of her what?" Jackson said innocently.

"You know what." She poked him in the ribs, and he laughed before grabbing her hand and kissing the knuckles.

"We'll make you come as soon as you're at our place. Now, should we go back and join the party? I think -"

"No, we're not going back to the party." Chloe's face was turning red. "We're going back to your place, right now."

"Whatever you say, honey," Jackson replied. "Did you drive here?"

"Yes. Give me your address and I'll meet you there."

Ian shook his head. "We drove here together, so Jackson will drive you to our place in your car. Okay?"

He didn't think Chloe would change her mind, but having Jackson in the car and - knowing him - talking dirty to her, would definitely make it more difficult for her to change her mind.

"I'm not going to change my mind," Chloe said.

He flushed a little. "Yeah, I know. The roads are icy though and I'd feel better if you let Jackson drive your car."

"I don't want anyone knowing that we're leaving together," she said.

He hesitated, and Jackson said, "Okay. I'll text you the address. We'll say our goodbyes now, you wait ten minutes and then leave. Sound good?"

"Yes," Chloe said. "Thank you."

"Drive safe, Chloe." Jackson pressed a kiss against her mouth before stepping back inside.

Ian stared down at Chloe, his stomach churning. If she

didn't show up, if she changed her mind, he wasn't sure he'd be able to stop from driving to her place and begging her to let them into her bed.

Chloe gave him a small smile. "I promise I won't change my mind, Ian. I'll see you in a little bit."

"Okay." He kissed her and squeezed her ass. "It'll be all about you, baby, I promise."

She made a soft shudder of need before smiling at him. "See you soon."

CHAPTER 8

S he didn't get nervous or second guess her choice at all on the drive over. Hell, she didn't even second guess when she walked into their modest home and, without a word, Ian and Jackson brought her straight to a bedroom.

But when she saw the bed, she faltered a bit. Jackson was removing her coat and he kissed the back of her neck. "It's okay, honey."

She looked to Ian, needing his reassurance as well. He smiled at her and squeezed her hand. "You have nothing to worry about, Red."

Easy for him to say. He'd done this before.

She took a deep breath. Okay, she could do this. She could be with two men at once and make both of them feel like sexy studs and…

Sexy studs? Christ, do not attempt to engage in dirty talk with them. Do you hear me, Chloe?

Agreed. Her dirty talk skills were, well, frankly they were non-existent. The one time she'd tried with her ex, he'd laughed until her embarrassment was almost painful.

She realized Ian had moved away from her. He was, in

fact, sitting down in a cozy looking armchair that was in the corner closest to the bed.

"Ian? What-what are you doing?" She asked.

"Just making himself comfortable." Jackson's arms slid around her waist and he pressed his cock against her ass.

"I thought," she tried not to rub her butt against his dick, but failed miserably, "we were all going to…you know."

"Ian and I talked on the drive over and we decided," Jackson cupped both her breasts, "that it would be best if Ian just watched this time. There's no pressure for you to please both of us, and it'll ease you into the idea of being with us both."

She didn't want to admit it, but the idea was appealing to her. She turned her gaze to Ian. "Are you sure?"

He nodded. "Yeah, baby, I'm positive." His gaze dropped to her tits, watching as Jackson cupped them gently. "I like to watch. Hop up on the bed and show me how you look with Jackson's dick in your pussy."

She shuddered all over as fresh wetness soaked her already-dripping panties. She didn't object when Jackson pulled her shirt over her head. He kissed her bare shoulder before swiftly and efficiently removing her bra, jeans, and socks. He left her panties on when she shook her head.

"Not yet, okay?"

"Whatever you want, honey."

She stood next to the bed, fighting her urge to cover her tits with her arms and staring at Ian as Jackson undressed behind her. Was she really going to do this? Was she going to let Jackson fuck her while Ian watched?

"You okay, Chloe?" Jackson slid his arm around her waist and nuzzled her neck. She leaned back against him, her gaze still on Ian.

"Yes. Maybe a little nervous."

"Don't be. I just want to make you feel so good."

She turned and smiled up at him. "I know you will. In fact, I... holy shit, are you kidding me?"

Her gaze had dropped to Jackson's cock and she took a step back. "Seriously?"

"What's wrong?" Jackson gave her a worried look before glancing at Ian.

"I mean, what are the odds that you'd have a magnum-sized dick too?" She turned to Ian. "Do you base your friends on who can match you in dick size?"

Both Ian and Jackson burst into laughter. She blushed but turned back to Jackson. "I'm serious. What are the odds of you both having abnormally large penises?"

"They're not abnormally large," Jackson said.

"Mine is," Ian replied.

"Shut up, Ian," Jackson said with a grin. He pulled Chloe up against him and kissed her. God, she loved the way he kissed. She loved Ian's kisses as well, but there was something about the way Jackson kissed that made her feel safe and protected and... horny as hell.

She returned his kiss, running her hands over the big muscles in his back as he cupped her ass through her panties and pressed her up against him. When Jackson trailed kisses down her throat, she glanced at Ian. He was watching them intently, one big hand rubbing his cock through his jeans. She gave him a shy smile before Jackson lifted her and set her down on the bed.

He laid next to her and she stared up at him as he traced one finger around her beaded nipple. "You're so beautiful, Chloe."

"So are you," she whispered.

He bent his head and licked her nipple before sucking it into his mouth. She moaned and clutched at his head, closing her eyes and arching her back as Jackson released her nipple with a wet pop, and moved to her left one. He teased it into an aching hardness, and she couldn't resist sneaking another look at Ian.

His big body was still reclined in the chair, one hand rubbing almost lazily at his crotch as he watched Jackson suck on her nipples. Fresh lust flared in her belly and when Jackson pressed his thigh between her legs, she rubbed her pussy against it.

His cock was pressed against her belly and she wrapped her fingers around it and stroked him from root to tip. He groaned against her breast before raising his head. "Fuck, Chloe, you've got me ready to explode. I want to taste you."

She lifted her hips and let him tug her panties down her legs. He dropped them over the side of the bed and studied her pussy until she blushed. "Jackson, are you…"

"Shh, honey, let me look at you first." He pushed on her thighs and she widened them, watching his face as he studied her wet pussy. "So pretty and wet."

He traced the tips of his fingers over her wet pussy lips before glancing at Ian. Chloe followed his gaze, her heart hammering in her chest. Ian smiled at both of them.

"Eat her pussy, Jackson. Make her come all over your face."

Jackson immediately moved down the bed. She braced her feet on the bed and kept her legs pressed tightly closed, feeling nervous and a little unsure. She barely knew Jackson. Was she really going to let him get up close and personal with her lady parts? Oral sex with her ex had always made her feel self-conscious and a bit weird, and that was after knowing him for years.

Jackson knelt at the end of the bed and rubbed his big hands up and down her thighs. "Show me your pussy, honey."

"Jackson, I'm not sure this is a good idea."

"Chloe."

Her gaze swivelled to Ian. He was leaning forward and he gave her a steady look. "Spread your legs and show Jackson your pussy."

Her legs parted almost immediately. Ian nodded in satisfaction and leaned back, his hand rubbing at his cock through his jeans again as she turned her gaze back to Jackson. He was staring at her pussy, and she chewed on her bottom lip.

"Jackson, you don't have – oh my God!"

Jackson had leaned down and licked her pussy from her aching hole to the top of her throbbing clit. He smiled up at her. "You taste delicious, Chloe."

"Again," she demanded.

He grinned and stretched out on his stomach between her legs, his hands sliding under her to grip her ass. His warm tongue settled on her clit, and she squealed with pleasure, her hands gripping his head.

Her self-consciousness, her worry that she would somehow mess this moment up, disappeared under an overwhelming tide of pure pleasure and need. She rocked her pussy against Jackson's face, his dark stubble a delicious burn against her wet lips. He sucked on her clit and she cried out, trying not to yank on his hair as her legs trembled and her body moved steadily toward her release.

As Jackson sucked on her clit and slid one thick finger into her pussy, she turned her head to the left. She sucked in a harsh gasping breath. Ian had unbuttoned his jeans and taken his impressively thick cock out. He was rubbing it with harsh strokes, watching as Jackson licked and sucked.

When his gaze lifted to her face and she saw the dark lust, she came immediately. She moaned Jackson's name and then Ian's, her hips rising and falling against Jackson's tongue as he licked her through her orgasm. She trembled wildly as Jackson straightened. He wiped his face on the sheet then reached into the nightstand and brought out a condom. She watched him roll it on and glanced at Ian again before giving Jackson a tentative smile. "Do you mind if I'm on top?"

Despite how wet she was, despite the ease with which she'd taken Ian's equally impressive dick earlier, she was still nervous, and she wanted to control the pace.

"No." Jackson relaxed on his back before patting his lap. "Climb on, gorgeous."

She smiled and straddled him. She grasped his cock and made a few long, firm strokes. Jackson groaned before pushing her hand away. "Sweetheart, I need to fuck you. Right now."

She rose up on her knees. Like Ian, Jackson helped lift her a little, the muscles in his biceps bulging. She grasped his cock and pressed the wide head against her opening. He slid in and she made a low moan of pleasure as she slowly sank down over his entire length.

"So good," she moaned.

"I want you to come on my cock, honey. Will you do that for me?" Jackson reached up and cupped her breast.

"Yes," she panted. "Yeah, I'd really like that."

He grinned at her and she gave him a shy smile before bracing her hands on his chest. He met each of her strokes with a hard thrust of his hips.

"Don't come, okay?" She couldn't stop the plea from slipping out. "I'll be quick, don't come."

"I won't," Jackson groaned. "Just fuck me, honey. Fuck me nice and hard."

She did as he asked, bouncing up and down as he thrust into her. His cock felt as good as Ian's, and she let her head fall back, staring wide-eyed at the ceiling as Jackson gave her every inch of his cock.

She lost track of how long he let her ride him, she forgot about Ian watching them fuck, she didn't care about anything but taking want she wanted from her. What only Jackson could give her.

She dug her nails into his chest and ground herself down on his hard cock. "Oh God, that's good," she whispered. "That's so good. I think, I think I …"

Her second orgasm was as intense as her first. She cried out, her knees squeezing into his hips as her pussy squeezed around his cock. Jackson moaned a curse and his fingers dug into her hips as he pumped hard and fast. He made another harsh cry and she stared down at him, her body trembling and her pussy milking his dick as he came.

He stroked her thighs with shaking hands and she leaned forward and rested her forehead against his chest. His harsh breath ruffled her hair and he stroked her braid. "God, Chloe, that was so good."

"It was," she agreed. She slid off of him and as he removed the condom and threw it into the wastebasket next to the bed, she suddenly remembered Ian. She whipped her head to the left, suddenly weirdly certain that he would be gone.

He wasn't. He was still sitting in the chair, still rubbing his cock, and the look of intense need on his face made her body react. Her pussy squeezed uselessly around nothing and a wave of longing washed over her. She wouldn't come again, her body was too sensitive, but she wanted Ian inside of her with a desperation she didn't quite understand.

"Ian," she whispered. "I want you too."

"It's fine." His voice was hoarse, his face a little crazed looking as he stared at her naked body and stroked his dick. "Next time, baby."

"No, now," she said.

He hesitated, but when Jackson reached into the night-stand and pulled out another condom, Ian stood and quickly undressed. He joined them at the bed, but when she started to sit up, he shook his head and pressed her lightly onto her back.

"I want to be on top," she said.

"Not this time, baby."

"Ian, I…" she glanced at Jackson. He was stretched out on his side on the far side of the bed, his head propped up in one hand, and he gave her a lazy smile.

"Trust him, Chloe. He won't hurt you."

She licked her lips before relaxing against the bed and opening her legs enough for Ian to kneel between them. She reached for Jackson's hand. "Don't leave, okay?"

"I'm not going anywhere, sweetheart."

She had a moment to think about how incredibly ironic it was that the thought of Jackson leaving while Ian fucked her was upsetting, before the head of Ian's dick pushing at her entrance snapped her attention back to him.

"Open your legs, Red. Let me in."

She let her legs drop open wide, shuddering with pleasure when Jackson's big, warm hand rubbed her inner thigh briefly. "That's a good girl, Chloe. Ian's going to make you come so hard, honey."

She stared up at Ian. She wouldn't come, and she hoped it didn't upset him. He smiled down at her as he propped himself up on his hands above her. His cock probed and pressed and then he was filling her up, stretching her inner walls even though she'd just taken Jackson.

"Fuck," Ian hissed out air between his teeth. "She's so goddamn tight."

"She is," Jackson said. "Tight and wet."

Ian pressed in more. Despite having taken him once before, she was weirdly nervous about him fitting. She pressed her knees against his hips and he shook his head. "No, baby. Wide open for me. Right now."

She immediately let her legs drop open again. He smiled his approval and with a low grunt, sheathed himself entirely. She squirmed at the thick invasion as her pussy tried to adjust again.

Jackson's hand cupped her breast, his long fingers playing with her nipples. "Relax, honey."

Her back arched and she clutched at Ian's naked back when Jackson pinched her nipple. It sent pleasure straight down to her pussy and she made a little squeal of surprise.

Jackson soothed her nipple with the ball of his thumb before moving his hand away. She stared up at Ian as he made a few slow and gentle thrusts. "Are you good?"

"Yes," she whispered. "Please."

He smiled at her and she clenched around him when he began a quick and steady pace. He thrust in and out, each thick slide of his cock sending fresh pleasure through her body. To her complete and utter shock, she could feel a third orgasm starting. Unlike the first two, this one was a slow and gradual ascent into pleasure.

As Ian thrust harder and faster, she wrapped her legs around his waist, resting her feet against the back of his thighs. She cupped his upper arms, her hands squeezing the hard muscles there as she met each of his thrusts. Her orgasm drew closer, and she gasped and bit down on her bottom lip when it washed over her in gentle, rhythmic waves that made her body tremble.

"You look fucking gorgeous when you come, Chloe."

Jackson's low murmur of approval made her reach for him with one hand. He held her hand as she stared up at Ian.

His eyes were closed and he made a low groan before thrusting deep and staying there. She watched his face as he came, loving the look of pure bliss on his face.

She'd done that to him. She'd brought him and Jackson as much pleasure as they'd brought her, and she was weirdly proud of herself. She made a soft grunt of pain when Ian collapsed on top of her.

"Jesus, Ian, don't crush her, dickhead." Jackson was shoving at Ian's arm. The big man rolled off of her and Jackson pulled her to the middle of the bed. Ian stretched out beside her, panting harshly and staring at the ceiling as Jackson pressed a kiss against Chloe's mouth.

"You okay, Chloe?"

She nodded and glanced at Ian. "Are you guys, uh, okay? I mean, was it good for you?"

"Fucking amazing," Ian said hoarsely. He slipped off the condom and chucked it into the wastebasket.

"What he said," Jackson said with a low laugh.

"Good. Um, should I leave now?" Chloe wasn't exactly sure what the rules were when it was just about the sex and nothing more. She was pretty certain though that sleeping over wasn't part of the deal.

"You are not leaving this bed." Ian scowled at her.

"What Ian means to say is that we would love it if you spent the night. If you want to stay with us." Jackson gave Ian a hard look when Ian opened his mouth.

Ian shut his mouth with a snap as Chloe gave him a tentative look. "If you're sure."

"We are." Jackson pressed a kiss against her forehead. "Are you thirsty?"

"A little."

"I'll get you some water." Ian stood up and headed for the

door. He paused in the doorway and said, "You're spending the night, Chloe. No arguments."

He left as Jackson made a low groan and threw one of the pillows at him. "Jesus, Ian, you can't go all fucking caveman on her."

He grinned at Chloe before kissing the tip of her nose. "You'll have to excuse Ian. Sometimes he thinks being a cop gives him the right to tell the rest of us what to do."

Chloe smiled and didn't object when Jackson tugged her up against his warm body. "That's okay. I'm glad you want me to spend the night."

Jackson pressed a kiss against her forehead and she snuggled closer to him. God, it felt so right to be in his arms.

When Ian returned five minutes later with not only water, but some fruit as well, she was sitting up against the headboard, tucked under the covers with Jackson on her right. Ian handed Jackson the tray before sliding into the bed on her left. She helped him arrange the pillow behind his back as Jackson opened a bottle of water and handed it to her.

She drank some water, and Jackson held out the strawberries. "Do you like strawberries?"

"Love them." She popped one into her mouth.

"How are you feeling?" Ian drank some water before resting one big hand on her thigh.

"Fantastic." She ate another strawberry before giving him a cheeky smile. "I came three times. Three times!"

Jackson laughed. "We remember."

"I've never come three times before. Usually I can barely come once. You guys have magic dicks."

Shit, her high from her orgasms was making her stupid.

"Uh, sorry."

"For what?" Ian rubbed her thigh.

"I'm talking like an idiot."

"You're not." Jackson ate a strawberry.

"I really enjoyed it," she said.

"We did too." Jackson kissed her forehead before popping another strawberry into his mouth.

They finished the fruit and their water in companionable silence. She leaned against the headboard staring at Ian's big hand on her thigh. When Jackson took her hand and squeezed it, she smiled up at him.

"Chloe, have you had anal sex before?"

"Jackson," Ian said. "you can't just open up with that. Jesus."

Chloe's face was bright red, but she shook her head. "No, uh, I haven't. I'm sorry."

Jackson smiled at her. "No need to apologize. Is it something you'd like to try?"

"Honestly, I've never really given it all that much thought. My previous partner never asked me for it and, so..."

She swallowed hard. "But, I guess if I'm going to be with both of you, that's something I have to do."

"No," Jackson said, "you don't have to do anything you don't want to do. There are other things we can do together. But, it's good to be open and have honest communication about what each person likes or doesn't like."

"Well, I don't know if I like it or not," Chloe said, "but..."

"But, what, Red?" Ian squeezed her thigh reassuringly.

"I've seen threesomes in, uh, porn, where the guys take her both at once and it looks...painful. They're always so rough and I don't want things wrecked down there."

"It wouldn't be like that," Ian said. "Jackson would be gentle."

She stared up at Jackson. "So, it would be you who, um…"

"Generally, yes," Jackson said. "Sometimes we switch it up. But I promise we wouldn't hurt you and we wouldn't be rough. I'll go slow and at the pace you need."

Chloe stared at the water bottle in her hand as Ian rubbed her thigh again. "You can think about it for as long as you need, Chloe. Okay? It isn't something you have to answer right away and if the answer is no, that isn't a problem."

She glanced at Jackson who nodded and said, "It won't be an issue if your answer is no. I promise."

"My answer isn't no," she said. "I want to at least try."

She could see the delight on Jackson's face and any lingering doubt disappeared. Ian rubbed her thigh. "Red, you don't have to say yes because you think that's what we want to hear."

"I'm not," she said. "I appreciate your concern, but I wouldn't do something I'm not comfortable with doing just to make two dudes I'm having sex with, happy. I want to try it."

Jackson cupped her face and turned her toward him. He pressed a kiss against her mouth. "Thank you, honey."

"You're welcome."

He kissed her again, this one slow and thorough. It brought on a new wave of lust and she arched her back when Jackson tugged down the covers and cupped her bare breast. He flicked at her hardening nipple with his thumb as he explored her mouth.

The feel of Ian's warm mouth on her back sent shivers up and down her spine. She moaned into Jackson's mouth as Ian pressed up against her. His cock was hard against her lower back and he slipped his hand under the covers and traced his rough fingers up and down one bare thigh.

When Jackson released her mouth, she turned her head,

wanting Ian's kisses. He kissed her, sucking on her bottom lip as Jackson bent his head and sucked on her nipple. She leaned against Ian's hard chest, spreading her legs eagerly when Ian pulled on her thigh. He rubbed her clit in lazy circles as he watched Jackson lick her nipples into hard buds.

She clutched at Jackson's head. "So, uh, you have lubrication for the, um, anal sex, right?"

He lifted his head and smiled at her. "Yes, but I'm not fucking your ass tonight, Chloe."

"I'm fine with it," she said. "I mean, I'm willing to try and…ohhh."

Ian had given her clit a delightful little pinch and she suddenly forgot what she was saying.

Jackson tugged on both her nipples. "Not tonight, honey. You need to be stretched first and that'll take at least a few days."

"How-how will you stretch…oh my God, Ian!" She squirmed against him when he pushed his thick finger inside of her. "Oh God, that's good."

"With my fingers and with plugs." Jackson licked around one throbbing nipple before sucking hard on it.

Chloe moaned happily when Ian rubbed her clit with his thumb. Jackson was still lavishing attention on her breasts, and she was completely overwhelmed by their touch and their scent and the warmth of their bodies. A girl could get used to this threesome thing very easily.

"Is she wet, Ian?"

Ian groaned. "So fucking wet. She's more than ready for your cock."

She whined in disappointment when Jackson moved away.

"Shh, Red," Ian said. "Come here."

He pushed the covers to the bottom of the bed before

spreading his legs. "Kneel between my legs, baby."

She did what he asked, kneeling between his thighs and feeling a remarkable lack of self-consciousness about her nudity. Ian found her beautiful. She knew he did. She stared at his thick cock. It rose up proudly from a nest of dark hair and she licked her lips as Ian reached out and tugged on the end of her braid.

"Unbraid your hair."

She yanked the hair elastic out, tossed it on the nightstand, and quickly unbraided her hair. Ian made a soft noise of approval. "Come here, baby."

She leaned forward, letting her breasts brush against his chest as he threaded his hand through her hair. He kissed her hard, angling his mouth over hers and forcing her mouth wide as he thrust his tongue between her lips. The head of his cock rubbed against her flat belly and she could feel his precum smearing across her skin.

He tugged her head back by her hair, running his thumb over her swollen bottom lip before smiling at her. "You're going to be a good girl and suck my cock, Chloe."

"Yes, Ian," she replied.

His nostrils flared, and he kissed her hard on the mouth again before leaning back against the headboard. She kissed across his chest, stopping to tease one flat nipple with her tongue. Ian growled and tugged on her hair. "My cock, now."

She wanted to tease and tempt, but the command in Ian's voice had her scooting back until her mouth was hovering over his cock. Still on her knees between his legs, she rested one hand on the bed next to his hip and gripped the base of his cock with the other.

He inhaled sharply at her touch and she smiled up at him before sliding her mouth down over his dick. When the head of his cock touched the back of her throat, she tightened her lips around him and sucked hard as she dragged her mouth back to the tip.

Ian hissed out a breath and when his hand tangled in her hair, she glanced up at him again. "Does it feel good, Ian?"

"So good, baby. You have no fucking idea. Keep sucking."

She glanced to her left. Jackson was standing next to the bed, his cock in his hand and he gave her a hungry look. "Suck his cock, honey. Right now."

She took his cock into her mouth again, hollowing her cheeks and sucking hard before tracing the ridge with tip of her tongue. Ian was moaning and panting, his hips rising up with every tug of her mouth. His hands were in her hair, holding it back from her face, and she loved the way it felt when he guided her mouth back and forth over his dick.

Her pussy was throbbing, and she reached between her legs, gasping when Ian gave her hair a particularly sharp yank. He pulled her mouth off his dick and shook his head. "No, baby. We're responsible for your orgasms. You don't touch yourself unless we say you can."

"Please, Ian." She licked her swollen lips.

"No," he repeated. "Keep your hands away from your pussy or I'll spank you, Red."

Fresh wetness dripped out of her pussy. Holy shit, was she turned on by that?

"Suck," Ian said. He wasn't gentle when he pushed her mouth back down over his cock and a small part of her was thrilled by it. She sucked on his cock, trying to ignore her urge to rub her clit. She gripped Ian's thigh instead, digging her fingers into it as she sucked and licked.

When she felt Jackson's hands grab her hips, she lifted her head. Ian let go of her hair and she stared at Jackson over her shoulder, one hand still gripping the base of Ian's dick.

"Jackson? What – what are you doing?"

He was kneeling behind her and he pushed her legs apart before rubbing her lower back. "Keep sucking Ian's cock."

"But, what -"

Ian's hands were back in her hair and he tugged her down to his cock. "Suck, Red. Right now."

She took his cock into her mouth, sucking hard as Jackson pressed up against her. She squealed around Ian's thick cock when the head of Jackson's dick pushed into her pussy. Her wetness smoothed a path for him and he pushed into her with one hard thrust.

She moaned again, and Ian tugged on her hair before reaching under her and pinching one nipple. "Keep your hot little mouth wrapped around my dick while Jackson fucks your pussy."

His crude words and the pinch of his fingers sent a line of fire from her breasts straight to her pussy. She wiggled against Jackson's cock, her mouth sucking hard on Ian's dick as Jackson drove in and out of her.

She moaned again when Jackson's fingers rubbed against her clit. She wanted to come desperately, but Jackson simply gathered some of her wetness before moving his fingers.

"Please!" Her voice was muffled around Ian's cock. He petted her hair and smiled at her.

"Not yet, baby."

She squealed again when Jackson's wet fingers rubbed against her back hole.

"Shh, honey," Jackson said. He gathered more wetness from her pussy and rubbed her tight little pucker before pressing his thumb against it.

When the tip of his thumb slipped inside of her, she stared wide-eyed at Ian. He gave her a distracted smile, his hips rising and falling with the rhythm of her mouth. "You're good, baby. It's good."

He glanced up at Jackson. "Fuck, I'm close. Make her come."

Jackson pushed his thumb in a little deeper. There wasn't any pain, but it felt strange to her. Still sucking Ian's cock, she wiggled a little bit and Jackson rubbed her ass. "Relax for me, Chloe."

She took a deep breath through her nose and tongued the head of Ian's cock as she relaxed her body. Jackson thrust a little harder, she could feel the beginning of her orgasm starting deep in her belly. Ian was thrusting hard into her mouth and she let him fuck her mouth as the pleasure of Jackson's cock distracted her from sucking.

"Fuck," Ian moaned. "Fuck, baby. Swallow all of my come. Swallow…"

His hand gripped her head tightly as his hips thrust up and his cock swelled. She swallowed eagerly when his hot come filled her mouth, and he made a low moan of approval. She pulled back and he wiped the come and spit from her lips before smiling at her.

"Good, baby. So good."

"Oh my God!" She cried out with pleasure when Jackson's hand wound in her hair. He pulled her head back and fucked her rapidly. She braced her hands on the bed on either side of Ian's big body, staring wide-eyed at the ceiling as Jackson took her hard and rough.

Her climax was building inside of her and she strained for it, the pleasure washing over her when Jackson pushed his thumb deep inside of her ass. She screamed, her body shaking and twitching as Jackson made a hoarse shout. He pushed in deep with his cock and his thumb, and she clenched around both as he shouted a curse and came. He thrust rapidly back and forth, his harsh breath blowing across her back, before he released her hair and eased out of her.

She immediately collapsed on top of Ian. He rubbed her back and brushed her hair out of her sweaty face. She watched as Jackson disposed of the condom before lying on the bed.

"Am I too heavy?" She mumbled.

Ian shook his head and she smiled dazedly at Jackson when he turned to face her. "That was super great."

He laughed, and she slithered off of Ian's body to the space on the bed between him and Jackson. Ian turned on his side and spooned her. Jackson pulled the covers up over all of them before sliding close enough that she could rest her head on his chest.

"Are you sure it's okay that I stay?"

Ian squeezed her breast and Jackson rubbed her hip. "You're staying right here with us. Go to sleep, Chloe."

"Yeah, okay." She yawned and snuggled closer to both men. It was ridiculously comfortable between their big bodies.

She yawned again. "Thank you. It was amazing."

"For us too. Go to sleep, baby." Ian pressed a kiss against the back of her shoulder.

CHAPTER 9

She eased quietly out of the bed. She had to pee like crazy, and she winced and rubbed at her thighs as she grabbed Jackson's t-shirt and slipped into it. There was no bathroom attached to the room, and she stepped out into the hallway. A bathroom was next door and she peed before washing her hands and staring at herself in the mirror.

She'd slept with two men last night. She'd sucked one man's cock while another fucked her, and she'd loved every single minute of it. She was tender this morning, and she resisted the urge to lift Jackson's shirt and study her crotch. Both Jackson and Ian were large, obviously she would be a little sore.

But you're still gonna let Jackson fuck you up the ass. If you think you're sore now, just wait.

She grimaced a little before smoothing her hair down. Even the thought of it being painful wasn't enough of a deterrent. It wasn't only about pleasing Jackson and Ian either. She wanted to try it, wanted to have both of them inside of her at once. She supposed that was a bit strange. Until last night, she'd never planned on sleeping with more than one man at a time, but now that she had the option... dammit, she wanted it.

She headed toward the kitchen. It was a little past seven and she had no idea if Jackson and Ian were morning people or not. But, she would make them breakfast as a way to say thanks for all the fantastic orgasms and then maybe they'd fuck her again. She smiled a little. She was already addicted to them and their big dicks.

Her purse was still sitting in the hallway and she snagged it as she walked into the kitchen. She grabbed her cell phone out of it, dismay filling her body when she saw the missed calls from her grandmother. She quickly called her back, pacing restlessly in the kitchen. The phone rang and rang and when the answering machine clicked on, she hung up and stuffed her phone back into her purse.

She ran back to the bedroom and grabbed her clothes from where they were scattered on the floor. She'd just gotten into her panties and bra when Ian sat straight up in the bed.

"What? What's wrong?"

His voice woke Jackson who sat up slowly and yawned. "Morning."

"Morning," Chloe said. "Um, I have to go."

"What? Why?" Ian threw back the covers and she shook her head.

"No, don't get up. It's still early, stay in bed."

She yanked her socks on and then tugged her jeans up. Jackson sat on the side of the bed, yawning and scratching his scalp as Ian ignored her and climbed out of bed.

"You don't have to leave, Chloe. If we said or did something last night that -"

"No, it has nothing to do with that. I – I have a personal thing that I need to take care of." She yanked her shirt over her head. "Thank you for last night, I had a good time."

"Chloe, wait," Ian said. "Tell us what's wrong."

She couldn't. She had shared all of her problems with Lori with her ex and look where that had gotten her. No, it was better to keep the family shit to herself. Jackson and Ian weren't interested in a relationship and if she shared too much, they'd drop her like a hot potato. They weren't interested in the personal problems of their fuck buddy.

"Have dinner with us tonight." Jackson was out of the bed now too, and she tried to ignore the way both of their cocks were standing at attention.

"Um, I'm not sure… can I, uh, get back to you on that?" She had no idea what was happening at her grandmother's or how long she would be there. Panic bit at her belly. Fuck, what if her grandmother was hurt? What if Lori had gone into a rage and Nana had tried to calm her down?

"I'm sorry. I have to go." Chloe grabbed her jacket and ran out of the room. She jammed her boots onto her feet and left the house. The air was bitterly cold, and she sprinted to her car, climbing in and starting it quickly. As she pulled out onto the street, she had one last glimpse of Ian, wearing a pair of shorts, standing in the doorway.

THE NEIGHBOUR TO THE RIGHT OF HER GRANDMOTHER'S house was sitting in a rocking chair on her front porch when Chloe parked in the driveway. As Chloe ran up the house, the woman yelled over, "I'm gonna call the cops next time! Do you hear me? I'll call the cops, I swear it."

"Nana? Are you okay?" Chloe used her key to open the front door. The odor of cigarette smoke and beer assaulted her, as well as the sour tang of vomit. She covered her nose, staring in disbelief at the living room. It was completely trashed, the books from the bookshelf covered the floor, her grandmother's ceramic figurines smashed in the fake fireplace. The couch cushions were on the floor as well and she studied the large cigarette burn in the closest one as panic clawed at her chest.

"Nana! Nana, where are you?"

She hurried down the hallway, glancing into the kitchen. It was trashed as well, dishes shattered in the sink and on the floor, food smeared on the walls and a large pool of vomit on the floor next to the stove.

"Nana! Nana, answer me!"

"Chloe, I'm here."

Relief washed over her, and she ran the rest of the way to her grandmother's bedroom. She tried the handle. It was locked, and she knocked on the door. "Nana, let me in."

She heard her grandmother shuffle across the room and the door unlocked with a quiet click. She opened the door and stared at her grandmother. "Nana, are you okay?"

Her grandmother nodded and then burst into tears. "Oh, Chloe, it was so awful. She was so-so angry last night. She scared me so bad."

"I'm sorry, Nana. I'm so sorry." Chloe hugged the old woman's frail body. Her grandma buried her face in her neck and sobbed.

"It's okay." She led her to the bed and sat down beside her. "Tell me what happened."

"She had a little too much to drink and she nodded off on the couch. Her cigarette burned the cushion and when I told her she had to pay to replace it, she got so angry." Nana's face was deathly pale. "She started screaming at me and then she-she broke all of my pretty figurines and she wrecked all the food I bought. I don't have any money for more food, Chloe. I spent all of it. What are we going to do?"

"It's okay. I'll buy you some more food," Chloe said. "Where's Lori?"

"She's in her room. I locked myself in here and she screamed and yelled for so long. Finally, when she stopped yelling, I checked on her. She was passed out in her bed, but I was afraid she was going to wake up, so I came back to my room and locked the door again."

She took a wavering breath. "Where were you, Chloe? I called and called and you didn't answer the phone. I was so afraid and you weren't there."

Guilt filled her belly.

"I'm sorry, Nana. I wasn't, uh, near my phone."

"I was so afraid," her grandmother whispered.

"I know. It's okay now." Chloe put her arm around her thin shoulders and rocked her back and forth. "It's okay. I'm here."

After a few minutes, she kissed the top of her grandmother's head. "Why don't you have a hot shower? I'll start cleaning up and then when I'm done, we'll go to the grocery store and pick up some more food for you. Okay?"

"Will you check on your sister first?"

Chloe sighed. "Yeah, I'll check on her."

She stood and helped her grandma to her feet. "Go and shower, Nana."

She left her grandmother in the bedroom and trudged down the hallway to her sister's room. The door was open, and she stuck her head into the room. Lori was lying face-down on the bed, one leg and arm hanging down over the side. She was wearing stained yoga pants and a ripped t-shirt, and her hair was a dirty, tangled mess.

She frowned and stepped into the room. That sour tang of vomit hit her again, and she grunted in disgust before picking her way across the clothes-covered floor. There was another puddle of vomit congealing on the floor next to Lori's bed. She grimaced and stared at Lori instead. Her face was pale and half-hidden by her dirty red hair.

She didn't seem to be breathing and a weird combination of alarm and relief swept through Chloe. Her hands shaking, she reached for Lori's neck. She made a soft shriek and stumbled back when Lori's mouth dropped open and she began to snore thickly.

Her heartbeat too fast and too high, Chloe stumbled back. She was alive. Of course she was alive. People like her didn't pass out and choke to death on their own vomit. No, they lived forever and continued to destroy the lives of everyone around them. They were too fucking selfish to die. Too -

Chloe, stop!

She caught sight of herself in the mirror and made a horrified little moan at the rage on her face. Oh my God, she didn't actually want her sister dead, did she? No, she didn't – couldn't – want that. It would make her a monster, if she did. She was just tired and upset and worried about her grandmother.

Weighed down by the guilt, she turned and staggered out of her sister's room.

"IAN, SHE DOESN'T WANT TO SEE US," JACKSON SAID. "SHE didn't answer any of my texts or yours. We're acting like crazy stalkers if we go up to her apartment."

Ian ignored him. He drummed his fingers on the steering wheel and stared at Chloe's apartment building. He was feeling unsettled and anxious, and the fact that Chloe had run out this morning and hadn't replied to any of their texts, was pinging every alarm bell he had.

"Something's wrong," he said to Jackson. "She was upset this morning when she left."

"Was she?" Jackson said. "She didn't seem upset to me."

Ian glared at him. "You don't pay attention to anything until you've had at least one cup of coffee. Trust me, she was upset."

"Okay, maybe she was. But, she obviously didn't want us to know what was wrong, or she would have told us," Jackson said. "Listen, I want to see her as much as you do, but we have to remember that she's sweet and a bit naïve. We probably overwhelmed her a little last night, and she needs some space to process. I'll talk to her on Monday and – Ian, Jesus, Ian, get back in the car."

Ian slammed the door shut and when Jackson got out and followed him, he locked the doors before shoving his car keys into his pocket. Jackson was still talking, but he ignored him and pushed the buzzer for Chloe's apartment.

After a few seconds, she said, "Hello?"

"It's Ian. Let me in."

"Ian? What-what are you doing here?"

"Let me in," he repeated.

"Is, uh, is Jackson with you?"

"Yes," Jackson said. "Hey, Chloe."

"Um, hi."

"Buzz us in," Ian said.

"Ian, cool it," Jackson said. "Chloe, would you mind if we came upstairs for a bit?"

There was silence and then she said, "I'm pretty busy right now. I've got some work to do, and I still need to cook supper and -"

"I'll cook you supper," Ian said. "Open the door, Chloe. I'm not leaving until you let us in."

"For fuck's sake, Ian," Jackson muttered. "What the fuck is wrong with you?"

The door buzzed, and Ian grabbed the handle, yanking it open quickly before Chloe could change her mind.

They rode the elevator in silence, but when the doors opened on her floor, Jackson said, "Ian, just be fucking cool, man. You're gonna blow it for us if you act like a goddamn jealous boyfriend."

"I'm worried about her," Ian snapped as he walked to her apartment. "Christ, aren't you?"

"She's a grown woman who doesn't need to be rescued," Jackson said. "I know you like helping and protecting people, but this is over the top, even for you."

"She needs us." Ian knocked on the door before Jackson could reply.

The door opened, and he stared at Chloe's sweet face. She was pale, and the skin under her eyes was puffy like she'd been crying.

"Hi," she said.

"Hi, baby."

Her eyes watered and without saying anything else, he stepped into her apartment and put his arms around her. She smelled like cleaning solution and he pressed a kiss against the top of head. "Tell me what's wrong."

"Nothing." Her voice was muffled against his chest and he resisted the urge to hang onto her when she pushed away from him.

She studied the floor as Jackson said. "Have you been crying? Tell us where you went this morning."

Ian resisted the urge to tell Jackson he told him so. At least his best friend was finally on the goddamn same page as him.

"I'm fine." Chloe backed away before heading down the

hallway to the kitchen. "I'm actually really busy tonight so if you don't mind, I don't have time for sex tonight. Maybe we can plan for this week sometime?"

"We're not here for sex." Ian followed her into the kitchen with Jackson right behind him. "We're here because we're worried about you."

"You don't need to be." Chloe was standing at the counter, her fingers gripping the edge of the sink and her back to them. "I'm perfectly fine. Maybe a little tired."

He could hear the tears in her voice and he glanced at Jackson. They crossed the kitchen and flanked her. Jackson rubbed her back and said, "Honey, tell us what's wrong."

"It's been a bad day, okay? And now I'm trying to work on my sketches for Amy because she wants them tomorrow and I can't – I can't do it and my chance to be a designer is over and-and-and..."

She burst into loud sobs. Ian pulled her into his arms and hugged her tightly as Jackson rubbed her back. She buried her face in his neck and he made soothing sounds while Jackson continued to rub her back.

"It'll be okay, baby." Ian picked her up and carried her to a kitchen chair. He sat down and set her on his lap. Jackson crouched next to them and rubbed her thighs as she leaned her head against Ian's chest and cried.

After only a few minutes, her crying stopped. There was a box of tissues on the counter, and Jackson grabbed the box and held it out to her. She took a few tissues and wiped her face before whispering, "Thank you."

"You're welcome. Do you feel better?" Jackson asked.

Chloe sat up on his lap and Ian stroked her pony tail before he cupped the nape of her neck, massaging lightly as she nodded. "Yes. I'm very sorry. I know this is hard to believe, but I don't normally cry this much. I'm not usually like this."

"We know," Jackson said. "Do you want to tell us why you're upset?"

She hesitated, her gaze meeting Ian's briefly before she stared at her lap. "No, I really don't."

"That's okay, you don't have to," Jackson said.

Ian glared at him and Jackson shook his head before squeezing Chloe's hand. "Do you want us to leave?"

"We're not leaving," Ian said before he could stop himself.

"Ian," Jackson's tone was full of exasperation, "knock if off, asshole. What are you going to do? Tie yourself to the damn chair?"

"I'm a cop, I'll just use my handcuffs," Ian said.

Chloe giggled, and relief swept through him at the sound. He held her a little closer as she said, "Now I have an image of you handcuffed to my kitchen chair."

"Kinky," Jackson said.

She giggled again, and Ian kissed her cheek. "Anytime you want to handcuff me to a piece of your furniture, just say the word. I'll hand them over."

This time she laughed and pressed a kiss against his mouth. "That's so sweet."

Jackson sat down in a chair across from them. "Hey, I'm willing to be handcuffed too, you know. Ian doesn't get to have all the fun."

"So tempting," Chloe said.

Jackson grinned at her and they lapsed into silence for a few minutes. Ian glanced at the clock on the microwave. It was almost six, and when Chloe's stomach growled, he kissed her forehead again. "Go sit on Jackson's lap, baby."

She stood and walked the couple of steps to Jackson. He

pulled her down into his lap and kissed her on the mouth. "Hey, beautiful."

"Hi." She put her arms around his shoulders and snuggled into him as Ian stood and opened the fridge.

"You don't have to make dinner," she said.

Ian shrugged. "I like cooking and Jackson and I haven't eaten either."

"Do you want us to stay?" Jackson said.

Ian wanted to smack him, but instead opened up the freezer and checked out its contents.

"Yes," Chloe said. "I do. But I really do need to try and work on the sketches for Amy."

Ian turned around. Chloe was staring at the sketch book on the table and he said, "Why don't you work on your sketches while I cook dinner."

"That's a great idea." Jackson patted Chloe's thigh. "If you don't mind letting me use your laptop, I could actually do a little work myself on the storefront. We can work while Ian does what he does best… cooks us dinner."

"Actually, what I'm best at is arresting people," Ian said. "Cooking is a close second though."

Chloe laughed, and Ian grinned at her. He wasn't used to making women laugh, it was Jackson's job to charm them, but he loved Chloe's laugh. Loved that he was helping cheer her up.

"What do you say? Sound good?" Jackson said.

"It sounds perfect." Chloe replied.

———

"THAT SERIOUSLY WAS THE BEST CHICKEN PARMESAN I'VE ever had." Chloe pushed away her empty plate and smiled at Ian.

"Thank you." He finished off his water before stacking the plates.

"I'll clean up," Chloe said. "You cooked, Jackson and I will clean. Right?"

She poked Jackson when he didn't reply. He had finished his dinner and was holding her sketch book, flipping through the pages. "These are really good, Chloe."

"Oh, um, thanks." She carried the plates and silverware to the dishwasher and loaded it as both Ian and Jackson studied the sketches she'd finished.

It had been weirdly comforting to have Ian and Jackson there while she worked. The only sounds were the tapping of her laptop as Jackson worked and the occasional low murmur from Ian. Secretly, she found it adorable that he talked to himself while he cooked. The drawings, which only half an hour earlier had been impossible to do, flowed easily and she'd created not only another two dresses, but a blouse and skirt combo that she'd been envisioning for a while. She needed to make a few more tweaks to the sketches, but they were designs she'd be proud to give to Amy tomorrow.

Ian moved up behind her and slipped an arm around her waist. He kissed the side of her neck. "You're really talented, Red."

She smiled at him. "I'm not sure about that. I didn't get accepted to a single design school. But, Amy's being really sweet and giving me a chance, and I appreciate it."

"Because she knows good work when she sees it." Jackson closed her sketchbook and set it on the table.

She flushed at their praise, or maybe it was the way Ian's big hand was rubbing her lower belly. When he slipped his hand inside her yoga pants, she parted her legs. He cupped her pussy through her panties and rubbed lightly. "Are you sore, baby?"

"A little," she admitted.

Ian turned her so she was facing Jackson. Jackson smiled at her, his gaze dropping to her crotch as Ian rubbed slow circles. "Maybe Ian should kiss it better."

She moaned when Ian sucked on her earlobe. "Would you like that, Red?"

"Yes," she whispered. Jackson stood and ambled over to them. He traced her hard nipple through her shirt and bra with one long finger.

She rubbed her ass against Ian's growing erection before cupping Jackson's dick through his jeans. He smiled at her and gave her nipple a little pinch. "I think it's time we got you naked and in your bed between us. What do you think?"

"I think that's a great idea." Her voice was breathless.

"Her panties are soaked," Ian said to Jackson.

"Well, that can't be comfortable," Jackson said with a small grin. "Let's get you out of those wet panties, and -"

Her cell phone rang and she stiffened against Ian.

"Ignore it, baby." He rubbed her pussy a little harder.

"I can't." She tugged on his arm. "Let go of me, please."

He released her immediately, and she walked away from both of them and grabbed her phone off the counter. Her stomach dropped, and she glanced at them. "Excuse me."

She hurried out of the kitchen and into the living room. Her apartment was on the smaller side and she kept her voice pitched low as she answered the phone.

"Hey, how are you feeling?"

"We're out of beer. You bought food, but no beer," Lori said petulantly.

"I told you before that I wouldn't buy booze for you."

"It's not for me, it's for Nana."

Chloe would have laughed if she hadn't felt so sick to her stomach. "Nana doesn't drink. Besides, the only reason I bought food was because you destroyed it all last night when you were drunk."

"I wasn't drunk."

"Lori," Chloe rubbed at her forehead, "you were passed out when I got there. There were pools of vomit all through the house, you destroyed Nana's stuff, including her figurines and her couch. You scared Nana badly. You have to stop drinking or you have to move out of Nana's place. She can't afford to -"

"I was sick!" Lori snarled into the phone. "I have the stomach flu, all right?"

"So, the stomach flu made you throw a fit and destroy all of Nana's stuff?"

"You're such a bitch, Chloe. You have all the fucking cash in the world, but you won't help our grandmother or -"

"I just bought her two weeks' worth of food, Lori. Don't talk to me about not helping. You could be helpful and quit drinking and get a goddamn job to help support her. But you won't because you're a selfish alcoholic who doesn't care about anything but how she can get her next drink."

"I have a job, you stupid bitch!" Lori shouted.

"Exchanging sex for booze is not a job." Chloe's voice was rising, and she tried to tamp it down as anger surged through her. "Prostituting yourself out is a new low, even for you, Lori. You need to get your shit together or move out of Nana's before you hurt her."

Lori burst into tears. "I would never hurt her. You're so awful, Chloe! Why are you so awful to me?"

Chloe rubbed at her temples. The anger, the fake crying, it was all a part of Lori's manipulation, and she wasn't at all surprised when her grandmother came on the line.

"Chloe?"

"Nana, put Lori back on the phone."

"I won't. You're so mean to her sometimes, Chloe. She's your sister."

"She's a drunk who is making your life miserable. You need to kick her out, Nana. If you don't -"

"Enough, Chloe," her Nana said sharply. "We're a family and in this family, we help each other."

"I am helping," Chloe said. "I came over and cleaned up the house. I bought you groceries. What more do you want from me, Nana?"

She hated the whine in her voice, hated how she craved her Nana's approval even now.

"I want you to be kind to your sister. I want you to recognize that she's doing the best she can."

"She isn't. She's not even trying, and you know that. She's dangerous to you, Nana. You have to kick her out before -"

"Stop it!" Now her grandmother burst into tears, but unlike her sister's, these were despairingly genuine. "Stop being so horrible, Chloe! Why would you be so hurtful to your own grandmother?"

"Nana, I'm sorry," Chloe said. "I'm not trying to hurt you, but you need to accept that it isn't good to have Lori around. She isn't going to change."

"Maybe you're ready to give up on your own sister, but I'm not," her grandmother sobbed. "I'm so ashamed of you, Chloe."

She ended the call before Chloe could reply. She stared at the screen of her phone before shoving it into her pocket and burying her face in her hands. Her cheeks were hot and the dinner she'd eaten was like a stone in her stomach.

She wanted to cry. She wanted to vomit. She wanted to forget that she even had a sister and just live her goddamn life.

"Red?"

She whipped around, staring in dismay at Ian and Jackson. They were standing in the doorway of the living room, and she backed up a step as shame and anger boiled together in her stomach.

"It's rude to eavesdrop," she said.

"We know you're upset about your sister. Do you want to talk about it?" Jackson said.

"No." She took a deep breath. "Let's go to the bedroom."

Jackson glanced at Ian, and she could almost see the silent communication between them.

"I don't want to talk about it, so let's finish what we started in the kitchen, okay?" She snapped.

Ian shook his head. "No, baby. Sex is the last thing you need right now. Come to the kitchen and we'll make you tea and you can tell us what happened."

"I don't want tea, I want sex," she said. "If you don't want to give that to me, then you should leave."

She waited for them to get angry and when they didn't, it only made her feel worse.

"Honey," Jackson said, "let us -"

Her fight with Lori, her grandmother's disappointment, and her own self-doubt over what was the right thing to do, was too much to handle. Their refusal to fuck her and let her forget about her goddamn sister for one night made her normally placid temper snap.

"Enough!" She glared at the both of them. "We agreed that this was just sex between us, remember? This isn't a relationship and I don't appreciate you trying to change the rules. I'm not looking for a boyfriend or *boyfriends*, okay? Either we go back to my bedroom and fuck, or the both of you can leave."

There was a moment of silence and then Ian said. "Good night, Chloe."

She folded her arms across her chest and kept her body ramrod straight as Jackson sighed and ran a hand through his thick hair. "Chloe, could you -"

Ian put a hand on his arm. "It's time to leave, Jackson."

Jackson studied her. "Yeah, okay. Good night, Chloe. I'll see you at the office tomorrow."

"Good night." She didn't walk them to the door. She couldn't. If she did, she might break down and beg them to stay. Might be tempted to tell them everything. They were so good at comforting her. She wanted their comfort, craved it, but if she told them what happened, she'd be letting Lori into their lives and nothing good ever came from that.

When she heard the front door shut, she sank to the floor and buried her head in her hands again. She wanted to cry, but the tears didn't come. They had left and it was her fault. She was trying to protect them from Lori and her toxicity, trying to keep her sister from ruining one of the few bright spots in her life, and in doing so she had destroyed it anyway.

She climbed to her feet and walked slowly toward the bedroom. She had wrecked her friendship with both Ian and Jackson, as well as her chance to keep sleeping with them, and she could only hope that Jackson would still be willing to work with her.

CHAPTER 10

"These look great, Chloe." Amy set down her sketch book as Chloe gave her a nervous look.

"So, will you be sending them in the package to Julien and Pierre?"

"Actually," Amy said, "Julien and Pierre will be here next week."

"Really?"

"Apparently they have some other business in the city and decided they'd drop in and meet with us as well. I'll show them some designs for the new casual line, yours included, and you and Jackson will join us for a meeting about the marketing plan and the storefront."

Amy turned to her laptop. "That reminds me, I need to schedule a meeting with Jackson and Luke this afternoon so we can give Jackson the heads up. I know Luke mentioned at family dinner last night that he was really happy with Jackson's plans for the website store, but he'll want to go over the details and maybe even have a test site they can show Julien and Pierre. Do you think Jackson could have something like that ready by next week?"

"Probably," Chloe said. "He's pretty fast."

"Good." Amy sat back in her chair. "How are things with you guys?"

"Fine," Chloe said quickly. "No problems."

She wasn't exactly lying. It was almost noon and she'd had no problems with Jackson. Of course, she hadn't seen him yet today. She knew he was in the office, his stuff was on his desk, but either he was deliberately avoiding her, or he had a bunch of meetings this morning that she knew nothing about.

"Chloe? You okay?"

"Fine," she said.

Amy hesitated. "Did you decide whether you were going to sleep with them yet?"

Chloe's cheeks flushed. "Yeah. We got together on the weekend."

Amy gave her a large grin. "And? How was it?"

"Amazing."

"Nice. Well done, you," Amy said.

"Thank you."

"Although, I would think you'd be more… giddy today? I mean, you did have amazing sex with two smoking hot men over the weekend."

Chloe forced herself to smile. "I had a really good time, but there was an issue with my sister and now I'm pretty sure that I won't be having sex with them again."

"Uh oh. Did she like show up in the middle of it or something?"

"No, nothing like that. She… it doesn't matter. It's hard to explain and you don't need to hear about my problems with my sister."

"I don't mind," Amy said.

"The thing is – I don't have a lot of friends and that's partially because of Lori, you know? I like you and I like your friendship and don't want to lose it so... I'd rather not bring my problems with my sister into the friendship. Okay?"

"Okay," Amy said.

Relief swept through her and she gave Amy a grateful smile. "Thanks, I appreciate that."

"You're welcome. But if you do need to talk about her, we can. Obviously, I can't relate exactly to what you're going through, but I'm a good listener."

"Thanks again."

"Of course. Do you want to have lunch with me and Jane?"

"I think I'll eat lunch in my office today," Chloe replied.

"Okay. If you change your mind, email me," Amy said.

"I will. Thanks, Amy."

"Hey, Chloe?"

She looked up at the knock on her door. Mark was standing in the doorway, holding a bottle of water and a plastic container with a fork balanced on top of it.

"Hi, Mark."

"Hi. Mind if I join you for lunch?"

"Uh, sure." Chloe gave him a bewildered look.

"Thanks." Mark set his stuff on her desk and rolled Jackson's chair over.

When she'd returned from Amy's office, Jackson still wasn't at his desk and his jacket was gone. She'd worked until noon and then heated up her lunch and brought it back to her desk.

"That smells good." Mark nodded to her container of food. "Is that chicken parmesan?"

"Yes." She poked at it with her fork. "Amy sent you here, didn't she?"

"She's worried about you," Mark said. "Do you want to talk about what your sister did?"

She poked again at her leftovers. Every Wednesday, she and Mark went to the same Al-Anon meeting. His troubles with his drug-addicted brother were similar to her problems with her sister and she supposed if she talked to anyone, Mark would understand best.

"You're kind of my boss now," she said.

"Not really. Luke's your boss." He ate a forkful of pasta. "Besides, it isn't like we don't share at Al-Anon."

She smiled a little. "True. I'll probably share on Wednesday night, so…"

"From the look on your face, I think waiting until Wednesday isn't the best idea," Mark said. "Why don't we have a mini meeting right now."

She sighed. "It would probably help to talk about it."

"It definitely would." Mark sat back in the chair. "Talk to me, Chloe."

"My sister got incredibly drunk Saturday night and basically destroyed most of my Nana's house and all of her food. I was, uh, busy and didn't get any of my grandmother's calls until the next day. When I went over, Lori had vomited and passed out, and my grandmother had locked herself in her bedroom."

"Was she okay?"

"Yeah. I guess Lori screamed a lot and threw a bunch of stuff, but Nana went to her room pretty quickly. She was really upset that I didn't answer my phone though."

"You're not responsible for your sister's actions," Mark said. "You know that."

"I know, but Nana was so upset... Anyway, I helped clean up the house and bought her new groceries. But, Sunday night Lori called me and she screamed at me for not buying beer with the groceries. I reminded her I wouldn't buy her booze and she flipped out. She was screaming and shouting and then she started that fake crying thing she does, and then Nana came on the line and was angry because I wouldn't support Lori."

Chloe took a deep breath before standing and pacing the length of the office. "I feel so guilty and I-I shouldn't. I'm allowed to have a life, right?"

"Yes," Mark said. "You are, Chloe."

"Only I fucking can't, because my sister worms her way into everything that might be good and destroys it. Jackson and -" She stopped, staring wide-eyed at Mark who gave her a curious look.

"Are you and Jackson dating?"

"No," she said quickly. "No... we were doing a work thing at my place and he overheard me talking to Lori. I'm embarrassed that he heard me. He's my co-worker, and I don't want him knowing my personal issues, you know?"

"I get it," Mark said.

"Anyway, I feel terrible about upsetting my Nana. I hate Lori for being a drunk and not getting her life together. You know, the usual."

"I do know," Mark said solemnly. "But again, it isn't your fault and Lori's behaviour is not a reflection on you. Nor are you responsible for your grandmother's decisions. I know it's hard, I know you want to protect her, but she's enabling your sister."

"I know." Chloe could feel the tears starting and she

blinked rapidly. They slipped down her cheeks anyway and she swiped them away. "I'm just tired, I guess. Tired of Nana always taking Lori's side, tired of having to clean up Lori's messes. Tired of my life being ruined because I can't walk away no matter how bad it gets."

She sniffed and wiped at the tears again. "She's prostituting herself out for booze."

"Shit. I'm sorry."

"Yeah, me too. It's like she's hit rock bottom and I can't do anything to help her." Her voice wavering, she said, "On Sunday when I went over to Nana's, Lori was passed out in her bed. But I – I couldn't tell if she was breathing, you know?"

She crossed her arms over her torso, hugging herself tightly. "For a moment, I really thought she was dead and I," she gave Mark a stark look of despair, "I was glad. Part of me was relieved that she was dead."

The tears were sliding down her cheeks now and Mark stood and crossed to her. He pulled her into a hug and she put her arms around his waist and rested her forehead on his chest. "I'm a monster."

"No, you're not." Mark said.

"I am," she whispered. "I was happy at the thought that my sister was dead, Mark."

"I think that's a pretty normal reaction," Mark said. "Lori has put you through a lot."

She lifted her head. "Are you sure? Because I think there might be something wrong with me."

"There isn't," Mark said. "I promise there's nothing wrong with you. I guarantee when you share this on Wednesday night, there will be other people who have felt the same way and won't hesitate to tell you that. You're not alone, Chloe."

"I feel alone," she whispered.

"You're not. You have me, and you have Amy and Jane now too. You're not alone." He gave her a quick peck on the forehead. "Any time you -"

"Am I interrupting something?"

She stepped away from Mark, staring at Jackson who was standing in the doorway. His usual affable tone was ice-cold and the look on his face as he stared at Mark, suggested he was about ten seconds from attempted murder.

"Nope. Just having lunch with Chloe," Mark said.

"I didn't realize you were friends." Jackson walked to his desk. His cheeks were red from the cold and he carried a paper bag from a nearby deli. He set it on his desk and shrugged out of his jacket as Mark glanced at Chloe.

She gave him a nervous smile and Mark turned to study Jackson. "Chloe and I have been friends for a while.

"Oh yeah?" Jackson stared at her instead of Mark. Alarm crossed his face and before she could stop him, he was across the room and pulling her into his embrace. He cupped her face and touched her tear-streaked cheeks before glaring at Mark. "Did you make her cry, asshole?"

"Jackson!" Chloe gasped.

"Did you?" He snapped.

"He didn't." Chloe squeezed his arm. "Mark was being a good friend. He was comforting me, okay?"

She gave Mark an anxious look. 'Jackson didn't mean to call you that. He's, um, it's really busy right now at work and he's under a lot of pressure."

To her immense relief, Mark gave her a small grin. "Yeah, he's calling me an asshole because of work pressure. That's the reason."

He grabbed his container from the desk and whistling softly, headed toward the door. "Talk to you later, Chloe."

"Bye, Mark."

She waited until he had left and closed the door before she whacked Jackson lightly in the chest. "What were you thinking? He's the boss, Jackson. You can't call the boss an asshole!"

Jackson stared at her. "You were letting him comfort you, but you won't let Ian and me comfort you?"

"I – I'm sorry, I don't want to burden you with my stupid issues, okay?"

"You're not." He was still holding her in his arms and he pressed his forehead against hers. "Just because we're not in a relationship, doesn't mean we don't want you to talk to us or share stuff with us, okay?"

"Yeah, okay." She leaned against Jackson. She knew she shouldn't, they were strictly co-workers now, but she couldn't help it. Jackson's embrace and the feel of his body against hers, comforted her in a way that Mark never could.

He rubbed her back and held her tightly. "Are you okay, honey?"

"Yes. I'm better now."

"Because of Mark?" His big body stiffened again and this time she was the one to rub his back.

"No, because of you."

He relaxed and pressed a kiss against the top of her head. "Ian and I are having dinner with my mom tonight, but will you come to our place tomorrow night?"

She stared up at him. "What? You want to keep, I mean... you still want to have sex with me?"

"Yes, if you want to. We're offering dinner as well." He gave her an adorable grin.

"Why?" She whispered. "I was – was awful to you last night. I yelled and…"

Jackson shrugged. "We could tell you were upset and

honestly, we pushed you too hard and we need to apologize for that. We have an agreement about this not being a relationship, and we acted inappropriately. On behalf of both Ian and me, I'm sorry."

She shook her head. "Stop it. You don't need to apologize. I need to say sorry for being such a jerk and saying horrible things."

"You didn't," he said. "Listen, can we forget about last night and start over? We promise we'll keep this casual, no pressure to talk about personal stuff or anything like that. Just three people having a good time together. Sound good?"

She nodded. "Yes, I'd like that."

"Good. So, then Tuesday night around six?"

"Sure. Should I bring anything?"

"Just your sexy self." Jackson gave her a flirty grin before returning to his desk.

She studied his broad back and headed to her own desk. She wanted to believe that Ian and Jackson were being honest about it being casual, but Jackson's reaction to Mark...

She sighed and picked up her fork. She would have to hope they meant what they said. She didn't want a relationship. Even if she did, a woman couldn't fall in love with two men, and there was no way she would ever try and choose between Jackson and Ian. She cared for both of them equally.

You're not supposed to care about them. This is sex only, remember?

She stabbed a piece of chicken. Yeah, she remembered.

FOR SOMEONE WHO WAS SUPPOSED TO BE KEEPING IT CASUAL, Jackson was way too excited about Chloe coming over. He checked his reflection in the bathroom mirror before walking to the kitchen. Ian had texted him that he would be late, and that he'd bring something home for dinner. Neither of them had even thought to cancel their plans with Chloe. After almost three days without her, both of them were dying to be with her again.

His cock was hardening at the thought of being in her tight pussy again, and he glanced at the small pink box sitting on the table. He had stopped after work and picked it up, and he hoped Chloe liked her present.

He adjusted the front of his jeans, trying to relieve some of the pressure. The doorbell rang, and he jumped up as eagerly as a kid waiting for Santa and almost ran to the front door. He opened it and smiled down at her.

"Hey, beautiful."

"Hi, Jackson. How are you?"

"I'm good. Come into the kitchen."

She took off her jacket and boots and followed him to the kitchen.

"Do you want a drink? I've got water, juice, beer."

"Water is good." She was staring at the box on the table. "Who's the present for?"

"As a matter of fact, it's for you." He placed the glass of water on the table.

"Really?" God, her grin was so cute. "Can I open it now?"

"Well, I was going to make you wait for Ian, but he's running late."

"I know. He texted me," Chloe said. "Please, may I open it now?"

He loved her sweet enthusiasm. "Yes, you may."

She grabbed the box and untied the ribbon before lifting the lid. She pulled back the pink tissue paper and stared at the object nestled in it. When she glanced up at him, her cheeks were delightfully red. "Is this a…"

"Say it," he said with a grin.

"Is this an anal plug?"

He nodded, and she burst into laughter. "You bought me a butt plug as a gift?"

"Best gift ever. Am I right?" He said.

"Oh, definitely." She picked up the plug a bit gingerly. There was a small bottle of lube in the box as well, and she glanced at it before studying the plug in her hand. "It's pretty small."

"You want to start small, trust me."

"I guess. But, I really want to…"

She flushed, and he gave her a flirty grin. "You really want me in your ass, is that it?"

"Yes," she said with uncharacteristic boldness. "I want you in my ass and Ian in my pussy."

Her face flamed an even brighter red almost immediately. "Sorry. I'm not very good at the dirty talk."

He moved to her and put his arms around her, palming her ass. "Trust me, that was hot."

"Yeah?" She gave him a pleased look.

"Yep." He stepped away and leaned back against the counter. "So, slight change in plans. Ian will bring home dinner since he's gonna be late. But if you're hungry, we can have a quick snack while we wait for him."

"Actually," she dropped the plug into the box, stepped closer to him and ran her hands across his chest, "Ian said we should start without him. So, I was thinking that maybe we could go to the bedroom and we can try out your new present while you fuck me. What do you think?"

Panic washed over him, his erection fled for the hills, and

he tried desperately to think of an excuse to wait for Ian. "Aren't you hungry?" He pasted a smile on his face. "I think we should eat first. I don't want you passing out on me in bed."

"I'm fine." She rubbed his cock through his jeans and more panic set in.

"What do you think?" She gave him a sweetly seductive look and rubbed a little harder.

"No."

She had a look of confusion mixed with embarrassment, and he tried to smile again at her. "We should probably wait for Ian. It doesn't seem fair to -"

"He was very clear that he didn't mind." She was starting to unbutton his jeans. "So, why don't you take me to your room and -"

He pushed her hand away a little harder than he intended. "I said no, Chloe."

She gave him a mortified look and stepped back immediately. "I'm so sorry, Jackson. I didn't mean to…"

He couldn't think of anything to say, and she gave him another look of shame. "I should go."

"No, it's not –

"No, it's okay," she said. "I, um, I'm pretty tired anyway and I'm sure with working late, Ian will be tired when he gets home."

She left the kitchen. Shit, she could move fast when she wanted to. She had her boots on and was zipping up her jacket by the time he got to the front door.

"Chloe, it isn't you. I'm just tired as well and –"

"No, no, you don't have to explain. I was totally out of line and I should have stopped the first time you said no. I'm sorry. I, um, if you get some rest and want to get together later this week, let me know."

"Chloe…"

She was out the front the door and hurrying to her car before he could say anything else.

He stood on the front step. "Chloe, -"

"Goodnight, Jackson. I'll see you at the office tomorrow." She waved, climbed into her car, and drove off.

He slammed the door shut and muttered a curse. Ian was gonna fucking kill him.

CHAPTER 11

"Are you fucking kidding me, Jackson?" Ian glared at him and dropped the bag of Chinese food on the table. "What the hell did you to say to her?"

"I didn't mean to upset her," Jackson said. "I was tired and I…"

"You were tired? You were tired?" Ian snapped. "So, you sent her home? I'm the one who worked late, I'm the one who had to chase a fucking drug addict on foot almost ten city blocks today, but you're the fucking tired one? Do you have any idea how much I was looking forward to being with Chloe tonight?"

"I fucked up, okay? I'll apologize to her tomorrow," Jackson said. "Can we just forget about it and eat dinner."

"No, we can't," Ian raged. "I want to know exactly what you said to her."

"She wanted to have sex. You told her we should go ahead and start without you."

"So what?" Ian said.

"You didn't even ask me what I wanted." Jackson glared at Ian. "Do you know how inconsiderate that is?"

"Am I in the goddamn *Twilight Zone*?" Ian gave him a look of exasperation. "We agreed on Sunday night that the only reason we were hanging out with Chloe was to have sex with her."

"I know!" Jackson said.

"So why the hell are you not having sex with her right now?" Ian said.

"Because I can't, all right!" Jackson yelled.

Ian blinked at him. "What do you mean, you can't?"

Jackson raked his hands through his hair. "I mean, I can't have sex with a woman unless you're there, Ian. I can't even get my fucking dick to twitch. It doesn't matter how hot the woman is or how much I want her, if you're not there watching or joining in, I can't get a fucking hard-on."

He stopped, panting harshly and scowling at his best friend. Ian gave him a cautious look. "Since when?"

"What does it matter?"

"How long, Jackson?"

"I don't know. Six months maybe."

"Did something happen or was there some kind of incident that -"

"Don't go fucking cop on me, Ian," Jackson said.

"I'm trying to figure out why this is happening to you," Ian said. "If we can figure out the cause, we can fix the problem. It'll be all right, Jackson. We just need to -"

"I know what the goddamn problem is," Jackson shouted.

He needed to shut his mouth, needed to stop talking, but now that he had started, it was like a dam had cracked in two and the words fell out of his mouth in a hot rush.

"I know you want to stop whoring around with me, Ian. I know you want a wife and kids and to start your life. I want you to be happy, I swear to fucking God I do, but the thought of us not doing, whatever the fuck this is that we're doing, anymore, makes me feel like shit."

He balled his hand into a fist and slammed it down on the counter. He ignored the pain that radiated up his arm. "Right or wrong, I don't want to sleep with a woman without you. It's so much better this way, and I can't go back to regular sex. Which means when you find the one, when you settle down and have kids and get married and live a normal life, I'll be fucking alone. I won't have you or anyone else, and I'll die old and alone and a goddamn monk."

He slammed the counter again and Ian shook his head. "Stop. You're gonna break your fucking hand. Sit down for a minute."

His heart racing, Jackson sat down in a chair, staring at the table as Ian sat down across from him. "Jackson, buddy, you're wrong. I'm not ready to settle down yet, okay? So, stop worrying about shit that hasn't happened yet."

"You're lying," Jackson said dully. "Don't do that, Ian. Don't lie to me."

Ian sighed. "Look, I haven't even come close to finding someone yet and besides, who the fuck is going to put up with me long term? I barely talk, I'm grumpy as shit most of the time, and I'm only two steps above being a goddamned hermit. Half the time I can't even get women to sleep with me unless you're there charming them, so you're fucking worrying for nothing."

"That's bullshit, and you know it," Jackson said. "You can get a woman on your own. You got Chloe, didn't you?"

"Yeah, because like I told you, I was in the right place at the right time. She was upset and wanted a distraction. The only reason we're sleeping with her now is because of you and your charm."

"Not true," Jackson said.

"Whatever. The point is, I may want a wife and kids, but it's doubtful it'll happen for me. So, you can stop worrying about never fucking a woman again, all right?"

"It'll happen eventually," Jackson said. "And now if it doesn't, that'll be my fault. Because you feel sorry for your bitchass friend, who suddenly can't fuck a woman without his best friend there to hold his hand."

"Since when did we start holding hands when we fuck a woman?" Ian said. "I mean, if you want to hold hands, I'll give it a try but…"

"Shut up, dickhead," Jackson said.

Ian grinned at him. "Listen, obviously you've got some fucking weird shit happening in your brain. And that's okay. We'll figure out together how to fix you so you can bang a woman when you're with me *and* on your own, all right? And if we can't fix you, then I'll have you committed. Easy-fuck-ing-peasy."

"Nice pep talk, Coach," Jackson said.

"You're welcome." Ian reached across the table and punched him in the shoulder. "In the meantime, we'll keep doing what we do best – fucking women together. Okay?"

"Yeah, okay. I'm sorry for fucking up your life, man."

"Hey, look at me."

He stared at Ian who shook his head. "You haven't fucked up my life, Jackson. I can't imagine not having you in my life and you will always be a part of it. I promise. Maybe we need to find a woman who will love us both and accept us as a package deal."

"Yeah, because it's so easy to find a woman who wants to live with and fuck two men for the rest of her goddamn life."

Ian shrugged. "She might be out there. We just need to find her."

"You want it to be Chloe, don't you?"

Ian didn't reply, and Jackson leaned forward. "I know you do."

"Yeah, maybe. I know we haven't known her long, but…"

"There's something special about her."

"There is," Ian replied.

"She doesn't want a relationship with us," Jackson said.

"Yeah, she's made that clear."

"Hell, after tonight, she probably won't have anything to do with us at all."

"Which is why you and I are going over to her place with gifts of Chinese food and," Ian studied the open pink box still on the table, "a butt plug, and you're going to get on your fucking knees and beg her to forgive you."

"I don't want her to know about my…issue. It's embarrassing."

"Then you'd better come up with something good for why you acted the way you did," Ian said.

Jackson sighed, and Ian reached over and squeezed his shoulder. "It'll be okay, man. I promise."

———

JACKSON WAS NERVOUS. IAN COULD SEE IT IN THE TENSE WAY he pushed the button to Chloe's apartment, in the small lines around his eyes. He shifted the bag of Chinese food to his other hand and squeezed Jackson's shoulder.

He was more freaked out by Jackson's confession than he let on. Everything Jackson had said about Ian wanting to start a family was true – shit, sometimes he hated that he was so transparent to him – but knowing now that Jackson was struggling with the idea of them living separate lives, was making his own stress levels rise.

He understood and could sympathize with him. Hell, he

wanted and preferred to have the two of them with a woman together as well, but the stuff he'd told Jackson was nothing more than platitudes to help him stop freaking the fuck out.

Finding a woman who would accept both of them for the rest of her life would be impossible. Which meant he would either need to sacrifice his own happiness or watch as his best friend spent the rest of his life miserable.

Fuck, what a goddamn mess. He had no fucking idea what to do.

You have to do what you said and help Jackson with his problem. Talk to Chloe. You've never seen Jackson this into a woman before. If anyone could help him, it would be her. Right?

Yeah, maybe. But that would mean telling Chloe what was wrong, and Jackson didn't want to do that.

If you don't tell her, you won't even have a chance at fixing Jackson.

That was true. Jackson really was into Chloe. He'd told Ian about walking in on Chloe and Mark hugging in the office. His jealousy had been obvious. Hell, Ian was jealous just hearing about it. He didn't want any man touching Chloe but him and Jackson.

She's the one for you. You know that.

He ignored his inner voice. Even if he did think Chloe was the one – which was ridiculous considering he had known her for less than two weeks – he could never do that to Jackson. Not now. Not when he knew how much he was struggling. Asking Chloe to consider being more serious with only him wasn't something he could even fathom doing. He might be falling for her, but he could never hurt Jackson like that.

"Hello?" Chloe's voice drifted out of the intercom.

Jackson gave him a nervous look. "Hi, it's Jackson. I'm so sorry."

There was silence and Ian could almost see Jackson deflating. He squeezed his shoulder again, but before he could say anything to Chloe, the door buzzed. Jackson pulled it open and gave him a look of relief.

"Thank fucking God."

Chloe had the door to her apartment open and was standing in the hallway when they got off the elevator. Jackson walked rapidly toward her and Ian watched as he pulled her into his arms and picked her up. She returned his hug as he kissed her neck.

"I'm sorry, Chloe."

"It's okay. I should have respected your boundaries and -"

"No, I felt weird about starting without Ian. I want you. I want you so much."

Chloe smiled at Ian over Jackson's shoulder. "I want you too. I want both of you. Come inside."

She giggled a little when Jackson carried her into the apartment instead of setting her down. She tapped his shin lightly with her foot. "I can walk, you know."

"Yeah, I know." Jackson set her on her feet but kept his arm around her.

Ian held up the bag of food. "Are you ready to eat, Red?"

She shook her head. "I'm not hungry. Let's just go to my bedroom, okay?"

Ian frowned. "You need to eat, baby."

"I will later. Please, Ian. I need you."

His resolve wavered and disappeared completely when Chloe stepped in close and wrapped her arms around his waist. She pressed a kiss against his chest. "Please, Ian. I'll put the food in the fridge for now, okay?"

"All right."

Chloe took the bag of food and disappeared into the kitchen. He removed his jacket and boots as Jackson did the same. Jackson was holding the small gift box in his right hand, but Chloe didn't seem to notice when she returned. She took Jackson's hand, pulling him down the hallway. They followed her to her bedroom and she flicked on the bedside lamp. She opened the drawer to the nightstand and brought out a box of condoms. She set it next to the lamp before grinning at them.

"I bought the magnum sized ones."

Ian laughed as Jackson studied her bedroom. "Your room is nice."

She shrugged. "It's small and it's only a queen-sized bed so…"

She eyed their big bodies as Ian smiled at her. "We'll make it work."

"Okay." She stripped off her shirt and reached for the button on her jeans.

Jackson took her hand, kissing the knuckles. "Hey, what's your hurry?"

"I want you," she said impatiently. "I want you and I don't…"

She had caught sight of the box in his other hand. Her cheeks turned a delightful shade of pink and Ian smiled at her when her gaze flickered to him.

"Did you like Jackson's gift, baby?"

She nodded as Jackson moved around behind her. Her hair was down, and he pushed it aside before kissing her neck. He tossed the box on the bed as Ian took off his t-shirt. Chloe inhaled sharply, and he stood in front of her.

"You're beautiful, Chloe." He stared at her pale skin before leaning down and kissing the freckles that were scattered across her upper chest.

"So are you," she whispered.

Jackson unhooked her bra and she let it drop to the floor. Ian studied her small breasts before cupping both of them. Her soft moan when he rubbed his thumb across her hardening nipples made precum leak from his cock. Fuck, he wanted her.

He unbuttoned her jeans, and he and Jackson stripped her of her pants, socks and panties. When she was standing naked between them, he studied her again. Jackson was rubbing her flat abdomen with one big hand, and she parted her legs when his fingers traced the patch of red hair at the top of her sex.

"Touch me," she said before rubbing her ass against Jackson's dick.

Jackson hissed out a breath, his other hand tightening on her hip.

"Not yet, baby," Ian said. He crossed over to the bed and grabbed one of the pillows. He dropped it on the floor in front of Chloe as Jackson pressed gently on her shoulders.

She giggled a little. "A pillow? You're adorable."

Ian grinned at her. "We want you to be comfortable when you're on your knees and sucking our dicks, baby."

Lust flared in her eyes and she knelt on the pillow immediately. Jackson groaned and quickly removed his clothes.

"Jackson first, baby. Show him how good you are at sucking cock," Ian said.

He unbuttoned his jeans, watching as Chloe eagerly sucked Jackson into her mouth. Jackson muttered a curse, burying his hands in her hair as she licked and sucked his cock.

"Fuck, that feels good," he moaned.

Ian shed the rest of his clothes before standing next to Jackson. He wrapped his hand around his dick, rubbing in firm strokes as he watched Chloe suck hard on Jackson's dick. She licked the head of his dick and smiled up at him. "Delicious."

"Christ," Jackson whispered when she gripped the base of his dick and pumped firmly as she sucked on only the head. "Fuck, I'm gonna blow my load if you don't stop."

"My turn, baby," Ian said.

Chloe immediately let go of Jackson and turned toward him. Ian smiled down at her, petting her hair as she leaned forward and licked the length of his cock. "Good. Lick me again."

She licked him repeatedly, cleaning away the precum that was on the tip as she stared up at him.

"Good, now suck."

She sucked, hollowing her cheeks and working her hot little mouth back and forth over his throbbing dick. When she began to stroke the base of him with her hand, he pulled it away and placed her hand on Jackson's dick.

"Touch him while you suck me, Chloe."

He loved the way she faltered a bit with her rhythm as she tried to please both of them at once. She couldn't quite focus on either one, and he could sense her growing frustration.

"You're doing so well," he praised. "Suck Jackson's dick, baby."

She released him with a soft pop and immediately took Jackson's cock into her mouth. She gripped Ian's cock and pumped back and forth without being told, and he stroked her arm before praising her again. "That's right, Chloe. Be our good girl and use your hands and your mouth."

She made a muffled sound of surprise when Jackson gripped her head tightly and thrust hard in and out of her mouth. Her hand tightened around Ian's dick and he had to work very hard not to come right then and there.

He moaned as Chloe pumped faster, staring up at Jackson

while he fucked her mouth with rough thrusts. He pulled back and she gasped in air when Jackson helped her to her feet. She let go of Ian's dick as Jackson kissed her roughly on the mouth, cupping her tit and pinching her nipple.

"Gentle, Jackson," Ian said.

"I need her," Jackson rasped. "Christ, Ian, I need her so bad."

"I need you too," Chloe whispered.

Ian moved to the bed as Jackson kissed her again. He pulled back the covers and took out the plug and the lube, setting them at the top of the bed between the pillows.

"Come here, Chloe."

Jackson released her and Chloe almost ran to the bed. She smiled up at Ian, and he bent and gave her a slow and lingering kiss as he cupped her ass and squeezed.

"Middle of the bed, on your side facing away," Ian said.

She did what he asked without hesitation, and Ian walked around the other side of the bed. By the time he'd rolled on a condom and slid into the bed, Jackson was already lying behind her with the bottle of lube in one hand. He reached between them and Chloe made a squeak of nervousness.

"Shh, honey," Jackson said. "Relax."

"It's cold," she said as Ian moved in close to her. Her breasts, their nipples hard as diamonds, pressed against his chest, and she didn't object when he lifted one creamy thigh and draped it over his hip. He moved down a little, until his cock pressed against her pussy. She moaned when he rubbed the head against her clit and rocked herself against him.

"Oh!" She gave him a startled look and he rubbed her clit again.

"Only my finger, honey," Jackson said.

"Please, I want you to fuck me," Chloe moaned.

"I will," Ian soothed. "Jackson's going to put the plug in first and then I'll fuck you. Relax, baby."

He continued to rub his dick against Chloe's swollen, wet clit as Jackson covered the plug with lube. He reached between him and Chloe again, and she tensed. Ian cupped her breast, caressing it lightly as Jackson kissed between her shoulders.

"Relax, Chloe. I want you to push back against the plug, all right?"

"I… are you sure it'll fit?" She moaned.

"It will," Ian said.

She moaned again, her eyes widening as Jackson pressed the plug against her asshole. "I – it feels too big."

"I know, but it isn't. Take some deep breaths and push back against me," Jackson said.

"I don't, I mean, I'm not sure I can -"

"Chloe, do what Jackson says," Ian said firmly.

She stared at him and he reached down and stroked her clit. "Be a good girl and take the plug."

"Yes, Ian," she groaned.

She pressed her ass back, her eyes widening again. Ian gave her clit a soft pinch to distract her. She moaned in pleasure when he rubbed it hard, and then made a low noise of surprise when Jackson said, "Good, honey."

"Is it in?" She blushed. "I mean, it's all the way in, right?"

"Yes." Jackson kissed her upper back again before reaching around and cupping her breast. "You did so well, honey. How does it feel?"

"Fine. It doesn't hurt, it feels a bit weird and I feel… full."

Ian smiled. Sweet Chloe was about to feel much fuller. He nodded to Jackson. Chloe's leg was still resting against Ian's hip and, without speaking, Jackson curled his hand around Chloe's leg and lifted until she was wide open to Ian.

She clutched at Ian's broad shoulders as he guided his cock to her narrow entrance. He pushed the head in and Chloe immediately tried to wiggle back.

"Too much," she moaned.

Jackson gripped her thigh tighter and she dug her nails into Ian's shoulder as she tried to pull her leg free. "Jackson, let go."

"No, honey. Stay still for us."

"Ian, it's too much, it's too…"

Her voice trailed off into a low moan as Ian pushed more of his cock into her. She was soaking wet and, despite her protests, it took less than ten seconds for him to be fully sheathed. Her hands clenched and unclenched around his shoulders as Jackson lowered her leg back down to Ian's hip.

"Good girl, honey," Jackson said. "How do you feel?"

"Like I'll never be able to take both your dicks at once," Chloe panted.

Jackson nuzzled her neck as Ian cupped her tits and squeezed lightly. "You will, baby. This is why we start with the plugs. Any pain?"

She shook her head. "No, but it doesn't feel nice, I mean, like, pleasurable either."

"No pain is what we're looking for right now," Jackson said. He turned her head and kissed her, swallowing her soft cries of pleasure when Ian fucked her slowly and rubbed her clit.

She moaned and cried out into Jackson's mouth, her body rocking forward to meet each of Ian's slow thrusts. God, he loved fucking her. Her pussy, so tight to begin with, was even tighter with the plug in her ass and he could only imagine how it would feel once Jackson's cock was in her.

He pushed a little harder and faster as Jackson released Chloe's mouth. She turned her head to face Ian again, biting at her bottom lip as he rubbed her clit in slow circles.

"Oh God, that's so good, Ian."

She reached behind her, fumbling for Jackson's cock. Jackson grabbed her hand and kissed the palm before resting it on her hip.

"I want you to feel good too," she panted.

"All about you, honey. Remember?" Jackson said.

"Doesn't seem…oh God…fair."

"Just concentrate on how good it feels," Jackson said.

He leaned forward a bit, watching Ian's cock slide in and out of her wet pussy. "So pretty, honey. I love watching you be fucked by Ian."

Ian groaned, and drove in and out of Chloe's hot, wet pussy.

"Fuck, Jackson," he muttered, "her pussy is so much tighter. I'm not gonna last."

He was about two minutes from coming and he rubbed Chloe's clit with a hard pressure. Her eyes were closed, and her slender body was rocking back and forth between his and Jackson's.

Jackson reached between his and Chloe's bodies and wiggled the plug in her ass. Chloe's eyes popped open, her hands dug almost painfully into Ian's chest, and she surprised both of them when her entire body stiffened and she came with a loud shriek.

"Fuck!" Ian shouted. Chloe's pussy clenched around him with exquisite tightness and he bellowed another curse as his climax, relentless and unstoppable, roared through him. He held Chloe in a tight grip, fucking her through her orgasm and his, until his body was too weak and shaky to move anymore.

He buried his face in Chloe's neck, as she patted his back with a shaking hand.

"Ian, move." Jackson's voice was desperate sounding.

He pushed himself back on the bed, rolling to his back and staring at the ceiling as Jackson said, "Chloe, on your hands and knees, sweetheart."

The mattress dipped and Ian patted Chloe's hand when she placed it on his chest for balance. Jackson was rolling on a condom and he quickly moved to the end of the bed, kneeling between Chloe's legs and nudging them farther apart with his thighs before he pressed his hand on Chloe's upper back.

She pressed her chest against the bed, turning her head to stare at Ian. She had a cat-like look of satisfaction on her face and Ian grinned at her.

"You okay, baby?"

"Yeah, I'm good. I feel so... oh fuck!"

Her back arched and she dug her fingers into the mattress. Ian tucked the pillow under his head and watched as Jackson pushed his cock deep into Chloe's pussy.

"Jesus, so fucking tight," he moaned before thrusting hard.

Chloe rocked back to meet him, spreading her legs even wider. Ian could see the end of the plug sticking out of her ass. When Jackson wiggled it with two fingers, she squealed and her entire body twitched.

"I – oh god, that – don't do that," she moaned.

"You don't like it, honey?" Jackson wiggled it again and Chloe shrieked before rearing up on her hands.

"Please, I can't come again like that. Please, I don't want... fuck!" She screamed again as Jackson fucked her hard and wiggled the plug in her ass relentlessly. He gripped her perfect ass with his other hand as Chloe cried out and squirmed and twisted.

Ian sat up and pressed hard on her back. She collapsed to the mattress, squealing into the pillow, and he held her down as Jackson fucked her. She was moaning and begging, and her ass bounced as Jackson slammed in and out of her.

Ian could feel the exact moment she came again. Her body tensed, her ass clenched around the plug, and Jackson shouted so loudly that Ian was certain the neighbours would call the cops on them.

Jackson pumped in and out of her furiously, the cords standing out in his neck as he came repeatedly. Chloe's body shook and quivered, and Ian released her and laid down again. He pushed her hair away from her hot face and rubbed her arm as Jackson eased out of her. She turned on her side, her body visibly trembling as she stared wide-eyed at Ian. "I, oh my God."

Jackson was pressed up against her back and he made a low moan. "Holy fuck."

Ian grinned at both of them. "That looked like a good one."

"You have no idea, man," Jackson muttered.

"I do," he said before kissing Chloe on the mouth. She rested her forehead against his chest and he rubbed her hip. The three of them laid silently for almost fifteen minutes before Chloe raised her head.

"Hey, doing okay?" Ian asked.

"Unbelievably good," she said. "You?"

"You were amazing," he said. "But we should probably get up, get some food into you, and think of an excuse for when the cops knock on the door."

She gave him a confused look and he laughed. "You and Jackson got real loud at the end there."

"Oh." She blushed before looking over her shoulder at Jackson.

"Couldn't help it," Jackson said. "Her pussy is incredible."

She blushed even harder and Ian rubbed her thigh. "Are you hungry, baby?"

"A little."

"Good." He sat up and removed the condom before heading toward the bathroom that was attached to her bedroom. "Jackson will help you remove the plug and then we'll wash up and eat some dinner."

He paused, happiness rushing through him when Chloe said, "Would you guys like to stay the night with me?"

He smiled at her over his shoulder, nodding in agreement when Jackson said, "We'd love to, honey."

CHAPTER 12

"Okay, Chloe, you can do this. It's just a plug that you're about to shove up your own ass. No problem. Completely a non-issue."

Chloe stared at the butt plug before staring at her reflection in the bathroom mirror. Last night, having Jackson insert the butt plug had seemed kind of sexy and erotic. But standing here in the harsh light of the bathroom, all alone, it was decidedly unsexy.

"You need to do this," she reminded herself. "If you want to be stretched enough to have anal sex with Jackson, you gotta wear the butt plug for a few hours every day."

This morning before Jackson and Ian had left, Jackson had told her if she wore the butt plug every day even when they weren't with her, it would rapidly decrease the amount of time it took before she could take his cock in her ass.

Still on a high from being eaten out by Ian and fucked by Jackson not twenty minutes earlier, she had agreed happily to wearing it every day. But she hadn't really thought about the fact that it meant inserting the damn thing herself.

"You can do this," she told herself again. "You got this."

She reached for the lube and hesitated. Fuck, this felt weird. She had spent most of her Al-Anon meeting tonight, thinking about the fact that she would be going home to stick a plug in her butt. She hadn't shared at the meeting and had barely even listened to the others share.

Mark had kept giving her little glances during the meeting and after, he'd immediately asked her why she hadn't shared. She'd given him an excuse that she was tired and had a headache before skipping the after-meeting coffee and heading home.

She thought about texting Jackson and asking him to come over and help her, but Ian was working which meant it would only be Jackson. Based on his reaction last night, being alone with her was obviously something Jackson didn't want.

Why is that? Maybe Jackson isn't as attracted to you as you thought. Maybe he's just doing this for Ian. Or, maybe, he's secretly in love with his best friend and can't get it up with you when he's alone because he really only wants Ian.

She sighed. Yeah, that was a distinct possibility. It was a thought she couldn't keep shoving aside, but for now, she would shelve it and concentrate on getting her damn butt ready for a ridiculously large penis. It was totally selfish of her not to consider Jackson's feelings, to use him to get what she wanted when he was probably not even into her at all, but here she was. Doing it anyway.

She really was a monster.

She reached for the lube again. Apparently, her desire to have sex with both Jackson and Ian outweighed her embarrassment at sticking a plug up her own ass. Her cell phone buzzed and, secretly thankful for the distraction, she dropped the lube and picked up the phone.

A giant grin crossed her face as she read the text. She

hurried to the front door and buzzed him in. When she heard his footsteps in the hallway, she yanked open the door and smiled at him.

"Hi!"

Ian smiled back. "Hi, Red. How are you?"

"I'm good. Come in."

Ian stepped inside and she resisted the urge to fling her arms around him like they were dating or something. Still, she couldn't hide her happiness when he hugged her and pressed a kiss against her mouth. "I'm sorry, I know it's late."

"It isn't," she said. "I just got home from a…meeting. How was work?"

"Busy." He took off his jacket and boots and followed her into the kitchen.

"Are you hungry? There's still some leftover Chinese food in the fridge."

"Nah, I'm good. Sorry for just showing up, I hope I didn't interrupt anything."

"No, I was…"

He gave her a curious look. "What?"

"Honestly? About to try and shove a plug up my ass. It isn't going well."

Ian gaped at her before bursting into laughter. She blushed and pushed him lightly on the chest. "No laughing at me."

"I'm not laughing at you, I'm laughing with you."

"I'm not laughing," she said and then ruined it by giggling.

He kissed the tip of her nose. "You're adorable. Do you want some help with the plug?"

She gave him a shy look. "The thing is, I don't think we should have sex without Jackson. I know he said he doesn't care, but last night, he was… I mean, it was obvious that he didn't want to have sex without you there. It doesn't feel right to me for us to have sex without him."

Ian smiled at her. "That's actually why I'm here. I want to talk to you about what's going on with Jackson. Why don't I help you put the plug in, without us having sex, and then we'll talk."

"I don't know," she said. "It's not exactly sexy to be all, hey shove this plug in my ass, would you?"

Ian laughed again, and she tingled all over at the sound. God, he was sexy. Even when he was talking about not very sexy things.

"I promise I'll still find you hot even after helping you put a plug in your ass."

"All right, but if there's even a hint that you're grossed out, I'm kicking you out and you never get to see my lady parts again."

He pulled her close and kissed her. "It would be my absolute pleasure to put a plug in your ass, Red."

"Oh God, such a sweet talker. How can I resist?"

He winked at her and she took his hand and led him toward the bathroom.

"How does it feel?" Ian asked.

"Like I have a plug in my ass?" She sat down gingerly as Ian laughed and turned the kettle on.

"I'll make you a cup of tea," Ian said.

"Why? Will it make me forget I have a plug in my butt?"

"It might."

She grinned at him and watched as he boiled the water and added tea bags to two mugs. He poured the water and grabbed the milk from the fridge before sitting next to her.

Shit, she could get used to having Ian in her kitchen every night.

She added milk to her tea and sipped at it. "It's good. Not 'forget that I have a plug in my butt' good, but good."

Ian just smiled at her. She reached out and took his hand. "Does Jackson know you're here?"

He shook his head. "No."

She frowned a little. "I don't want to come between you and Jackson, Ian. Ever. If this is what's happening, then -"

"No," he said quickly. "What's happening is me trying to help Jackson. And I need you to help me do that."

"All right. Tell me what I can do."

Ian sighed and studied their linked fingers. "Last night when I got home from work and found out you'd left, I was pissed at Jackson. We had a small fight and he finally admitted that he can't have sex with a woman unless I'm there."

"Yeah, I kind of suspected that," Chloe said.

"It's been happening for about six months now, and he kept it from me because he thinks that I want to settle down with a woman and have kids and…start my own life. He doesn't want to ruin it for me."

"Is that what you want?" Chloe's stomach clenched. Why did the thought of Ian sleeping with another woman make her feel nauseous?

Ian shrugged. "Maybe. I don't know. It's…complicated. Anyway, I want to help Jackson figure this out and help him to start having sex with a woman on his own again."

"Ian," Chloe gave him a hesitant look, "do you think, maybe, Jackson can't sleep with a woman without you there because it's you he's attracted to?"

Ian shook his head. "Nope. That's not it, Chloe."

"Are you sure? I mean, he may not even be consciously aware of his attraction to you. It might be -"

"That isn't it, Red."

"But how do you know?"

"Jackson and I first started sleeping with women together about five years ago. Jackson was dating this chick, nothing serious, but it was more than obvious that she was into me as well. One night she proposed a threesome and we were like, why the hell not? It was good, really good, for all of us."

He drank some tea and then took her hand again. "She and Jackson only dated for about another month or so. The three of us slept together probably about another five times during that month. When they broke up, Jackson suggested that we bed another woman together, just to see if it was as good. It was."

She smiled at Ian. "So, that's when you started always banging women together?"

"For the most part," Ian said. "The first year or so it was about fifty/fifty, I guess? Jackson is excellent at charming the ladies and has no trouble picking them up. I'm not so great at it."

She smiled again. "You were pretty charming the night we met."

"Thanks. Anyway, Jackson and I had an agreement that we wouldn't try to date any of the women we slept with. Neither of us were ready to settle down at that point anyway, and," he paused and gave her a brief look that she didn't understand, "what woman would want to spend the rest of her life with two men? About a year after we started having threesomes, one of the women we were with wanted Jackson and me to, uh…"

"Be intimate?" Chloe suggested.

Ian nodded. "Yeah. We figured why not give it a try. We

did some kissing and touching, but it didn't do anything for either of us."

"Nothing?" Chloe said. "You're sure?"

"Yep," Ian said. "Both of us lost our erections almost immediately and the woman got super annoyed and left."

"Things didn't get awkward between you and Jackson after that?" Chloe asked.

Ian gave her a puzzled look. "Why would it? We've been best friends for years."

"Sometimes that sort of thing can make it weird between friends, especially for guys," Chloe said.

Ian shrugged again. "We're not like that. We might not be attracted to men, but men with men doesn't make me or Jackson feel weird."

"All right. So, then it isn't because Jackson is secretly attracted to you," Chloe said.

"It isn't. He just needs to work some shit out, you know? He's worried that he's going to wreck my life – which he isn't – and I was hoping that maybe you could help him work through this."

"I can try," Chloe said. "I don't know if I can help him or not though."

"I think you can," Ian said. "Jackson trusts you and he... he likes you. If you go to him, if you tell him that it's not a big deal if he doesn't get an erection, maybe it'll help with the mental block, you know? Like, right now, he can't be with a woman alone because he's embarrassed that he doesn't get hard. But, he could take it slow with you, right? If it doesn't work the first time, you can try again another time with no expectations or shit like that."

Chloe nodded slowly. "That might work. Does Jackson know you're talking to me about this?"

"No," Ian said. "I'm not trying to hide it from him, but I

figured I would talk to you first and see if you even wanted to help."

"Of course I do," Chloe said.

"Good. If you want to tell Jackson about our conversation, I'm fine with that. We don't have any secrets between us, and if Jackson gets pissed off with me for talking to you," a smile crossed his face, "he'll let me know."

"He might not want my help," Chloe said. "You know that, right?"

"Yeah, I know. But I think he'll be willing to try," Ian said.

Chloe squeezed his hand again. "You're a good friend, Ian."

"Thanks, Chloe. So are you."

She smiled and released his hand, staring down at her tea so he wouldn't see the disappointment on her face. She was perfectly fine being just friends with benefits with Ian and Jackson. It was what she wanted, what she told *them* she wanted, so being upset that Ian thought of her just as a friend was incredibly stupid.

She was getting exactly what she wanted. So why was she so unhappy about it?

"YOU WERE RIGHT, THE FOOD IS DELICIOUS." CHLOE SAT back in the booth and smiled at Amy. It was Thursday night and both Ian and Jackson were working. She'd felt a little guilty about leaving Jackson in the office alone, but what he was working on wasn't anything she could help him with. She'd run down to the café and brought him up something to eat before she left.

He'd been sweetly appreciative, and she couldn't help

stealing a couple kisses from him before she'd headed toward the elevator. She'd run into Amy in the parking garage and, before she knew it, she was following her to a restaurant for dinner.

"Isn't it? It's my and Mark's favourite place to eat. Speaking of which," Amy glanced at her phone, "Mark might join us when he's finished his meeting. If you're okay with that?"

"Of course." Chloe ate a few bites of potatoes. "So, do you have all the designs ready for Julien and Pierre?"

"Yes," Amy replied. "I've included four of your designs with mine and another couple from Rachel. Have you met her yet? She's on the design team and super talented. Anyway, we'll see what they say when we meet with them next week. But, I don't want to talk about work. I want to talk about the two delicious men you're banging."

Chloe flushed before poking at her chicken. "It's really great."

"Yeah? Good, I'm glad. Care to share the dirty details?" Amy grinned at her over her glass of wine.

Chloe probably shouldn't be telling Amy anything about her relationship with Jackson and Ian, but she couldn't help it. It felt so good to have a friend to confide in again. Even after all this time, she missed her best friend Kandace with a fierce ache.

"They're both amazing in bed. Like, crazy good. And I was worried that I wouldn't be able to, uh, you know, please them both, but they're so sweet about making it all about me. I mean, they have a good time too, but I don't feel any pressure to make them feel good."

"Awesome," Amy said. "Do you sleep with them separately too, or always together?"

"Always together," Chloe said. "It's my preference and

theirs as well." She wouldn't tell Amy about Jackson's issue, it wasn't her issue to share. "That could change in the future, but for now…"

"So, this is serious?" Amy said. "I thought it was just a fling."

Chloe shrugged. "It is. They're not interested in anything more and I feel the same way."

"Do you?" Amy cocked her head at her.

Shit. Amy was already good – too good - at knowing when Chloe was lying.

"Honestly? I don't know."

"Are you more attracted to one than the other? Maybe eventually you can date only one of them?"

Chloe shook her head immediately. "No, I can't. I couldn't choose between them. They're so different from each other, but they both have qualities that I admire and want. Like, Ian is quiet and a bit of an introvert, but I feel protected and safe with him. Jackson's a total extrovert, and so sweet and funny and caring."

"Is Ian a Dom? Did you find out for sure?" Amy asked.

"I haven't talked to him about it yet, but I'm pretty sure he's at least close to being one," Chloe said. "Like, he's usually the one, uh, telling us what to do and stuff in bed, so…"

"Dom," Amy said with a grin, before drinking some more wine. "Sounds like you kind of like it though."

"I like everything they do to me in bed. I like being with them outside of the bedroom too. We agreed that it was just casual, but we almost always have dinner beforehand and we always spend the night together. The idea of being with the two of them long-term is intoxicating. In fact, I think I'd love to date both of them, but…"

"Dating two men isn't exactly a socially accepted norm," Amy said.

"No, but I don't actually care about that," Chloe said. "It's more – how Jackson and Ian feel about it. Ian and I kind of talked about it last night, actually. He seems ready to settle down and start a family, but Jackson definitely isn't, and like I said before, I won't choose one over the other. I can't. It makes me feel sick to even -"

"Chloe?"

Her heart dropped into her stomach at the sound of her sister's alcohol-rough voice. She turned and stared at Lori as her sister, holding a bottle of beer in one hand, weaved toward their booth. Already the strong scent of beer clung to her and Chloe grimaced when she had to grab their table to stop from falling.

"Lori, what – what are you doing here?"

"Enjoying a night out with my friends. I got friends too, you know." Lori made a petulant jerk of her head over her shoulder. "Shove over."

"Lori, I'm in a work meeting. I can't -"

"Shove over, I said." Lori pushed her way into the booth beside Chloe.

She took a swig of beer before eyeing Amy. "I'm Lori – Chloe's big sister."

"Hello, Lori," Amy held out her hand. "I'm Amy."

Lori shook her hand, her chipped and dirty nails and nicotine-stained fingers a stark contrast to Amy's perfectly groomed nails. "Nice to meetcha'."

"Lori, I'm actually in a meeting and -"

"You dress pretty fancy," Lori said to Amy. "Where'd ya get that suit?"

"I designed it actually," Amy said. "Your sister and I work together at a clothing company."

"Oh yeah?" Lori took another drink of beer. "Chloe likes to draw clothes and shit, but she wasn't never good enough to get into school for it."

She laughed so loudly that the people at the table closest to their booth stared at them. "How many schools did you apply to again, Chloe? Like five?"

She leaned over the table and gave Amy a conspiratorial grin. "She got rejected from all of them. She cried so hard that summer. Swear to God, Nana's house was almost washed away from all the cryin' she did. Ain't that right, Chloe?"

"You should go back to your friends now, Lori."

"Hold your fuckin' horses, *Sis*." Lori gave her an angry look. "I'm talking to my new friend."

She turned to Amy and shook her head. "Jesus, she's always tried to tell me what to do. It's a real pain in my ass, to tell you the truth. She thinks she's better than me, but," she drank a swallow of beer before wiping her hands across her lips, "she ain't. She ain't nothin' special. Couldn't even get into design school."

Lori snorted laughter before slamming her beer bottle down on the table. She scanned the restaurant. "Fuck, where's the goddamn waiter? I need another beer."

"No, you don't," Chloe said. "Go home, Lori."

"Shut up, Chloe." Lori kept her gaze on Amy. "Hey, what did you say your name was again?"

"Amy."

"Right. You look like you do all right for yourself, think you could buy me a beer?"

"Lori, no. Amy is not -"

Lori elbowed her so hard in the ribs, that Chloe's eyes watered. "Shut up, I said. What do you think, Amy? You wanna be nice to your friend's sister and buy her a drink?"

"No," Amy said.

Lori's lip curled. "Why not? You think you're better than me too? Is that it? You think -"

"Hey, sorry I'm late."

Chloe's shame grew when Mark slid into the booth next to Amy. He kissed Amy's cheek and smiled at her. "Hi."

"Hi, Mark," Amy said.

Mark tugged at his tie before smiling at Chloe. "Hey, Chloe."

She nodded to him as Lori gave Mark a delighted look. "Well, ain't you a handsome man."

"I'm Mark." He held out his hand, tugging it free when Lori shook it and then ran her fingers suggestively over his wrist.

"Lori. It's good to meet ya, Mark."

"You're Chloe's sister," Mark said.

"That's right." Lori glanced at Chloe. "How do you know my sister? You ain't datin' her, are you?"

"No," Mark said. "We're friends."

"That's real good to know." Lori poked Chloe in the ribs again. "A guy like you is way too good lookin' for my sister. She couldn't even keep her man. He dumped her like a piece of garbage a few months ago, isn't that right, Chloe?"

She didn't reply. Her cheeks were painfully hot, her dinner was sitting like a hard stone in her belly, and she wanted to sink under the table with shame.

"Did you ever meet her fiancé?" Lori asked Mark.

Mark shook his head, and Lori finished off her beer and reached across the table to stroke his arm. "He wasn't nearly as good looking as you. In fact, he was kind of a weenie. Like," Lori made a jacking off motion with her hand, "I actually think he was gay and my sister was his beard. I bet they didn't even fuck. Did you, Chloe? Did you fuck him?"

"Enough," Chloe snapped. "Go home, Lori. Right now."

"Shut up," Lori said dismissively. She took Mark's hand. "Hey, you wanna go somewhere quieter and have a drink with me?"

She glared at Chloe when Chloe pulled her hand away from Mark's. "Mark and Amy are dating, Lori."

"What?" Lori gave Amy an incredulous look before her gaze skipped to Mark. "No, that ain't fucking true."

"It is," Chloe said through gritted teeth. "C'mon, let's go. I'll give you a ride back to Nana's and -"

"You," Lori pointed one finger at Mark, "are dating her?" She pointed at Amy, her hand shaking unsteadily.

"Yes," Mark said politely. He took Amy's hand and squeezed it.

"But – but look at you," Lori said. Her mouth was open, and she had a look of genuine astonishment on her face. "You're fucking hot and she's a goddamn fatty."

"Lori!" Anger shot through Chloe and without stopping to think about it, she shoved Lori out of the booth. Her sister landed on her ass on the floor, bellowing a curse as the babble and murmur of voices cut out and the restaurant turned deathly quiet. She could feel everyone's eyes on them as she slid out of the booth and grabbed Lori's arm, hauling her roughly to her feet.

"Get up," she snarled at her when Lori stumbled. "Get up right now."

"You're hurting me!" Lori whined. Chloe dug her fingers into her arm.

"Shut up," she said into Lori's ear. "Just shut your fucking mouth for once in your goddamn life."

She never cursed at Lori, never allowed her anger at her sister to overwhelm her, but she couldn't help it. Lori gave her a startled look as Chloe grabbed her purse and her jacket from the booth. Without looking at Amy and Mark - she *couldn't* look at them, couldn't bear to see the anger on their faces – she mumbled, "I'm really sorry. I – I need to get her out of here. I'm so sorry."

Still holding Lori's arm, she marched her toward the door of the restaurant, past the staring patrons, past the hostess standing silently near the front door. For once, her sister didn't argue or complain, just followed her out the door and to her car.

She yanked open the passenger door. "Get in."

Lori climbed into the car and Chloe slammed the door shut before stalking to the driver's side. She started the car, put on her seatbelt and pulled out of the parking lot.

"You know, you didn't -"

"No!" Chloe held her hand up but refused to look at her sister. "Sit there and keep your goddamn mouth shut. If you say another word, I swear I will take you directly to the bus station, buy you a ticket to the farthest destination they have, and fucking tie you to the bus seat. Keep your mouth shut, Lori."

Her sister grunted angrily but didn't say anything. Chloe drove through the darkened streets, trying not to cry as her anger pulsed and thumped inside of her. Lori had ruined another friendship. No, make that two friendships. Neither Mark nor Amy would ever have anything to do with her after this. It was fucking goddamn Kandace and Adam all over again.

She rubbed a shaking hand across her forehead. It was worse. At least with Kandace, all she'd lost was friendship. By this time tomorrow, she would most likely be unemployed. Amy was a nice lady, but holy shit, Lori had hit on her man and called her fat to her face.

She wanted to weep, but instead she hit her hands on the steering wheel. She drove another ten minutes, trying to calm down before she spoke to Lori. If she didn't, the conversation would delve into a screaming match.

She took a deep breath and stared at the road as she drove. "Lori, what you did back there was unacceptable. Amy is my boss and my friend, and you cannot insult the people in my life like that. Do you realize that you've probably gotten me fired? I love my job, and you've ruined it. You, Lori. No one else."

There was no reply. Steeling herself, she glanced over at her sister. Lori was passed out, her head lolling on the seat, her mouth open and a thin line of drool running down her chin. She made a loud snoring noise before grunting and farting.

Chloe turned her gaze back to the road. The tears leaked down her cheeks as she drove toward her Nana's place. Lori had fucked up her life again. She would always fuck up her life. Thinking she could have friends, or a job she loved, or a relationship with Ian and Jackson was a pipe dream.

Lori would always be there. Waiting and watching like a rattlesnake hidden in the tall grass. Striking and pumping Chloe full of her poison when Chloe least expected it.

CHAPTER 13

Chloe took a deep breath. It was Friday morning and she'd barely sat down at her desk before she'd received the email from Amy. She'd read the request to come to Amy's office with an utter lack of surprise. She was very glad that Jackson wasn't in the office yet. If he'd been there, she would have been tempted to crawl into his damn lap and sob.

She closed her eyes, straightened her skirt, and knocked on Amy's office door. She wouldn't cry, she told herself. She wouldn't cry or beg for her job. She would tell Amy that she understood and apologize once more for her sister's behaviour before walking out of the office with her head held high.

"Come in."

Amy's voice made the acid in her stomach bubble up to her chest. She swallowed hard and stepped inside Amy's office, closing the door behind her.

"Hi, Amy. You wanted to see me?"

"Hi." Amy walked across the office and stopped in front of her. "How are you?"

The compassion in Amy's face made her voice falter a little. "Uh, I-I'm fine. I would like to apologize for my sister's behaviour last night. She was drunk and it's not an excuse, but…"

She took another deep breath. "I want to say I'm sorry and that I've really enjoyed working with you these past couple of months. Having you choose some of my designs was the best moment of my life and I can't thank you enough."

"Chloe, are you - are you quitting?" Amy gave her a confused look.

Chloe blinked at her. "I – you're firing me."

"I'm not firing you."

"Of course you are. I – my sister hit on your boyfriend and called you fat."

Amy shrugged. "It's not the first time I've been called fat and it won't be the last. Chloe, I called you up here to make sure that you're okay. I was worried about you."

Chloe stared at her in astonishment. "You're worried about me?"

"Yes, I am." Amy took her arm and tugged her toward the beanbag chairs in front of her desk. "Sit down."

She sat, sinking into the soft leather as Amy sat in the beanbag chair beside her. "I wanted to call you last night, but Mark said it was best to give you time to decompress. Considering he's gone through the same shit with his brother, I figured he knew what he was talking about. Was he wrong though? Should I have called you last night?"

"Why – why are you being so nice to me?" Chloe said.

Amy reached out and snagged her hand, squeezing it tightly. "You are not to blame for your sister's actions, Chloe."

"Yeah, but…"

"But what?" Amy said. "You can't control what your sister says and does, just like Mark can't control what Michael says and does. They're addicts, and neither you nor Mark can fix them."

Chloe's lips trembled, and she pressed them together. "You're serious."

"Yes. You're not fired, Chloe. In fact, why don't you take the day off. No offense, honey, but you look terrible. Did you sleep at all last night?"

"Not much," Chloe said. "I really am sorry, Amy."

"You have nothing to apologize for." Amy squeezed her hand again before releasing it.

Chloe knotted her hands together in her lap, staring at her fingers. "I used to have a best friend named Kandace. She was married to a guy named Adam. They'd only been married a year or so, and Lori, she... she seduced Adam and they slept together. Lori didn't look, uh, as rough as she does now. But she was still drunk most of the time and she didn't care who she hurt. Kandace found out they'd slept together and she blamed me."

"I'm sorry," Amy said.

Chloe shrugged. "She was right to blame me. I dragged Lori into her life, you know? But Kandace and I had been friends since school and I never thought that Lori would do something like that. She knew how much Kandace meant to me. She knew and she still... anyway, Kandace and Adam divorced and Kandace refuses to have anything to do with me. We were friends for years and years, and in one single night, Lori ruined it. She cost me my friendship with Kandace and, even worse, she destroyed Kandace and Adam's relationship."

She pressed her lips together again before whispering, "Why can't I just walk away from her, Amy? Why do I let her keep hurting me and dragging me down into her fucked-up life?"

"It's hard to give up on the people we love," Amy said. "I'm no expert on this, but I've seen what Michael has done to Mark over the years. I see how Mark is now that he doesn't have any contact with his brother, and the difference is astonishing. I know it's not the same, Michael is in prison and it's easier for Mark not to be around him, but maybe you need to take a break from Lori for a while."

Chloe nodded. "Yeah, I know, but my nana won't agree to it, and I can't leave her to deal with Lori alone."

Amy sighed. "That does make it more difficult."

Chloe cleared her throat. "Anyway, this really isn't your problem and I'm sorry I dragged you into it."

"You didn't," Amy said. "Chloe, I know we work together, but we're friends too. And I promise you that Lori can't say or do anything to ruin that friendship, all right? Calling me names and hitting on Mark doesn't even ping on my anger scale. I'm a laid-back hippie, remember?"

Chloe smiled a little and Amy reached out and patted her knee. "Why don't you take the day off? Go home, have a hot bath and a nap and then watch really bad daytime television."

"I appreciate the offer, but I'll sit and mope all day if I do that. It's better for me to stay busy. Besides, Jackson will be crazy busy today trying to get the software finished for the new digital storefront, and I want to be there to help him if he needs me."

"All right. But if you change your mind, email me. I'll let Luke know I gave you permission to take the day off."

"Thanks, Amy. I appreciate it."

"CHLOE?" JACKSON OPENED THE FRONT DOOR. "WHAT, UH, what are you doing here?"

"Can I come in?" She was shivering, and he studied her before nodding and stepping aside.

Anxiety was already brewing in his belly, and, hoping she didn't hear it in his voice, he said, "Ian is working tonight."

"I know." She took off her boots and handed him her jacket. He hung it in the closet and followed her to the kitchen.

"Sorry I was in a bad mood all day," she said before sitting at the table.

He joined her. Part of him was thrilled that Chloe was here, and the other part was terrified that she was going to ask him for sex. "Honestly, I was so busy that I didn't really notice. Thanks for grabbing some lunch for me, by the way. That was really nice of you."

She smiled at him. "You're welcome."

There was silence that wasn't quite awkward, but not as comfortable as he wished it would be. "So, uh, is everything okay?"

"Yes. I came by because I was thinking maybe we could watch a movie together or something until Ian is finished work."

"Of course, I'd really like that." He hoped like hell that 'watch a movie' wasn't code for banging.

"Also, I was hoping you could help me with something," Chloe said.

"What's that?" Shit, he was growing more anxious by the minute.

Relax, dude. If she wants sex, you can bluff your way through it. Just eat her out, make her come a few times and then she'll fall asleep. You can tell her you were being a

*gentleman and letting her sleep. By the time she wakes up,
Ian will be home.*

Right. Excellent plan.

He gave her a more natural smile. "Is it work related?"

She laughed. "Not exactly." She reached into her purse
and pulled out the small pink box that held the anal plug. "I
was hoping you could help me put this in. I've gotten it in the
last couple nights, but it's been a real struggle. Think you
could help me out?"

Relief washed over him. "Of course."

"Great." She jumped up and still holding the box, headed
toward his bedroom. He followed her, flicking on the beside
lamp as she paused by the bed. "We'll put this in and then watch
a movie? Unless you have other plans. Shit, I should have texted
or called you first. I'm sorry. That was really rude of me."

"No, it's fine. Really. I'm glad you did." Now that his
anxiety had eased, he took a good look at her. Her face was
pale and there were lines around her eyes. She looked tired
and a bit upset, and he pulled her up against him. "Hey,
what's wrong?"

She smiled at him, but he could see her eyes watering.
"Nothing. It's been a long day and last night was…rough."

"Why? What happened?" He sat on the side of the bed
and pulled her down onto his lap.

For a moment, she almost looked like she was going to
tell him, but then she glanced away and shook her head.
"Nothing important."

"Honey," he said, "you can talk to me about it."

"I know." She sighed and rested her head on his chest. He
rubbed her back and kissed the top of her head. God, she
smelled good. He craved her touch almost constantly now,
craved her warmth and her softness.

After about ten minutes, she said, "Thanks, Jackson."

"I didn't do anything."

She sat up and cupped his face. "You did. I feel better already."

She studied his mouth before kissing him. He returned her kiss, stroking her tongue with his and wishing like hell his goddamn cock would do something. He tried to ignore the way it stayed limp as Chloe stroked his chest through his shirt.

She kissed him again before kissing his throat. When she sucked on his earlobe and her hand wandered down his stomach, he grabbed her wrist. "Chloe, wait."

She stopped and leaned back a little to look at him. "It's all right, Jackson."

"No, it isn't." Anxiety made his voice irritable. "I don't feel like having sex right now."

"Because you don't want me or because you need Ian here?"

He froze and gave her a cautious look. "How do you know that?"

She rubbed the line of his jaw with her thumb. "I suspected it after Tuesday night. Ian dropped by Wednesday night and confirmed it."

"Asshole," Jackson muttered. "I told him not to say anything."

"I'd pretty much figured it out anyway," she said. "And he told me because he's worried about you and was hoping I could help you."

"Well, you can't," he said.

She shrugged, not put out by his tone. "You don't know that for sure."

"I do," he said flatly. "I can't get a fucking erection

without Ian in the room, okay? We've been kissing for how long and there's nothing."

She refused to get off his lap. "So, we try a little longer."

"And when it doesn't work?" He snapped. "When I can't get a fucking hard-on, then what do we do?"

"You put the plug in my ass for me, and then eat me out and make me come," she replied.

He stared silently at her. She kissed his chin. "It doesn't always have to be about the actual sex, Jackson. If you don't get an erection now, you'll get one later when Ian's here and we'll fuck then. It doesn't make a difference to me if we fuck now, or later when Ian is with us."

She smiled at him as he continued to stare at her. Her body language was relaxed, and she was giving him an honest and open smile.

"You really mean that, don't you," he said.

"Yes. We'll try tonight and if it doesn't work, no problem. We'll keep trying until it does work. It's not the issue you think it is, Jackson."

He had no sense that she was saying it just to appease him but still, he had to say it. "I may never get an erection without Ian around."

She shrugged. "Maybe you won't."

"That doesn't upset you?" He said.

"Why would it? I know you want me, you've made that more than clear," she said. "You've got a bit of a roadblock at the moment and I get it. So, stop worrying about your dick right now and just concentrate on making me feel good. Okay?"

"Yes," he said.

"Great, but first, let's get that stupid plug into my ass."

He laughed, and she giggled before kissing his thick neck again. "Ian helped me put it in on Wednesday night, but I did it myself last night. It was kind of awful doing it alone, even if it did seem to go in much easier."

She gave him a bright smile. "That being said, I think I prefer having it put in while I'm horny."

"In that case," he cupped her breast and teased her nipple with his thumb, "maybe I should make you horny?"

"Yes, please." Her voice was already a little breathless and needy.

He tugged on the bottom of her shirt and she lifted her arms over her head so he could pull it off. She was wearing a pale blue bra and he traced the silk cups before pressing a kiss above her breasts. "I love your tits."

She giggled. "No, you love my ass. Admit it."

"I do love your ass." He reached beneath her and kneaded one firm ass cheek. "I can't wait to fuck it."

She unclipped her bra and dropped it over the side of the bed. He bent his head and sucked on one tight nipple as she let her head fall back. "Mmm, that feels so good, Jackson."

"Stand up, honey."

She stood and he quickly stripped her of the rest of her clothes before taking off his own shirt. He kept his jeans on. He believed Chloe when she said she didn't care if he got an erection or not, but that didn't mean he wanted her seeing little Jackson just hanging limp.

She didn't comment on the fact that he kept his pants on, just climbed into the bed when he pulled back the covers. He took the plug out of the box and grabbed the lube from the nightstand drawer. She was lying on her side and he left the plug and the bottle of lube on top of the nightstand before spooning her.

He kissed the back of her shoulder before sliding his hand down between her legs. She parted them immediately, leaning back against him and lifting her top leg to give him better access to her pussy.

"Touch me," she moaned. "Please."

She was dripping wet and he made small circles on her swollen pussy lips. "Look how wet you are, sweetheart."

He showed her the tips of his fingers, lust coursing through his belly when she grabbed his hand and brought it to her mouth. She sucked his fingers clean before licking her lips and smiling at him.

"Fuck," he muttered before reaching between her legs again. He rubbed her perfect clit until she was moaning loudly and rocking her pelvis against him. When her body tensed and her nails dug into his wrist, he pulled his hand away.

She mewled in disappointment and rubbed her ass against his crotch. "Jackson, no!"

"Shh, honey. Time for the plug."

She muttered a curse but waited patiently as he covered the plug with lube. He reached between their bodies and squeezed and kneaded her ass cheeks for a few moments before saying, "Spread your ass for me, honey."

She rolled to her front and reached behind her to spread her cheeks. He stared at her tight little hole, another surge of lust making his fingers tremble a little, as he pressed the plug against her hole, working it in slowly. It slipped past her tight ring of muscle and she made a whine of pleasure as he pushed it all the way in. He wiggled it a little and she reared up, gasping for air.

"Oh God. I'm gonna come."

"Not yet," he said. He pulled her back against his body, her ass snug against his crotch, his hand reaching around to cup her tit. Her body stiffened, and she peered over her shoulder. He didn't understand the look on her face.

"Honey, what's wrong?"

"Um, unless you've got a banana in your pocket, you're *really* happy to see me," she said.

He stared at her before leaning back a little and staring down at his crotch. "Holy shit."

She laughed, a full-throated laugh that made his erect cock grow harder. "So, not a banana then?"

"I can't fucking believe it," he said. He reached down and touched himself through his jeans, as if he thought his erection would just magically disappear. He groaned when Chloe reached behind her and her soft hand rubbed him through the denim.

"Fuck, that feels good," he said.

"Would probably feel better if you took your pants off," she said. "I mean, it's only a suggestion, but..."

He gave her a light smack on the ass, making her squeal, before sliding out of the bed. He undressed in record time and quickly rolled a condom onto his dick. He was as giddy as a kid in a fucking candy store, as he climbed in behind her again and rubbed his dick against her ass. It pushed on the plug and she made a happy little moan before reaching between her legs and rubbing her clit.

"Stop that." He pulled her hand away.

"I want to come," she said.

"I know you do." He cupped her pussy, his fingers rubbing in slow circles against her. He let his fingertips graze over her clit, loving her reaction.

"Jackson, don't tease."

"I love teasing you, honey." He nuzzled her neck. "I love making you beg to come."

"I'm begging now," she said. "I don't want to wait."

"You need to be fucked. Is that right?"

"Yes," she moaned.

His cock was like a fucking rock and he needed to be inside her tight pussy right fucking now.

He reached for her leg but before he could lift it and slide his dick deep inside of her, Chloe said, "Jackson, wait."

He groaned but stayed still as she studied him over her shoulder. "I want you to fuck me in the ass."

His cock twitched against her ass, it liked that idea very fucking much, thank you, and she grinned at him. "You want that as well."

"Of course I do," he rasped, "but we can't. You're not ready yet."

"I think I am," she said. "I want to try. Please, Jackson? I'd rather try having anal sex on its own first before I take both of you at once. This is the perfect opportunity to try."

He hesitated, and she squeezed his hand. "If it isn't going to work or it hurts too much, we'll stop, all right? We can try again later."

"You've only been wearing the plug for a few days," he said.

"I know," she said, "but I think it'll be okay. It – it feels really good when you touch the plug or move it. Please, let's just try."

"Do you promise to tell me if it hurts too much?"

"I promise," she said.

She smiled when he sat up and coated his cock with lube. He reached between them and traced the plug in her ass. She pressed against his erect cock and he pulled out the plug, tossing it to the end of the bed, before squeezing more lube onto his fingers and sliding them into her. He stretched her a little more with his fingers then pressed the head of his dick against her hole. He rubbed her hip when she tensed a little.

"Breathe out and push back against me, honey," he said.

She nodded and took a deep breath, releasing it as she

pushed back against him. He eased forward, groaning when the head of his dick pushed past her tight muscle. She clenched around him and he groaned again.

"Fuck, honey, don't squeeze. Christ, don't squeeze."

"Sorry," she panted. "I didn't mean to do that."

"I know, but try to relax or this'll be over before it even starts."

She smiled a little and he breathed a sigh of relief when she relaxed. "Good, honey."

"Is it all the way in?"

He shook his head. "No, sweetheart. Just the head."

Her eyes widened. "Just the head? I think I might have been a little too hasty in suggesting we try this right now."

"Does it hurt?" He rubbed her hip and thigh again.

"No, but I, uh, I feel really full, Jackson. I'm not sure I can take any more of it."

"You can." He kissed her shoulder before taking her hand and guiding it between her legs. "Touch yourself."

She licked her lips and nodded before rubbing a bit tentatively at her clit. He waited patiently, rubbing her hip, ignoring his throbbing cock and his almost irrepressible need to slide his dick all the way into her magnificently tight ass.

It only took a few minutes for her to start rocking her body against him as her pleasure grew. She took an inch of him without even realizing it, as she pressed back against him and rubbed hard at your clit.

"Feel good, honey?" He said as he reached between them and pushed apart her ass cheeks.

"Yes," she panted. She made a squeal of pleasure as she rubbed her clit with firm circular strokes. "I'm close."

"Good," he said. "Come for me, honey. I want to see you coming all over your fingers."

She cried out and her body arched as she pinched her clit.

RAMONA GRAY

He pushed in fully as her orgasm consumed her, moaning loudly when her ass clenched around his dick while she climaxed.

She panted and moaned and rubbed at her clit as he slowly slid in and out of her ass with short, gentle pushes. She collapsed against him, panting loudly and he palmed one small breast before kissing her neck. He continued to thrust in and out, his hand moving to her hip to hold her steady.

"Jackson," she moaned.

"Yeah, honey?"

"It feels…good."

He smiled and kissed her shoulder again. "Spread your legs for me."

She did what he asked, and he slipped two thick fingers into her tight pussy as he thrust a little harder. She cried out, her pussy and her ass clenching around him. He groaned into her ear. "Fuck, honey, you're gonna make me come."

"I want you to," she whispered.

"Soon. I want you to come again first."

"Oh God," she shivered against him as he thrust his fingers in and out of her pussy and his cock in and out of her ass. "It's so….good."

He groaned when she began to meet each of his thrusts. "Your little ass is so tight," he panted. "So fucking tight. That's right, honey, take my cock in your ass."

She moaned, her hips rocking back and forth, her ass smacking against his pelvis in a quick, hard rhythm. He stroked her pussy harder and faster and when she made a harsh cry and came again, he thrust deep and allowed himself to come as well. Her ass clenched around him and he shouted her name as he pushed in and out. He was almost crushing her into the bed, and he forced himself to withdraw slowly before collapsing on his back. She stayed on her side, her body trembling, as he disposed of the condom before spooning her again.

"Honey? Are you okay?" He could hear the worry in his voice. He'd been so rough at the end, had almost lost control.

"I feel awesome," she said. "How about you?"

"Incredible."

She rolled to face him and he palmed her ass, squeezing it lightly, as she ran her fingers through the hair on his chest. "I'm sorry if I was too rough."

"You weren't," she said. 'I mean, I'll probably be a little sore, but I think that's to be expected, right?"

He nodded and she smiled at him. "Thank you, Jackson."

"I should be the one thanking you," he said. "I just had sex without Ian. Do you know how long it's been since that happened? Over six months."

"Congratulations." She yawned like it was no big deal and he laughed before kissing her on the mouth.

"Seriously, Chloe. Thank you."

"You're welcome. I'm going to have a quick shower." She kissed his chest. "I'll be back in a bit, okay?"

"Okay." This time he yawned, and as she slid out of the bed and walked naked to the bathroom, he threw his arm over his eyes and grinned. He'd had sex with Chloe. He'd had sex without Ian there and maybe, just maybe, he wasn't about to screw up his life and Ian's.

CHAPTER 14

I an couldn't stop the eager grin on his face as he slipped into the house. Chloe's car was in the driveway and just seeing it had immediately put him in a good mood. The house was dark and quiet, and he quickly walked upstairs. He could hear the shower and the bathroom door was partially open. Steam drifted into the hallway as he eased the door open further and stepped into the room.

His cock hardened almost immediately, and he was stripping off his clothes before he even really thought about it. Chloe, her naked body wet and slick, was standing under the spray of water, letting it beat down on her upper back. Her hair was up in a messy bun and he stared at her delectable ass as the soap sluiced away from her perfect pale skin.

He slid open the shower door. Chloe didn't turn, but he could hear the smile in her voice. "Decided to join me, big guy?"

He put his arms around her and pulled her back against his chest. "When I come home to find a naked woman in my shower, I absolutely have to join her."

She jerked in surprise and then giggled before smiling up

at him. "How often do you come home to find naked women in your shower?"

"You're the first." He turned her around and kissed her, reaching down to cup her ass as she rubbed her tits against his chest.

When he finally pulled back, she was breathless and her mouth was red and swollen. She gave him a sweet smile. "Hi, Ian."

"Hi, baby. How are you?"

"Glad you're home."

"Me too." He nuzzled her wet skin. "Where's Jackson?"

"Sleeping."

He frowned when he squeezed her ass again and she flinched slightly. "What's wrong?"

"My butt is a little sore," she said.

"Your butt is sore," he repeated.

"Yep." She gave him a cheeky grin. "Yours would be too if you just had anal sex."

His eyes widened. "You and Jackson… he got an…and you were able to…"

"Yes, and yes," she said.

He hugged her hard, kissing the side of her neck before saying, "Thank you, baby. Thank you so much."

She shrugged. "Honestly, I don't really think it was me. It was like you said, he just needed to know that the woman he was with didn't care if he got an erection or not." She gave him another adorable cheeky grin. "I told him it was all about me anyway and ten minutes later, he was good to go."

He laughed before cupping her hips and kissing her again. "You're amazing."

"Amazing because I could have anal sex with a huge penis after only a few days of plugs? Because, yep, I'm seriously impressed with myself over that. I mean, it hurt, don't get me wrong, but not nearly as much as I thought it would, and after I adjusted to the feel…holy moly, it felt really good. Like…weirdly good."

He loved how open and honest she was about sex. "I'm glad you liked it, baby."

"Me too." She reached down and rubbed his erection. "I can't wait to have sex with both of you. Maybe we should head to Jackson's bedroom and -"

He shook his head. "Not tonight, Red. You need some recovery time."

She pouted at him and ran her thumb over the head of his dick. "Well, you're no fun."

He gave her a mock scowl. "No fun? You're lucky I'm in a good mood or else your sore butt would be getting a spanking."

She giggled. "Promises, promises."

He cupped her firm breast and turned their bodies so they were both being hit by the hot spray. She leaned against the shower wall, her slender body arching as he bent and ran his hot mouth over both her perfect tits. He sucked on her nipples, nipping at them until she clutched his head and made a low cry of need.

"How long have you been in the shower?" He lifted his head.

"Um… I dunno, ten minutes maybe? Why?"

"Just wondering if we have enough hot water to last while I fuck you."

She bit her bottom lip as lust crossed her face. "I think we should definitely try and find out, officer."

"Yes, ma'am." He kissed her again, pressing her slick body up against the wall as he skimmed his hand down her hip. She spread her legs and he slipped his hand between her legs. He rubbed her clit, watching her face as she grew wet.

Her hands squeezed his arms and she gave him a lazy smile full of need.

"I want you, Ian."

"I want you too, Chloe."

They kissed repeatedly, and she reached down and stroked his cock with her soft hand. "You can't come inside of me, okay? I'm not on birth control."

"I won't," he said. "I promise."

She cupped his face and gave him a sweet kiss. "Fuck me."

He cupped her hips and lifted her. She wrapped her legs around his waist as he braced her body against the wall. She reached between them and he hissed out a breath when she guided him into her wet pussy. Taking her bare, feeling her wet walls squeezing and rippling around him with no barrier, was a fucking dream.

He hadn't fucked a woman without a condom in years, and he gritted his teeth and thought about the mountain of paperwork sitting on his desk to try and control himself. Fuck, not using a condom was a very bad idea.

"Ian? What's wrong?" She stroked his wet back.

"This was a bad idea," he gritted out. "You're so wet and tight."

She smiled at him and traced a lazy circle on his back with her finger. "Control, Officer Aldrin. You need to have control."

"Fuck," he muttered before thrusting twice into her.

She moaned, her fingers digging into his back and her legs tightening around his waist. "Oh, oh God, that's nice."

"You need to come for me quickly," he moaned. "I'm sorry, baby, but – but this has to be quick. You feel so good without a condom that I can't…"

"Hard and fast is good," she whispered into his ear. "Whatever you need, Ian."

He groaned and drove into her with hard, deep strokes. She clung to him, moaning his name as he fucked her. His need for her was spiraling out of control, and he almost lost his goddamn mind when she came around him. Her pussy squeezed him tight, milking him with rippling little pulses that threatened to make him break his promise to her.

With a low groan, he pulled out of her and set her on her feet before she even finished coming, using one hand to steady her as his other hand pumped his cock rapidly. He moaned her name, arching his back as he came all over her flat stomach. Breathing harshly, he pressed his body against hers and rested his forehead on the tile wall. She stroked his back and kissed his chest. Her body was trembling, hell, *his* body was trembling, and he smiled down at her.

"That was amazing, baby."

"It really was." She kissed his chest again. "C'mon, let's get cleaned off before we completely run out of hot water."

He held her close when she tried to slip past him. "Are you staying the night?"

She nodded. "If that's okay?"

"Yes. We want you to stay with us, baby. Always."

Even he could hear the tenderness in his voice, and he winced when she stiffened a little and said, "Ian, this isn't -"

"For the night," he said hastily. "We always want you to stay the night when you come over? Okay?"

She studied him before nodding. "Yeah, okay."

He let her go and watched as she washed away the evidence of his need for her. He had to stop mooning over her, had to stop acting like they were in some kind of relationship. She'd made it perfectly clear what this was, and just because she was the perfect woman for both him and Jackson, didn't mean he could force her to be in a relationship with them. She didn't want that and he would damn well respect what she wanted. Even if it was fucking killing him.

———

WAKING UP TO THE SMELL OF BACON AND COFFEE WITH A warm, hard body tucked against her back was the best way to wake up, Chloe decided.

She stretched lazily, smiling a little when Jackson made a soft snoring sound behind her. Was it bad that she could tell Ian and Jackson apart just by the sound of the snoring? She giggled to herself before reaching for her phone on the nightstand. After she and Ian showered together last night, she'd sat with him while he'd warmed up some dinner and ate. She'd grabbed her cell phone, and they'd climbed into Jackson's bed with him. He hadn't woken, and tired and feeling deliciously satisfied, Chloe had fallen asleep between the two men.

There were no missed calls from her grandmother and she relaxed in the bed, scrolling through Facebook for a little while before the need to pee had her sliding out of bed. She slipped on Ian's t-shirt and used the bathroom, then headed downstairs.

"Morning." She kissed Ian's bare back as she slipped by him and grabbed a mug. She poured herself a cup of coffee before squeezing his ass through his track pants.

"Morning," he said. "Sleep well?"

"So good." She poured some milk into her coffee and sat down at the table. "How about you?"

"Like a rock." He grinned at her as he turned a piece of bacon, then winced. "Ow, shit."

He rubbed at his abdomen and she laughed. "Cooking bacon half-naked is the worst idea ever, Ian."

He winked at her. "Maybe you should give me my shirt then."

"Yes, because your neighbours want to see me walking around naked in the kitchen."

"We'll close the blinds," Ian said with another grin.

"Morning." Jackson, yawning hugely and wearing a pair of sleep pants and t-shirt, wandered into the kitchen. "That smells really good."

"Thanks. Start the toast, would you?"

"Sure." Jackson leaned over and kissed Chloe before lifting her mug to his mouth and taking a drink.

"Hey, get your own." Chloe poked him in his flat stomach and he grinned at her before moving to the toaster.

"What can I do to help?" Chloe asked.

"You could set the table," Ian said. "But can you grab the eggs for me, first?"

"Sure." She brought Ian the eggs before beginning to set the table. She had to admit that it was kind of nice to wake up on a Saturday morning with Ian and Jackson instead of alone. She knew she'd been lonely since John had left, but she hadn't realized how lonely until now.

Stop it, Chloe. These two are not your boyfriends. Don't start thinking they are. You get close to them, you let them into your life and Lori will ruin it for you. This is about fucking and nothing else. Don't forget that.

Her good mood was threatening to deflate like a balloon. She hated that it had to be this way. Hated that she had to constantly keep a part of her life hidden from the people she cared about.

"What are your plans for today?" Ian asked.

"Uh, I'm not sure. Why?" She arranged the silverware next to each plate, hating the wariness in her voice.

Ian gave Jackson a deceptively casual look. "We wondered if you wanted to hang out with us today. I'm off and we thought it would be nice to spend the day together."

"Um, I'm not sure… I mean…"

Jackson turned and smiled at her. "It's not a date, Chloe. Just three friends hanging out. We have a couple of errands to run and then we thought we'd go to a movie. You're welcome to join us, or not. Totally up to you. But," he wiggled his eyebrows at her, "you should know that Ian is planning on making his infamous chicken pot pie for dinner, *and* we'll let you ride our cocks for as long and hard as you want, if you stay."

"Hmm," she said, "I do love chicken pot pie."

Both Ian and Jackson laughed, and she grinned happily at them. "I'd love to hang out with you guys. But we need to stop at my place on the way to do errands, so that I can change and brush my teeth."

"We can do that," Ian said.

"And," she stole a piece of bacon when Ian set it on the table in front of her, "I get to pick the movie."

"She drives a hard bargain," Jackson said to Ian.

"Do we have a deal or not?" She blew on the bacon and crunched it down as Ian and Jackson smiled at each other.

"Deal," they said in unison.

"I had a really great day today, Ian. Thank you." Chloe slid her arms around Ian's waist and kissed his back through his shirt. She could hear Jackson climbing the stairs to the bedroom, and lust swept through her.

She realized Ian had stiffened and she kissed his back again. "What's wrong?"

"You said that like you're leaving." He stared out the kitchen window.

"I'm not," she said. "I want to spend the night."

He relaxed, and she ignored the tendrils of unease starting to replace the lust. She'd had an amazing day with Ian and Jackson, one of the best days of her life, and they hadn't even had sex once today. Running errands, going to the movies, hell, picking up groceries for supper tonight shouldn't have made her so happy, but they did. Even doing mundane things with Ian and Jackson made her feel content.

You're letting them get too close, Chloe. You need to pull back, need to re-establish the ground rules, before it's too late.

She ignored her inner voice. Not that it wasn't right, but tonight wasn't the time to think about it. Tonight, she wanted to forget about everything but the need to take both Ian and Jackson at once.

Her pussy made a hard flutter and she squeezed Ian's waist. "Come to bed, Ian."

He turned and slipped his arms around her before giving her a solemn look. "Baby, you know you don't have to take both of us tonight, right? You're probably still a little sore, and both Jackson and I don't mind waiting. It's not as important to us as you think it is to fuck you at the same time. Really, it isn't."

"I know. I want this," she said. "I want this a lot. If it's too painful or I don't think I can do it, I'll ask you to stop. Okay?"

He studied her. "Will you?"

"Yes. I'm not gonna wreck my lady parts over this. If I can't do it, I'll be honest about it."

He was still studying her gravely and she reached between their bodies and rubbed his dick. "I promise, Ian."

He kissed her and stroked her hair back from her face. "All right. Let's go upstairs then."

He flicked off the kitchen light and she followed him up the stairs and to his bedroom this time. Jackson was already naked and pulling back the covers to the bed. She giggled when Ian said, "Christ, Jackson, could you at least try and play a little hard to get?"

"Chloe likes seeing me naked," Jackson said cheerfully. "Don't be jealous of that."

Ian rolled his eyes as Chloe walked to Jackson and squeezed his naked ass. "You *are* really hot."

"Right?" Jackson pulled her up against him and palmed her ass. "Now, let's get you naked too."

"Yes, let's." She glanced over at Ian. "Get naked, mister. Right now."

"Yes, ma'am." Ian gave her a little salute before undressing. Jackson helped her strip out of her clothes and the three of them climbed into bed.

She smiled a little. Already she was more comfortable with her nakedness with Ian and Jackson than she'd ever been with her ex-fiancé.

She laid on her back in the middle of the bed, smiling at her men when they stretched out on their sides on either side of her. Ian smoothed a hand over her belly as Jackson cupped her breast and kissed her collarbone.

"You're so beautiful, Chloe," Ian said.

"Thank you," she whispered. She arched her back and spread her legs, silently begging for Ian to move his hand to her pussy. He ignored her and stroked her smooth thighs before kissing her.

"Please" she said. One hand moved restlessly in Jackson's

hair as he sucked on her nipple, the other dug into Ian's broad back.

Ian smiled and shook his head. "We have plenty of time, Red."

"I want you right now," she said.

He moved to the end of the bed and she spread her legs eagerly when he stretched out between them and kissed her inner thigh. Jackson kissed her, and she cried out into his mouth when Ian's wet tongue licked up her slit. He lingered on her clit, teasing it lightly as Jackson sat up. He stood next to the bed and she leaned forward eagerly when he cupped the back of her head and guided her mouth to his cock.

She sucked him hard, loving his taste as Ian nibbled on her pussy lips before sucking on her clit. Jackson was moaning quietly, and he wound his fist in her hair, tugging lightly as she slid her mouth back and forth over his cock.

Ian laved her clit with his tongue. He slid one thick finger into her pussy and she took a gasping breath before sucking Jackson's cock again. God, it felt so damn good, so...her body stiffened and then relaxed when Ian slid his finger into her ass.

"Okay, baby?"

She nodded around Jackson's cock, staring up at Jackson as he smoothed her hair back from her face. "Ian's going to stretch you a little, honey."

She relaxed her body as Ian slid another finger into her ass. He stretched her gently, distracting her from the discomfort by licking her clit.

She wanted to hold back, knew she probably should hold back, but when Ian sucked on her clit again and wiggled his fingers in her ass, she was powerless to stop her climax. She shrieked around Jackson's thick cock, her hands fisting in Ian's hair as she ground her pussy against his mouth. Her body shook and, feeling weak and unsteady, she collapsed on her back as Ian licked her clit a final time.

She moaned and watched through half-lidded eyes as Jackson quickly rolled on a condom before tossing one at Ian. Ian ripped his open and slid it on, then laid on his side next to her again as Jackson stretched out on her right side.

"How you feeling, Red?"

"Super," she mumbled.

Ian and Jackson laughed, and she gave them a lazy smile. "I want you both to fuck me."

"Are you sure?" Ian asked.

"Yes," she replied.

Ian glanced at Jackson and another one of those silent communications rippled between them.

"Straddle Ian, honey," Jackson said.

She sat up and slung her leg over Ian before straddling his waist. He rubbed her hip bones with his thumbs. "Put my cock in your pussy, Red."

She giggled a little at the way he said it so sweetly, and he circled her belly button with his thumb. "Go on, baby. Do what I tell you."

"Yes, sir," she said.

That earned her a light slap on her butt and she squeaked and moved back until her pussy was resting against Ian's hard cock. She rose up on her knees and slid him into her, moaning a little at the delicious stretch. Ian rubbed her hips.

"Good girl." His voice was hoarse, and she rested her hands on his chest before smiling at Jackson.

"Now what?"

"Now you let Ian fuck you," Jackson said. He was standing next to the bed again and he made no move to join them as Ian took her arms and tugged her down. She braced her hands on either side of his head and rubbed her tits against his chest.

He groaned with pleasure, cupped her ass, and drove in and out of her pussy. She made her own moan of pleasure, her ass bouncing as he fucked her with long, deep strokes. She shifted a little, making a loud squeal when the head of Ian's dick rubbed against her g-spot.

She met each of his strokes with renewed excitement, squealing happily each time his cock hit that magical spot. "Oh God," she moaned. "That feels so fucking amazing."

Ian didn't reply, and she scowled at him when he slowed to a stop. "No, don't stop."

"Shh, baby, wait a minute."

"No!" She wanted to smack his chest and settled for digging her fingers into the covers and making her own hard thrusts against him. "I don't want to stop."

She muttered an angry curse when Jackson's heavy hand centered on her back. She didn't even realize that he had moved onto the bed and was kneeling between Ian's open legs. He held her against Ian's body easily, preventing her from moving, and she glared at him. "Move your hand."

"In a minute, honey," he said.

"No, now. I want to come."

He ignored her, and she squeezed Ian's hips with her knees. "Ian, make him let go."

Ian grinned at her and she was getting ready for another angry retort when the cold lube dripped down the crack of her ass.

"Cold!"

"Sorry." Jackson's fingers massaged her ass, warming the lube up. He slid his fingers into her, adding more lube and gently massaging her until she relaxed.

"Good, baby," Ian said. He petted her hair and kissed her throat. "Are you ready for Jackson's dick?"

"I'm ready to come," she said grouchily. "I was about to have a g-spot orgasm, which I've never been able to do before, and you guys ruined it by... oh!"

Her body tensed and then relaxed as Jackson pressed the head of his dick against her anus and pushed. She blew out her breath and pushed back, her gaze on Ian's face. As Jackson worked his way past the tight ring of muscle, she tried not to moan. It hurt more than before, but she shook her head when Ian said, "Do we need to stop?"

"No, I'm good," she panted. "It's just... a lot."

That was the understatement of the year. Between her pussy being full of Ian's giant dick and Jackson's equally giant dick slowly sliding deep into her ass, she had never felt fuller in her life. She tried to move forward a little to ease some of the pressure and Jackson's hand pressed on her lower back.

"No, honey. Stay still." He pulled back a little and then pushed forward again. "You're being so good. You've almost taken all of it."

She moaned as the sweet burn intensified. "I don't think – I can't... ohhh."

Ian had reached between them, wiggling his fingers between the tight fit of their bodies and was gently circling her clit. "Better, baby?"

"Yeah," she panted, "yeah, that helps. Thank you, Ian."

"You're welcome." Ian's voice was a little strangled sounding and he groaned when Jackson made a final push and Chloe squeezed her pussy around his cock. "Christ, baby, try and relax. Please. You're gonna make me come before we even get started."

Jackson's harsh breath blew across her back as he rubbed her ass. "Fuck, that's goddamn tight."

"Yeah." Ian's voice was barely recognizable.

She raised up a little and stared down at him. He looked like he was on the brink of his control already and she smiled at him. "You okay, Ian?"

He made a clipped nod of his head. "Jackson, you ready?"

"Yes." Jackson's voice sounded as unsteady as Ian's.

She twisted her head, staring at Jackson's face as he gave her a strained smile. "You're so tight like this, honey."

She gave him a shy smile, digging her fingers into the covers again when Ian started moving beneath her. After a few seconds, Jackson moved as well, the two of them sliding in and out of her in a perfect rhythm. She arched her back a little, as the feeling of fullness increased.

She took a deep breath, closing her eyes and letting the sensations overtake her. She was impaled on two dicks, both Ian and Jackson were fucking her at once, and it felt... her eyes popped open. It felt fucking incredible.

The warmth she was feeling was growing, threatening to burn her up, as Ian and Jackson moved harder and faster. Exquisite pleasure was radiating throughout her lower body and her soft cries and gasps competed with the men's low grunts and hoarse noises of ecstasy.

Their previous slow and measured pace was giving way to a rough and hard, almost out of control rhythm. She clung to Ian's broad shoulders, letting her body move between them, reaching for that pinnacle that was growing closer.

Both men were close, she could tell in the way their bodies moved, in the raspy sound of their groans. When Jackson shifted her slightly and Ian's cock rubbed against her g-spot, she made an inarticulate scream before coming so hard that stars burst into light behind her tightly-closed eyelids.

Dimly she was aware of Jackson's hoarse shout of pleasure, of Ian's hands digging into her hips as his body drove up into hers, but their pleasure was overshadowed by the pure intensity of her own orgasm and the feeling of utter connection with both men. Her climax went on and on, her body shaking and shuddering between the two men, and when Jackson eased out of her and helped her lie on her side next to Ian, she continued to shake and twitch.

She kept her eyes closed as both men crowded in close. They rubbed her body with their warm hands, whispered praise into her ears, kissed her and soothed her and told her repeatedly how beautiful she was.

She sunk into their embrace, feeling cherished and protected and...loved. Her body wanted to tense, her inner voice told her to flee, but she was too weak, too sated, and too overwhelmed to move.

"Okay?" Ian whispered into her ear.

"Better than okay," she replied. "It was amazing. I'm just really tired now."

"Go to sleep, honey." Jackson nuzzled her bare shoulder. "We've got you."

CHAPTER 15

"How was she today?" Ian was barely in the kitchen before he was giving Jackson an anxious look. "Did you talk to her?"

Jackson shook her head. "She was the same as she's been. Busy, distracted sad. And I've been so fucking busy myself that I really haven't had the time to talk to her, Ian."

"Fuck." Ian slammed his fist on his own thigh. "I sent her a text earlier before I finished work, asking her to have dinner with us, but she said she had plans. This is our fault, Jackson. We pushed her too soon to have sex with us both."

"It isn't," Jackson said. "Look, I know she's been avoiding us for a bit, but -"

"A bit? It's *Wednesday*, Jackson," Ian said. "She hasn't been with us since Saturday night. Hell, she'll barely talk to you at work and she doesn't respond to half my texts. I knew we should have waited longer to both have sex with her. What if we hurt her? What if we did something she didn't like and now she hates us both? Did you think of that?"

"Ian, dude, calm down," Jackson said. "She was the one who pushed for sex with both of us, remember?"

"Yeah, but -"

Jackson leaned against the counter and rubbed his forehead. "Look, I know you don't want to hear this, but it has nothing to do with the both of us fucking her at once, and everything to do with her being afraid to get close to us. She's pushing us away because she's scared of what she's feeling for us."

He huffed out a laugh. "Hell, I don't blame her. That night with her, Ian …it was powerful and special and… I don't even know how to explain it, but I know you felt it too."

Ian nodded before sinking into a chair. "I'm in love with her, Jackson."

He could feel Jackson's startled gaze but didn't look up from his hands. "And you are too."

Jackson was silent, and Ian waited a moment before looking up at him. "Admit it."

"I care for her a lot, but I haven't known her long enough to be in love with her, and neither have you." There was low-grade panic in Jackson's voice. "You're just high on whatever the hell that connection was with her on Saturday night. Nothing more."

"That connection you felt? That's called love," Ian said.

"Stop it." Jackson's voice was harsh. "Don't start acting like what we have with Chloe could be something more. She's a great girl and I like her a lot, but she does not want a relationship with us. She's made that clear. Besides, even if she did, what would we do? The three of us move in together and be one big happy family? We both knew that fucking women together had an expiration date, but it doesn't end because we both get the same woman. It ends because we find separate women and build separate lives with them. One woman falling in love with two men is a fucking fairy-tale, Ian. It's a fairy-tale! Do you hear me?"

"Yes." Ian could hear the pain in Jackson's voice, and guilt coursed through him. "I – you're right, okay? I know you're right. But for now, I'm really worried about Chloe. I know you think her blowing us off doesn't have anything to do with what happened Saturday night, but what if you're wrong? We need to find out."

"We can't force her to have dinner with us."

"No, but we can go by her apartment, ask her to give us five minutes to talk to her."

"We can't keep showing up at her place," Jackson said with an exasperated sigh. "Christ, Ian, you're a cop. How do you think it'll look when Chloe puts out a damn restraining order against us?"

"Don't you think you're exaggerating a little?" Ian said. "Chloe doesn't hate us, she -"

"She's just finished with us." Jackson paced back and forth in the kitchen. "Look, you haven't seen her, okay? I have. She's done with us. She barely looks at me. If I even get close to her, she tenses up, and she turns into a goddamn mute if I ask her anything that isn't work-related. You need to accept that what we had with her is finished and she isn't going to show up on our doorstep anytime soon."

The doorbell rang, and Jackson stared blankly at him. Ian, his heart pounding, strode out of the kitchen and down the hallway. He threw open the front door, burying his immediate need to yank Chloe into his arms when he saw her standing on the front step.

"Hi." She gave him a timid smile. "Sorry to come by without calling or texting, but, uh, do you mind if I come in?"

He shook his head, stepping aside so she could walk past him. Her arm brushed against his chest and he inhaled her sweet scent as Jackson stuck his head into the hallway from the kitchen.

"Chloe?"

"Hi, Jackson. Sorry to stop in like this."

"It's fine. Come in to the kitchen."

She gave Ian a nervous smile before walking to the kitchen. He followed her, fighting the urge to pick her up and carry her straight to the bedroom. Not for sex...no, just so he could wrap his arms around her, could hold her against his body and try and fix whatever was wrong.

Something *was* wrong. Something terrible. He could see it in the way she kept her arms crossed against her torso, in the dark circles under her eyes, and the sadness that practically seeped from her pores.

She slid into a chair, staring at the floor as Ian and Jackson sat down on either side of her.

"Do you want some tea?" Jackson asked.

She shook her head. "No, I can't stay long. I wanted to come here and apologize for how I've been behaving the past few days. I've treated you both horribly, and I'm very sorry."

"Did we upset you?" Ian asked. "On Saturday night, did we do or say anything to you that -"

"No," she said quickly. "No, it has nothing to do with either of you. I enjoyed Saturday night, so much."

"Baby, look at me." Ian took her cold hand and she raised her gaze to his. He could see she was holding back tears and he squeezed her hand. "Tell us what's wrong."

"I had a really bad day with my grandmother and my sister on Sunday. I went there for the afternoon, and Lori has a new boyfriend and he was awful and he -"

"Did he do something to you?" Ian's voice was tight. "Did he touch you or hurt you?"

"Ian," Jackson said, "relax, man."

"Did he?" Ian ignored his best friend. "Answer me, Chloe."

"No," she said. "He's a drunk like her and the two of them together were awful. I was afraid to leave Nana alone with them, so I stayed until they passed out and it was really…exhausting. Nana called Monday night because he was there again, and she was afraid. I went over after work and stayed until they drank themselves unconscious at about three. Last night they went out, thank God, and stayed who knows where, but I was still up most of the night, worrying that they'd come home and scare Nana or-or hurt her."

She took a deep breath, staring at the floor beneath their feet. Her voice was dull and robotic, and Ian had the idea that she'd forgotten where she was and who she was talking to. "Anyway, I went to Al-Anon tonight and I wanted to share, but I couldn't even do that. Nana left this morning on some senior's trip with her church group. She's not back until Saturday which means I at least have a small break, but as soon as she's back, it'll be the same old thing. I'm so tired and upset and worried and I felt terrible about how I've been treating you guys, but once again, Lori fucking takes up all of my energy and I'm so fucking tired all the time. I just wish she would -"

She suddenly stopped and yanked her hand away from his. She gave him and Jackson a horrified look. "Oh my God, I am so sorry. I didn't come over here to tell you this. I came by to say that I'm sorry for avoiding you and for being rude, and to let you know that it has nothing to do with you. I'm truly sorry."

She stood up and both Ian and Jackson stood as well. Ian stepped in front of the doorway. "Don't leave, baby. I'll make you something to eat, okay? When was the last time you ate?"

Chloe shook her head. "I'm not hungry. I should go. I'm really tired and I'm embarrassed and -"

"You don't need to be embarrassed," Jackson said. "You can tell us whatever you need to, honey. You don't have to hide or hold back when you're upset. Let us help you with your sister, maybe if we talk to her -"

It was the wrong thing to say. Chloe's eyes went wide and her face paled until she was the colour of fresh snow. "No! No, you don't go anywhere near her. Do you hear me? Stay away from Lori, Jackson. She's poison, and I don't want you or Ian going anywhere near her. Promise me!"

"Okay," Jackson said immediately. "Okay, we won't. I promise. But, honey, you can't deal with this all on your own. We want to help you."

"I can't let you do that." Chloe turned to Ian and gave him a pleading look. "Please try and understand that it has nothing to do with you. Lori is toxic – *I'm* toxic – and I don't want you to be a part of that. It's why I can't be in a – it's why this has to stay simple and uncomplicated between us. Okay? Please?"

"What if we want more?" Ian said softly.

Tears dripped down her cheeks. "I can't do that. I'm sorry. I need to go."

She tried to push past Ian, pressing on his chest when he put his arms around her and hugged her. "I have to go, Ian."

"Don't go, baby."

"I can't give you what you want. I'm sorry, I wish I could, but I can't. You have to believe me when I say it's better that you don't get too close to me. I'll destroy your lives, I will."

Being without her would destroy him, but Ian kept his mouth shut as Jackson rubbed Chloe's back. "It's okay, honey. We won't ask you for anything else, all right? We'll take whatever you can give us. That will be enough."

"Will it?" Chloe's voice was muffled. She lifted her tear-streaked face to Ian's and he made himself smile at her and lie.

"Yes, Red. It will."

She studied him for a few minutes before nodding. "Okay. Uh, thanks, you guys. I'd better go."

Ian told himself not to beg, but he couldn't quite unwrap his arms from around her slender body. He glanced at Jackson who said, "Stay with us tonight, Chloe."

"I can't. I don't want to give you the wrong idea anymore and staying the night -"

"Staying the night doesn't give us the wrong idea," Jackson said. "Besides, we want you to stay the night only so we can do dirty, wicked things to you."

He was lying, Ian knew him well enough to see it immediately, but Chloe relaxed in his arms and gave Jackson a tentative smile. "Oh, well in that case…"

Jackson grinned at her. "Good. Now, I know you said you weren't hungry, but you should at least have some toast or something. I'll run you a bath to soak in for a while and then we'll go to bed. Okay?"

Chloe gave Ian a tentative look. He leaned down and pressed a kiss against her mouth. "Say yes, Red."

"Yes, Red," she whispered.

He hugged her again and she buried her face in his chest as he met Jackson's worried gaze.

"You ready to be hit on by a couple of horny Frenchmen?" Amy sat down next to Chloe in the boardroom.

"So ready," Chloe said.

Amy laughed. "Where's Jackson?"

"He's on his way. He and Luke were going over some last-minute stuff on the website in our office."

"How are things going with him and Ian?" Amy asked.

"Fine."

"Just fine?" Amy arched one eyebrow at her.

"It's complicated."

"I imagine it is. Sleeping with two guys at once, there are bound to be some jealousy issues or some weird third-wheel feelings."

"There isn't," Chloe said.

"Really? Like, at all?"

"No." Chloe ran her fingers over the smooth surface of the boardroom table. "There really isn't. I don't think either Ian or Jackson have a jealous bone in their body. Being with both of them feels right and… natural, you know? I've had sex with both of them separately and while I like it a lot, it doesn't feel right. Like something is missing when I sleep with just one of them."

"Interesting," Amy said thoughtfully. "So, what's complicated then?"

"They want more," Chloe said. "They want a relationship with me. They deny it and pretend they're fine with keeping it casual and uncomplicated, but I can see it in their faces. Ian's especially. I think Jackson wants more but is in a bit of denial about it, but Ian definitely isn't."

"You don't want more?" Amy said.

Chloe hesitated. "No."

"You hesitated."

"I didn't."

"You did. You want more too."

Chloe scowled at Amy, but the pretty blonde just shrugged. "I call it like I see it."

"We can't have more, okay?" Chloe said.

"Because of your sister."

"Yes. You've met her, you've seen what she's like. She'll wreck everything that's good between me and Ian and Jackson. They're good guys, but even good guys have their limits. Eventually, they'll get tired of the way I blow them off whenever something happens with Lori or my Nana, and they'll ask me to make a choice just like John did."

"It wouldn't make you a bad person to choose them over your sister," Amy said gently.

Chloe chewed on her bottom lip. "History has proven that I'm incapable of not choosing my sister."

Amy nodded. "I get it. I couldn't imagine ever giving up on Luke. But, you also have to remember that you're not responsible for her, and being kind to yourself and making choices that bring you happiness is not wrong."

"I know. Anyway, even if my sister wasn't an issue, there are other things to consider. Being in a committed relationship with two men isn't exactly accepted by society. I'm sure our families would freak out, and forget getting married or having a family."

"Screw what society or even your friends and family say," Amy said. "Do what makes you happy. Do you think my family would find it acceptable that I have a master/slave relationship with Mark? Or that I let him flog me and spank me until I have bruises? They wouldn't, but I don't care. I want those things, I *need* them, and having Mark fulfill those needs for me is incredible. What we do in our private lives is no one's business, but ours."

"It's a lot easier to keep what you do with Mark private, then it would be to keep a threesome relationship private," Chloe said.

"Fair enough. But, hell, life is short, Chloe. Do you really want to spend it apart from the men you love just because of what a few strangers might think?"

"I don't love them," Chloe said quickly.

"You sure about that?" Amy said.

"Yes. I like them a lot. They're great guys who are unbelievably sweet and kind and they make me laugh and feel good, and I love spending time with them, but I'm not..."

Amy laughed. "Nope, not in love with them at all."

Before Chloe could reply, the door opened and Luke and Jackson walked in. They sat down across from them and Jackson grinned at Chloe. She smiled back, feeling the same surge of warmth she always felt now when she saw either him or Ian.

She had gone to their house after her meeting Wednesday night not only because of her guilt over how she'd been treating them, but because she'd been so miserable and upset for the last few days that she'd needed to be with them. Needed the comfort and the distraction that only they could give her.

She wanted sex. She wanted to use it to forget about her anger and her fear, and she was ridiculously relieved when they'd asked her to stay. Only, they didn't have sex that night. They'd told her they would, but Ian had made her eat some toast while Jackson drew her a bath. She'd relaxed in the tub until the water cooled and then Jackson brought her to Ian's bedroom. The heat from the bath, the stress, and the late hour had all combined to make her almost stupidly tired.

She'd climbed naked into Ian's bed and both men snuggled her, Ian at her back and Jackson at her front. Their gentle touch and the combined heat of their bodies lulled her to sleep in less than five minutes.

Last night, she'd invited them over to her place. She was determined to have sex with both of them, determined to keep it casual and fun. Except, they'd taken one look at her, announced she was still obviously exhausted, and made her have another hot bath while Ian cooked dinner.

She'd tried to lure them to her bedroom after eating, but there was some survival reality show season finale that Jackson wanted to watch. She'd found herself sandwiched between them on her tiny couch, the three of them tucked under a blanket, with her head on Jackson's shoulder and her feet in Ian's lap. By the time the show ended, she could barely keep her eyes open. Ian had carried her to the bedroom and the two of them undressed her before tucking her under the covers. They'd stripped off their clothes and joined her, but like before, she'd fallen asleep before she could even attempt to seduce them.

Jackson had left early in the morning to go home and shower and change for work, but, Ian, about to start evening shifts at the station, was still sleeping in her bed when she'd left. She'd left her spare key on the nightstand for him, trying to ignore the weird excitement that action brought on. It wasn't like Ian would keep the key, she would get it back from him this weekend.

"Chloe?"

She realized two things at once – Luke had been talking the whole time and she was staring at Jackson like a love-struck moron.

Her face turned bright red and she gave Luke a mortified look. "I'm sorry, I was, uh... sorry, what did you say?"

"I was saying that Julien and Pierre's plane is delayed so they'd like to move the meeting to this evening over dinner. Are you available?"

"Yes, of course."

"Jackson?" Luke asked. "How about you?"

"I am," Jackson said.

"Great. So, Amy, you'll talk to Mark and let him know about the change in plans, and I'll get my PA to book us a reservation." Luke's glance slid to Chloe again. "As usual, if anything they say or do makes you uncomfortable, Chloe, don't hesitate to speak to me about it. I realize that with them investing in the company, you may feel like you can't speak up. It isn't true. We take harassment very seriously here and if, at any time, you're uncomfortable or want to end contact with them, we'll be on your side. Clear?"

"What are you talking about?" Jackson asked.

Luke cleared his throat. "Julien and Pierre have a bad habit of hitting on our employees. Chloe has met with them before and she's aware of what they're like, but I wanted to be clear that we are fully on her side."

"I know, Luke," Chloe said. "It'll be fine, honestly. Besides, they'll probably mostly hit on Amy. They're way more into her than me." She grinned at Amy who rolled her eyes.

"They know she's dating Mark now, so they'll probably focus their attention on you," Luke said.

Amy stared at him. "What? How do they know I'm dating Mark?"

"I might have mentioned it," Luke said.

"Luke! My personal life is no one's business, least of all Julien and Pierre's."

"Sorry, Ames, but I can't sit through a meeting watching two men try and convince my baby sister to sleep with both of them at the same time. It's too gross."

Amy shrugged. "You need to accept that I'm gorgeous and men are gonna hit on me, big brother."

"Gross," Luke said.

Jackson was staring intently at her, completely ignoring Luke and Amy's bantering. She stole a quick glance at Luke before mouthing 'What?' at Jackson. He frowned, but before he could say anything, Luke stood up.

"Jackson, can you come back to my office? Now that we've got some more time before the meeting, I wouldn't mind implementing a few more changes to the storefront.

"Of course." Jackson stood as Luke checked his watch.

"Good. Amy and Chloe, we'll meet at the restaurant at six. Sound good?"

They nodded, and Ian and Jackson left the boardroom. Amy leaned back in her chair and grinned at Chloe.

"What?"

"Did you see the look on Jackson's face when Lukie was talking about the boys hitting on you?"

"He didn't have a look on his face."

"He totally had a look on his face. I think you're wrong about your boys not having a jealous streak."

Chloe pushed back her chair and stood. "Maybe he had a slight look on his face, but it doesn't mean anything. I'd better get back to work. I'll see you at six."

"Jane!" Chloe smiled happily at the slender brunette who was standing inside the front door of the restaurant. "I didn't know you would be at the meeting."

"I wasn't supposed to be." Jane glanced over to where Luke was speaking with the hostess. "But, Luke has this weird idea that if he isn't home to cook me dinner, I'll starve. So, here I am."

"I'm glad you joined us," Chloe said.

"Me too," Jane replied.

Luke joined them. "Our table is almost ready. Hi, Chloe."

"Hi, Luke." She shifted her laptop bag to her other hand.

"I brought my computer in case Julien and Pierre wanted to go over the marketing presentation I sent them last week."

"Good idea. They did email me and tell me they thought the marketing plan looked good, but better to have it and not need it, right?" Luke said.

Chloe nodded as Jane grinned at Luke. "Do you think they'll even be able to concentrate on the meeting with three ladies at the table?"

Luke grimaced. "I told them that Mark and Amy were dating and I also," he turned a little red, "might have mentioned that you were living with me now."

Jane laughed. "Of course you did."

"But that does mean that Chloe's gonna get the full brunt of their…charm," Luke said. "Remember, Chloe, if they say or do *anything* -"

"It'll be fine, Luke. I can handle their flirting, I promise," Chloe said.

The door opened, bringing a gush of cold air. Julien and Pierre swept into the restaurant, identical smiles on their faces.

"Bonjour, mon amies," Julien said. He shook Luke's hand before pressing a kiss against Jane's cheek. "You look magnifique, Jane."

"Thank you, Julien." Jane smiled at him before turning to Pierre. "Hello, Pierre."

"Bonsoir, Jane." Pierre kissed her cheek and stepped back, a small grin crossing his face when Luke put a propri-etary arm around Jane's waist. "It is a pleasure to see you again."

"You as well," Jane said as Luke shook Pierre's hand.

"Julien and Pierre, you remember Chloe," Luke said.

Chloe took a deep breath as Pierre and Julien turned toward her. They both stared her up and down, blatant appreciation on their faces. She held out her hand and Julien took it first. He brought her hand to his mouth and kissed her knuckles.

"Of course. How could we forget such a beautiful ange roux, such as Chloe."

Pierre took her other hand before stepping close and brushing his lips across her cheek. "You are even more beautiful than we remember, ma chérie."

"Thank you," Chloe replied.

Julien stepped closer as Pierre's gaze dropped to her tits.

"Are you still single, mon ange?" Julien asked.

From the corner of her eye, she could see Luke rolling his eyes. She smiled at Julien. "I am."

"I am happy to hear that." He kissed her knuckles again.

"We are here for the weekend, sweet Chloe," Pierre said.

Shit, they were already trying to charm her into their bed.

"Perhaps you would care to join us for drinks later this evening at our hotel room?" Julien said. "Our room has a beautiful view of the city, and -"

"Jackson, any trouble finding the restaurant?" Luke suddenly said.

Chloe automatically pulled her hands free of Pierre and Julien's and took a step back as Jackson moved into her view.

"No trouble at all." Jackson shook Luke's hand without taking his eyes off of Chloe. She could feel the heat rising in her cheeks. There was something in Jackson's eyes as he studied the way the two Frenchmen stood so close to her. A hint of jealousy perhaps, or proprietorship, maybe.

Her stomach flip flopped lazily, goosebumps rising to her skin when Jackson joined them and his hand pressed lightly against her lower back. That light touch through her suit jacket made her more aware of her body than any touch from Pierre and Julien ever would.

Her legs trembled as Jackson stared down at her. That taste of jealousy had disappeared, if it had even been there in the first place, and in its place was pure lust. Her body reacted immediately, trembling even more as Jackson's hand dipped a little lower to rest against the top of her ass.

She had no idea what was going on with him, but holy crap, if he didn't stop looking at her the way he was, she'd be trying to lure him into the bathroom for a quickie before the appetizers even arrived.

"You must be Pierre and Julien. I'm Jackson Black."

"It is nice to meet you in person, Jackson." Pierre held out his hand and Jackson shook it before shaking Julien's hand.

"You as well," Jackson replied.

There was awkward silence. Pierre and Julien glanced at each other before studying how closely Jackson was standing next to her. She tried to sidle sideways and Jackson's hand slid to her hip. He held her against him and smiled stiffly at the investors.

"Mr. Dawson? Your table is ready." The hostess touched Luke's arm. "If you'd follow me, please."

As Luke, Jane and Amy followed the hostess, Jackson gave the Frenchmen another stiff smile, his arm still holding her firmly. "After you."

"Merci," Julien replied. He and Pierre started after the others. The moment their backs were turned, Chloe elbowed Jackson lightly in the ribs.

"Knock it off."

She expected Jackson to give her his usual flirty grin and some teasing remark. Instead, he scowled, bent his head and placed his mouth at her ear. "Remember that you belong to me and to Ian, Chloe."

She elbowed him again. "Since when did you get all caveman possessive, Jackson? I don't belong to any guy."

He nipped her earlobe, sending a hot shiver down her back. "Just know that even thinking about sleeping with them will earn you a spanking."

Okay, so Jackson's sudden possessiveness was not turning her on. It absolutely wasn't. Lots of women had the sudden urge to drag their man to the car for a quickie, right?

Her cheeks were warm, and her breathing was starting to get a little shallow. Ignoring the lust zipping up and down her body, she said, "Our very important investors who are the reason we both have jobs with Dawson Clothing, are going to spend the entire night flirting with me and attempting to convince me to fuck them both. You'll need to trust that I'm not interested in them and keep your inner caveman under wraps. Basically," she stroked one finger across his flat stomach, "behave yourself or *you'll* be the one who gets the spanking tonight."

His tense body relaxed a little and he gave her an adorable grin. "Does that mean you're coming over tonight?"

"I was thinking about it," she said tartly. "If you behave yourself at dinner."

"In that case, I'll be the perfect gentleman." Jackson held out his arm. She tucked her hand into the crook of his elbow and allowed him to guide her toward the others.

IAN UNLOCKED THE FRONT DOOR. A BLAST OF ROCK AND ROLL washed over him as soon as he opened the door, and he glanced at his watch before walking to the kitchen. It was one-thirty in the morning and unusual for Jackson to be up this late, even on a Friday night.

He stopped in the doorway and a happy grin crossed his face. Chloe was standing in the middle of the kitchen, shaking and shimmying her hips to the music. Jackson leaned against the counter, a beer in his hand and a smile on his face, watching her dance.

She clapped her hands and popped her hips to the beat. Ian's gaze drifted to her denim covered ass. Fuck, Chloe really did have an amazing ass. That amazing ass wiggled, and he adjusted his suddenly hard cock as she twirled in a circle. She caught sight of him and made a happy squeal of excitement before launching herself at him.

He caught her and she planted a kiss on his mouth. "Hi, Ian."

"Hey, baby. You're in a good mood."

"I am." She danced away, moving her hips seductively and winking at him over her shoulder. "How was work?"

"Fine." It had actually been a shitty night, but coming home to find Chloe dancing in their kitchen had erased every bad moment. She was usually so solemn, so worried and anxious about her sister and her grandmother, and to see her happy and carefree made his love for her grow by the damn second. "How was your meeting?"

Chloe grinned at Jackson who tipped his beer to her. She turned back to Ian. "It was most excellent. Julien and Pierre were very impressed by my marketing plan and Jackson's plans for the new digital storefront. Weren't they, Jackson?"

"They were," Jackson confirmed.

"That's great." Ian grabbed a beer from the fridge and twisted it open. He clinked his beer bottle against Jackson's. "Congratulations, man."

"Thank you." Jackson took a drink of beer. "Tell him the other part, Chloe."

Chloe placed her hands on her hips and pretended to walk the runway in front of them, tossing her hair and exaggerating the sway of her hips. "They," she swung around, tossing her long red hair behind her again, "loved my designs. Loved them."

"I knew they would," Ian said.

"You don't understand," she said excitedly. She ran forward and pressed her body against his, wrapping her arms around his neck and smiling up at him. "They didn't even know they were my designs. Amy showed them the portfolio and they specifically pointed out two of my six designs and said they loved them. Two of my designs, Ian! Two!"

"Congratulations, baby." He tried to kiss her, but she was still talking.

"When Amy told them they were my designs, they were so complimentary. I mean, probably about sixty percent of it was them just trying to get me into their bed, but that still leaves forty percent of them actually being impressed with my designs. I'll take forty percent."

"Wait, what?" Ian's body stiffened, and he automatically put his arm around Chloe's waist, pulling her in tight against him. "They tried to get you in their bed?"

"They're total horndogs," Chloe said airily. "They try to get every single woman that crosses their path into their bed. They want me to meet them for drinks tomorrow night, but -"

"No." Ian's hand tightened on her hip. "No way. Absolutely not, Chloe. You are not having drinks with them."

"Ian," Jackson nudged him, "I wouldn't, man. I tried that approach earlier and she threatened to spank me."

Ian was barely listening to him. He stared down at Chloe. "You're not having drinks with them. I won't -"

Chloe poked him hard in the chest. "I already told them no. One, I wouldn't sleep with investors in the company I work for, and two, I'm not interested in them. Why would I be? I've got my own two very naughty boys to do very naughty things with."

He relaxed a little. "As long as you realize that you belong to -"

"Don't you start that with me too," Chloe said. "Maybe some women are into the 'you're my woman, hear me roar, grunt, grunt' behaviour from their men, but I'm not one of them."

"Aren't you?" Jackson said.

She stuck her tongue out. "No."

"I'm just saying," Jackson gave her a lazy grin, "that you got a little flushed when I talked about you belonging to us and mentioned spanking you."

She reached over and poked him in the chest this time. "It's very rude of you to mention that."

Jackson laughed. "Maybe you like the caveman behaviour a little more than you're pretending."

Ian squeezed her ass before giving it a hard spank that made her squeal. She glared at him and he grinned at her. "Just testing the waters."

She wiggled out of his grip, taking a step back and staring at them both. For a moment, he worried that he'd gone too far, until her lips curved up in a smile. "Both of you naked and in the bedroom. Now."

"Yes, ma'am," Ian drawled.

"She's kinda bossy, but I dig it," Jackson said. When Ian didn't move, Jackson made a forward motion with his arm. "Our lady requires servicing. Get a move on, my good man."

CHAPTER 16

M*iss me yet?*

Chloe read the text from Jackson, smiling to herself, before texting back.

I left your place four hours ago.

His reply came less than a minute later.

Have you eaten? It's after six and I'm starving. Have dinner with me. We'll watch a movie and then bang like bunnies until Ian is finished work.

She giggled and clutched at her phone like she was a stupid teenage girl. She wanted to say yes. God, did she ever. Guilt plucked at her. Her grandmother was back from her trip today and Chloe was just leaving to stop in and check on her. Her plan was to treat her with a dinner out, maybe try and talk to her about not letting Lori's new boyfriend come to the house. Her nana needed to establish ground rules for Lori, and maybe being away for a few days had helped her gain some perspective.

She sent another quick text to Jackson.

Taking my grandmother out for dinner. Can I come by after?

Yes. Come by whenever, will leave door unlocked.

She smiled and was about to toss her phone into her purse when it rang. She hit the answer button. "Hi, Nana. How was your trip? I'm on my way to your place to take you for dinner. Don't bother saying no, you deserve to be treated to a night -"

"Chloe! Chloe, you have to come over here right now!"

The panic in her grandmother's voice sent fear shuddering down her spine. She grabbed her purse and her keys and ran for the door, not bothering to grab a jacket. She ran down the hallway and into the stairwell.

"Nana? I'm on my way. What's wrong?"

"He's killing her, Chloe! Please hurry! Please!"

The line went dead and her heart went into overdrive. Fear blasting crater-sized holes in her gut, she burst into the lobby of her building and headed for the parking lot in a dead run.

"I CALLED THE COPS! DO YOU HEAR ME? I CALLED THE DAMN cops! I'm sick of this shit!"

The neighbour next door was standing on the porch and screaming at her. Chloe barely heard her over the terrified screams of her sister and the angry shouts of her boyfriend coming from within the house. She tried to open the front door to her Nana's house, cursing when it was locked. Her sister screamed again, and Chloe jammed the key into the lock and twisted it open. She threw the door open and charged down the hallway.

"Nana! Nana, where are you!?"

"Chloe!"

Her grandmother was standing outside of her sister's

room. Her wrinkled face was deathly pale, and she staggered back as Chloe skidded to a stop in front of her.

"Nana!"

"He's hurting her! Chloe, he's hurting your sister!"

"Lori!" Chloe pounded on her sister's door when the handle wouldn't turn. "Open the door! Lori!"

"Go away, you fucking bitch!"

"Get away from my sister, you asshole!" Chloe shouted. Adrenaline pumping through her body, she slammed her slender frame against the door.

It shuddered and there was a sharp crack. She hit it again, the cheap frame splintered, and the door popped open. She almost fell into the room, her heart stopping in her chest when she saw her sister lying on her back on the bed with her boyfriend straddling her prone body.

He smacked her hard in the face. "You gonna cheat on me again, you stupid cunt? Are you? I swear I'll cut your face to shreds if you even think of fucking around on me again."

He raised his hand again, this time curling it into a fist. Terrified he was going to kill her sister, Chloe ran forward. She snatched up the lamp sitting on the night table, ripping the cord from the wall, and smashed it over his head.

He groaned and staggered back, blood pouring down his face from a cut to his temple. He touched the blood, staring at the red liquid on his fingers before giving her a dazed look. "You – you cut me?"

"Get away from my sister," Chloe said.

He stumbled toward her and she backed away. The scent of whiskey was overwhelming, and he took another step before dropping to his knees.

"Fuckin' bitch, hit me…" he slurred, before his eyes rolled up in his head and he fell face-forward into the worn carpet.

Chloe made a shuddering sigh of relief. "Lori? Are you okay? Are you?"

"What did you do?" Her sister slid off the bed and wobbled toward her. Chloe winced at the ripe mixture of body odour and beer. "You killed him! You killed Ron!"

"I didn't kill him," Chloe said. "Lori, sit down and –

Her sister's fist smashed into her stomach, driving the air from her lungs. She doubled over, gasping for breath as her sister grabbed her and threw her up against the wall. "You bitch! You killed my man!"

She punched her in the belly again and pain flared in Chloe's side. Still gasping for air, she tried to push Lori back, but her sister slapped her hard twice across the face. Her ears rang, and she grabbed at Lori's hands when Lori wrapped them around her throat.

Chloe's eyes bulged as her air supply was cut off completely. She tried to claw at Lori's face, and her sister kneed her in the stomach before squeezing brutally around Chloe's throat.

"I am so fucking tired of you ruining my life," Lori wheezed booze-scented vitriol into her face. "Always so fucking perfect, always so righteous. I hate you. I should have fucking killed you the day mom and dad brought you home from the hospital."

"Lori! Stop!" Her Nana's hands wrapped around Lori's arm, tried to tug them away.

Lori snarled at their grandmother, baring her teeth at her before shoving her away with her body. "Get out of here, Nana. This is none of your fucking business. Go to your room, right fucking now."

"Lori, let her go." Her grandmother cried. "Let her go right now!"

"I said fucking leave, Nana!" Lori screamed.

Black roses bloomed in Chloe's vision. She clawed at Lori's hands, kicked at Lori's legs as the sound of her sister's voice grew fainter. When the bruising pressure around her throat was suddenly gone, she slid down the wall, coughing and choking and gagging in air.

"Please don't hurt her! Don't hurt my Lori!" Her nana's voice was wavering and thin, panic infused throughout it.

"Nana, it's…" Chloe's voice dissolved into a coughing fit as pain scorched like fire across her throat.

"Move back, ma'am. Right now."

Chloe squinted in front of her. Her sister was lying face-down on the floor and a cop was kneeling on her back and holding her hands behind her. She was twisting and squirming and screeching expletives. When one flailing hand broke free of the cop's grip, she tried to scratch him across the face.

"Ma'am, stop resisting!" He shouted. "Police! Stop resisting!"

Lori screamed at him and he pressed his knee into her back. He caught her hand and latched one cuff around her wrist before latching the other cuff to her second wrist. He stood, wiping the sweat from his face as Lori screamed again.

A second cop, his broad back oddly familiar looking, placed his hand on her grandmother's arm. "Ma'am, I said, move back, please."

"Ian?" Chloe's voice was hoarse, barely audible above the sounds of her sister's pig-like squeals of outrage, but the officer stiffened and whipped around.

"Chloe!" He ran forward and knelt beside her, putting his arm around her and lifting her to her feet. "Baby, are you all right?"

"I'm okay."

"Jesus, your throat." He touched her throat before glancing at the other cop. "Tony, radio in for medical – now!"

He pulled Chloe into his arms, rubbing her back as she coughed harshly. "It's okay, baby."

"I think I killed him," she whispered.

He stared at the unmoving man on the floor before booting him hard in the ass. The man groaned, and Ian shook his head. "You didn't."

"I'm sorry. I'm so sorry," Chloe whispered.

Ian cupped her face and pressed a kiss against her mouth. "It's all right, baby. I've got you. You're safe now."

"Ian! Where is she? Where's Chloe?" Jackson grabbed his best friend's arm. Ian had called him and, despite his assurances that Chloe was okay, Jackson's fear had turned to outright panic in the half hour it took him to drive to her grandmother's house.

"She's okay, Jackson. She's inside." Ian grabbed his arm before he could rush inside the house. "Listen to me for a second, okay?"

"What?" Jackson gave him an impatient look before studying the cop car parked in the driveway. A woman, her red hair hanging in her face, was sitting in the back seat. Jackson inhaled sharply when she glanced at him through the window.

"That's her sister, isn't it?"

"Yes." Ian pulled him back when Jackson tried to walk to the car. "What are you doing? You can't go near her."

"She almost got Chloe killed," Jackson snarled.

"Stop it." Ian shook him roughly. "I called you because I need you to be here for Chloe and that doesn't include yelling at her sister. She needs you, Jackson. I can't stay, I'm on fucking duty for God's sake. She needs you, so get your fucking shit together."

"Yeah, okay," Jackson said.

"You good?" Ian eyed him.

"I'm good." He followed Ian into the house. Chloe was sitting on a chair in the kitchen. An EMT was packing up her bag and Chloe smiled at the woman.

"Thank you." Her voice was hoarse, and Jackson could see the dark bruising already starting to show on her throat.

He clenched his hands into fists as the EMT nodded. "You're welcome. If you start to have difficulty breathing or the bruising and swelling doesn't go down in a couple of days, go to the hospital. All right?"

Chloe nodded and the EMT brushed past Jackson and Ian without saying a word. Chloe's face fell when she saw Jackson. "What are you doing here?"

"I called him," Ian said as Jackson pulled up a chair beside her. He put his arm around her and kissed her mouth.

"Honey, are you okay?"

"I'm fine." She stared at Ian. "You shouldn't have called him."

"Yes, he should have." Jackson ignored the hurt that trickled through him.

She sighed and rubbed at her forehead. "I'm okay, Jackson. Don't worry about me, all right? Go home and -"

"You're coming with me," Jackson said.

"No, I'm staying here with my grandmother."

"Chloe, it isn't safe. You and your grandmother can both stay at our place," Jackson said.

Chloe laughed bitterly. "No. Nana can't know where you live. Knowing her, she'd tell Lori and then…fuck, she'd probably show up on your doorstep."

"We don't care," Jackson said. "Honey, it isn't safe for you here."

"It's perfectly safe. Lori's boyfriend is going to jail for the night at least. Right, Ian?"

Jackson frowned at him. "Just for the night?"

"My sister won't press charges against him," Chloe rubbed her stomach gingerly. "She says she will, but she's lying."

"All the more reason for you to stay with us," Jackson said.

"I can't," she whispered.

"You can." His frustration was growing but, Jesus, he was scared to death for her. "Honey, you -"

"Chloe?"

Jackson glanced up. An old woman, her fine silver hair sticking up in short spikes was standing in the doorway. She pulled nervously at the sleeves of her sweater as she stared at Jackson. "Who is this?"

"He's a friend, Nana," Chloe said. "Go back to your room, okay?"

Her grandmother stepped into the kitchen. Jackson had to fight his urge to block the old woman from touching Chloe when she sat down on the other side of her. She took Chloe's hand. "Sweetie, are you all right?"

"Yes. Are you? Did Lori hurt you?"

"Of course not," her grandmother said. "She didn't mean to do it, Chloe."

"Bullshit," Jackson spat. He pointed to the bruising on Chloe's throat. "She choked her. She choked her until her skin bruised."

"Jackson, hush," Chloe said. She squeezed her grandmother's hands. "Nana, she's sick. I know you don't want to believe it, but she needs help. If I press charges, she'll stay in jail for a while. If we don't pay bail, the judge won't release her. It'll help her dry out, right? And maybe if she's sober for a week or two, we can convince her to go back to rehab."

"You can't. Oh, Chloe, you can't do that to my baby girl." Big fat tears dripped down her grandmother's face, but Jackson didn't feel an ounce of sympathy for her. He couldn't – not when Chloe could barely speak above a whisper and her slender throat was covered in dark mottled bruising.

"I know it's difficult," Chloe said, "but it's the right thing to do. Please, Nana."

"No, Chloe. Please, honey, please don't do this. You can't press charges against your own sister. She needs our love and our help, not our -"

"What she needs is to be locked up so she can't hurt Chloe again," Jackson said.

Ian's hand squeezed his shoulder, but he shook his best friend off. He glared at the old woman. "Lady, I don't know what your problem is, but your precious granddaughter is a drunk."

"How dare you," the old woman said. "How dare you speak to me that way when you don't even know me."

"I know you don't give one flying fuck about the woman who's sitting beside you. She's your granddaughter too, and she needs you just as much as Lori does. You're wasting your time trying to save a drunk who tried to kill her own sister, instead of -"

"Jackson, enough!" Chloe's voice rose in a hoarse and horrified shout. "Stop it, right now!"

He shut his mouth with a snap as Chloe's grandmother burst into tears. She stared at Chloe, her thin body shaking. "What kind of friends do you have, Chloe? They're trying to turn you against your family. Against your own sister. Is that what you want? You're going to let your sister rot in jail because your friends think it's a good idea?"

"No, Nana," Chloe said wearily. "Jackson means well, he's just…"

"He doesn't understand," her grandmother said. She took Chloe's hand and squeezed it before giving her a pleading look. "No one understands. Please, Chloe. If you let Lori stay in jail, it'll kill me. Is that what you want?"

"Stop manipulating her," Jackson said. "She isn't going to - "

Chloe pulled away and glared at him. "This is none of your business. You need to go home, Jackson."

This time he couldn't hide the hurt. "None of my business? Chloe, I want what's best for you and -"

"I appreciate your concern, but you still need to leave."

"So, that's it? You're gonna brush me off like I mean nothing? Like I don't care for you or lov -"

"Don't!" Chloe's voice cracked. "Don't you dare say it, Jackson. Not now. You knew what this was. Please go. I'll – I'll call you later and -"

He stood up, shaking off Ian's hand again when he felt it on his shoulder. "Don't bother, Chloe. There's nothing left to say."

Ian squeezed his arm. "Jackson, man, just -"

He brushed past Ian and stalked out of the house. Before he could open his car door, Ian was grabbing his shoulder and spinning him around.

"What the fuck, asshole? I called you so you could comfort her, you dick. What the fuck was that?"

"She's not going to press charges and her bitch of a sister will be right back in the house. You know she will, Ian. What happens if she gets drunk and tries to kill Chloe again, huh?

What happens if the goddamn neighbour doesn't call the cops the next time? Chloe will be dead," he shoved Ian in the chest, "the woman we *love* will be dead. Is that what you want?"

"You know it isn't," Ian said. "But Chloe is a grown woman and we can't tell her what to do."

"She needs us. She needs our help and," Jackson raked his hand through his hair, "she keeps pushing us away. Why is she doing that?"

Ian grasped his shoulder and squeezed. "She's tired and afraid and thinks we'll make her choose between us and her family. Which, frankly, you just about fucking tried to do back there. You screwed up, asshole."

"Fuck! I know." Jackson slammed his fists against his car door. "You think I don't know that? But I'm fucking scared, Ian!"

"I know, me too. But, Chloe needs time, okay? We'll give her a few days and then we'll talk to her."

"What happens if her sister or that asshole boyfriend tries to kill her again?"

"The boyfriend has about five warrants on him. He won't be getting out anytime soon. Lori won't get out of jail for a while either, even if Chloe doesn't press charges. She didn't cooperate when Tony was cuffing her, he'll back me up in charging her with resisting arrest which means she'll need to be bailed out. Chloe told me earlier that she won't pay for Lori's bail, and her grandmother just bailed her out not that long ago. She won't have the money to do it again so soon. Chloe will be safe until we talk to her."

"Are you sure?" Jackson asked.

Ian nodded. "I'm sure. Go home, okay?"

"I should stay."

"It's too late. Chloe is pissed at you, and she's not going

to leave her grandmother anyway. Go home and I'll see you when my shift is over."

"I'm sorry, Ian."

"It's all right, man. I feel the same way you do. But we'll fix this, okay? Chloe loves us, I know she does. She just needs some time to figure things out."

CHAPTER 17

"You look like shit," Luke announced as he strolled into Jackson's office.

Jackson leaned back in his chair. "Thanks."

Luke sat down in Chloe's empty chair. "Seriously, are you sick? Do you need to go home? You share an office with Chloe, maybe you've caught the same stomach flu she did."

Jackson shook his head. It was Wednesday morning and neither he nor Ian had spoken or seen Chloe since Saturday night. She had replied to one of Ian's texts, telling him she was fine and not to worry. She hadn't picked up any of Jackson's calls and finally, in desperation, he had texted her an apology. She'd replied back with a short 'it's fine', and he had no fucking idea what to do with that.

When she still hadn't shown up for work by Tuesday, he'd convinced himself that going to her house after work was the right thing to do. Too bad Ian had shown up at the office at the end of the day. Jackson didn't *think* his best friend could read his actual thoughts, but Ian had taken one look at him and shook his head. "No. Do not go to her house,

Jackson. She needs a bit of space. C'mon, we're going for a beer."

Now, Luke tapped his fingers on Chloe's desk. "So, I was thinking for the storefront that we should -"

"Jackson?" Amy, her cheeks pale and her eyes worried, darted into the office.

"Ames? What's wrong?" Luke stood up and Jackson did the same.

"It's Chloe, she needs you," Amy said to Jackson.

"Where is she?" Jackson asked.

"The hospital. She -"

Cold fear sliced into Jackson's stomach. He stared wild-eyed at Amy. "Is she hurt?"

Amy shook her head. "She's okay, she's not hurt. Her sister got out of jail last night and sometime early this morning, she burned down her grandmother's house."

"What? Was Chloe there? Are you sure she isn't hurt?"

"She wasn't there," Amy said. "I just got off the phone with her. The firefighters got her grandma and her sister out, but her grandmother's been admitted to Mercy General because of smoke inhalation."

"Fuck." Jackson grabbed his jacket and his cell phone.

Amy gave him a worried look. "She didn't ask me to tell you, but I – I think she needs you and Ian. She sounded so… lost and scared on the phone."

"Thank you, Amy," Jackson said as he rushed by her. He ran for the elevator as he called Ian.

"CHLOE?" THE NURSE PATTED HER ARM. "YOU SHOULD GO home and get some rest. Your grandmother is resting comfortably, and I doubt she'll wake up until later."

"I don't want to leave her alone," Chloe said. "If she wakes up and I'm not here, she'll be afraid and confused."

Her voice trembled, and the nurse said, "We'll explain what's going on to her if she wakes up. But, most likely, you'll be back before she even wakes."

"I'll stay a little longer. Just in case," Chloe said.

"All right. There's a coffee machine and cold drink machine down the hallway if you want something to drink." The nurse eyed the bruising around Chloe's throat. "Have you had that bruising looked at?"

Chloe nodded. "Yes."

"Okay. I'll come back in a little bit and check on you."

"Thank you."

She stared down at her grandmother's hand, stroking the thin skin as she blinked back the tears. She really should go home and try and sleep, but she wouldn't. She couldn't. Being alone in her apartment was the last thing she wanted.

Call Jackson and Ian.

She used her knuckle to rub away the tears. She couldn't call them. She had blown them off for the last three days, and they'd be pissed with her. Hell, they'd probably already written her off as a lost cause. She'd chosen her sister over them, just like she always did and always would, and –

No. Not this time. You're done with her, Chloe.

She almost didn't recognize her inner voice. There was a cold flatness to it that made goosebumps rise on her skin.

Enough is enough, Chloe. You're not helping her. You're enabling her.

Yes, she was enabling her, and it ended right now. She couldn't save Lori, no matter how hard she tried, and it was time she started taking care of herself. She needed to call Ian and Jackson, needed to try and make amends with them before it was too late. She'd get on her knees and beg them for a second chance if she had to.

She stood up abruptly. Coffee first. She needed a coffee before she keeled over from exhaustion right there. She had barely slept or ate since Saturday night. She would use the boost of caffeine to clear her muddled thoughts, and then try to call Ian or Jackson.

She started toward the door of the room, her steps faltering when she saw who was standing in the doorway.

"What-what are you doing here?" She whispered.

Ian stepped into the room and gave her a sweet smile, "Hi, baby."

She burst into tears and stumbled across the room toward him. He met her halfway and wrapped her in his embrace. She buried her face in his chest and clung to him as he rubbed her back and pressed kisses against the top of her head.

She lifted her head and stared at him. "How did you know I was here?"

"Jackson called me," Ian said.

"Jackson? Is he – where is he?"

Ian stepped to the side. Jackson was standing behind him and Chloe stared silently at him as he gave her a brief smile. "Hi, honey."

"Jackson, I…"

"If you want me to leave, I will, but I -"

"Don't leave." She threw herself at him, plastering her body against his. She heard him mutter, "thank fucking, God", before he was holding her tight and kissing her.

"I'm sorry," she whispered. "I'm so sorry."

"I'm the one who needs to apologize. I stepped over the line on Saturday and I -"

"No," she shook her head. "No, you were trying to help and I – I was awful."

She reached for Ian's hand, squeezing it hard as she stared at the two men. "I'm so glad you're here."

"We'll always be here for you, Chloe," Ian said. "We love you and we're not going anywhere."

"I love you too," Chloe said as tears streamed down her cheeks. "I love both of you and I'm so sorry that I pushed you away, and that I chose my sister over you."

"Shh, honey." Jackson pulled her close again. "We love you and we understand, okay?"

She sniffed and wiped at her face before glancing at her grandmother. "Nana is still sleeping. Will you come to the cafeteria with me? I need coffee and maybe something to eat."

"Of course," Jackson said.

She took his hand and, still holding Ian's hand in a tight grip, led them out of the room.

"How did you know I was here?" Chloe blew on her coffee before taking a sip.

Beside her, Ian was buttering a muffin and he handed half of it to her. "Eat, baby."

She bit into the muffin as Jackson said, "Amy told me. What happened, honey?"

Chloe washed the bite of muffin down with another sip of coffee. "Nana bailed her out again."

"How?"

She shrugged. "I don't know. She wouldn't tell me. I stayed with Nana until yesterday afternoon. I went out to pick up some groceries and when I came back, Nana was gone. She returned about an hour later with Lori."

Ian put his arm around her and kissed her temple. She

277

picked at the muffin in front of her. "Lori didn't even remember what she did to me. She was blackout drunk that night and doesn't remember anything. Nana had to tell her what happened and even then, she didn't really apologize. Just said that she'd had a little too much to drink and it wouldn't happen again."

She leaned against Ian as Jackson reached across the table and took her hand. "I told Nana that either Lori left, or I was leaving. Nana chose Lori."

"I'm sorry," Jackson said.

Chloe sighed. "I knew she would. Lori's had her wrapped around her baby finger since birth. Anyway, I went home, and the hospital called me at about four this morning. I guess Lori went out to the bar after I left and came home drunk around one. Nana went to bed as soon as Lori got home. About one-thirty, the neighbours saw smoke drifting out of Nana's house, and called 9-1-1."

"Where is Lori now?" Ian said.

"I don't really know," Chloe said. "Nana's been sleeping since I got here. She inhaled a lot of smoke. The doctor said she would recover, but if the neighbours hadn't seen the smoke…"

Tears splashed onto the muffin half and she pushed it away. "Nana's nurse looked up Lori's name and she was brought here as well. She's alive and fine, that's all I know. I don't know if she's still in the ER or if she's been discharged and I don't care."

Jackson squeezed her hand. "It's okay that you don't, honey."

Chloe stared into her coffee. "I'm done with Lori. No more choosing her over everyone else, no more coming to her rescue or-or trying to save her from herself. I'm done."

Ian kissed the top of her head. "You're exhausted, and it's been a difficult morning. You don't have to make any decisions right now, baby. You can -"

"No," Chloe said. She stared at both of them, feeling a wave of love that was almost overwhelming in its intensity. "I'm done. She tried to kill me Saturday night, and she almost killed Nana last night. I don't want anything to do with her ever again."

Jackson leaned in close. "Honey, there's still your grandmother to consider. Lori will use her to get to you."

Chloe laughed bitterly. "No, she won't. I talked to my dad this morning. He's flying in tonight and as soon as Nana can travel, he's taking her back to Iowa. He's been trying for years to get her to move in with him and my mother, but Nana refused to leave her home. But, now that Lori's burned it to the ground and she has no place to live, she doesn't really have a choice."

She sighed and rubbed at her forehead. "My mom is an alcoholic. Did I tell you that?"

Ian and Jackson shook their heads and she said, "She is. Recovering, and has been for a while now, but it's one of the reasons that they moved to Iowa. Dad moved her to this teeny little town in the middle of goddamn nowhere, so she wouldn't have so many bars to go to."

She studied the cafeteria table. "I told him he was being crazy, told him that drunks like her would always find bars. But he didn't listen. It's good that he didn't. I mean, she still had to do a rehab stint in Iowa for nearly four months, but it worked. She's been sober ever since. I think my grandma thought that if my mom could beat it, so could Lori."

She gave both Ian and Jackson a look of sorrow. "But she's wrong. Lori can't be helped until she wants help and, I don't think she ever will. I don't want to try anymore. I'm not going to try. I'm choosing me and my happiness instead."

She thought she might cry or feel guilty but there was nothing but relief. She took a deep breath. "I should feel horrible about it, but I don't. I feel… relieved."

"I think that's a normal reaction," Ian said.

"Yeah, maybe. Anyway, I know I've been really awful to the both of you and I'm so sorry. If you'll give me another chance, I'll make it up to you."

"You have nothing to make up for," Jackson said. "We love you, Chloe, and if you change your mind about your sister or, if in the future you want to try and help her again, we will be right here with you. Always. You don't have to deal with any of this alone."

Chloe gave him a trembling smile. "I love you, Jackson."

"I love you too."

She turned to Ian. "I love you, Ian."

"I love you, Red."

She smiled at the nickname before resting her head on Ian's shoulder. "So, I guess we're in a relationship now, huh?"

"Guess so," Jackson said.

"It's not going to be easy," Ian said. "Chloe, are you sure that you really want to be in a relationship with both of us?"

"Ian, dude, I love you, but shut up," Jackson said.

Chloe couldn't help her soft laugh. "Yes, I want to be in a relationship with both of you. I know it's different and weird, and we'll probably lose some friends and maybe even family over it, but I don't care. I love you both equally and I'm not choosing one or the other. I'm all in – with both of you."

Ian and Jackson gave her identical grins of happiness. God, she really did love them.

"You should know," Ian said with a grin at Jackson, "that

once you say you're ours, we don't plan on ever letting you go. You'll be ours forever, Chloe Matthews."

The sounds of the people around them faded to a muted hum as happiness rushed through Chloe. She smiled at both of her men. "I'm yours."

END

THE ASSISTANT EXCERPT

"Ms. Jones! My office, immediately."

His harsh and demanding voice spilled out of his office and I sighed before standing up from my desk. Smoothing my skirt, I entered his office and smiled at my boss.

"Is there a problem, Mr. Wright?"

"Shut the door," he barked.

I shut the door and sat down in one of the leather chairs across from his desk. I crossed my legs delicately and his eyes drifted to my short hemline before he glared at me.

"As a matter of fact, there is a problem. A rather large one."

I pasted my best 'what can I do to help' look on my face and folded my hands in my lap.

He raked his hand through his hair before his gaze dropped to my chest. "Your outfit, Ms. Jones."

My cheeks flamed immediately, and I pulled self-consciously at my too-tight blouse. "Wh-what do you mean?"

"You know exactly what I mean, Ms. Jones." He leaned forward and folded his own hands on the top of his desk. "It isn't work appropriate. What do you have to say for yourself?"

"Laundry day," I whispered.

He frowned. "What?"

"It was laundry day yesterday and I didn't have any quarters for the washing machine." I cleared my throat nervously. "I didn't have anything else to wear."

I was nearly sweating with embarrassment. I had hemmed and hawed over my outfit this morning for half an hour but left without much choice, had decided to just go for it. I knew what I looked like. The shirt was much too tight. It hugged my large breasts and clung to my curves and the skirt, well... let's just say that bending over was not an option.

"How long have you worked for me, Ms. Jones?"

"Three years."

"I would think that after three years you'd have a better understanding of the office dress policy. Wouldn't you?"

My temper flared and I scowled at him. "I'm not breaking any rules. My skirt is well within the regulation length."

He scowled back. "Is it? Then explain why I got an eyeful of your garters when I walked by your desk. And I'll bet you a thousand dollars that the first deep breath you take, your buttons on that shirt pop open. Showing your tits is a definite infraction, Ms. Jones."

I gaped at him. "Did you just talk about my tits?"

He sat back in his chair and I watched wide-eyed as his hands moved to the buckle of his belt. "As I was saying, you've created a large problem and it's up to you to solve it."

As he was speaking, his hands were unbuckling, unbuttoning, and unzipping.

A small gasp escaped my throat when he tugged his cock through the opening in his pants. It was long and thick and hard as a rock, and my mouth dried up as I watched him stroke it firmly.

"Come here and solve the problem, Ms. Jones," he commanded.

Like a woman in a dream, I rose to my feet and crossed around his desk. I couldn't take my eyes off of his cock. As moisture dampened my panties, I unconsciously rubbed my thighs together in an effort to quell the throbbing that was starting between my legs.

"On your knees, Ms. Jones." He rolled back his chair and I knelt obediently between his legs.

My mouth was in front of his cock now and I watched his hand slide up and down his thickness before he wound his other hand in my hair and pushed me toward the head of his cock.

"Open," he said.

I opened my mouth and moaned in sheer delight when he guided his cock past my lips. I closed my mouth around his throbbing length, my stomach tightening with pleasure when I heard his harsh moan.

"Good girl," he whispered. He petted and stroked my hair as I sucked enthusiastically. His hips were rising in his chair and he was thrusting more firmly into my mouth. I made a soft humming noise and he groaned again before pulling on my hair.

"All of it. I want you to take all of it."

ABOUT THE AUTHOR

Ramona Gray is a Canadian romance author. She currently lives in Alberta with her awesome husband and her super cute dog. She's addicted to home improvement shows, good coffee, and reading and writing about the steamier moments in life.

For more information about Ramona, check out her website at

www.ramonagray.ca

facebook.com/RamonaGrayBooks

twitter.com/RamonaGrayBooks

instagram.com/ramonagrayauthor

amazon.com/Ramona-Gray/e/B00OD26SAM

bookbub.com/profile/ramona-gray

ALSO BY RAMONA GRAY

Individual Books

The Escort

Saving Jax

The Assistant

One Night

Sharing Del

Filthy Appeal

Forbidden Bliss

Shadow Security Series

Dead of Night

Edge of Night

Dark of Night

Undeniable Series

Undeniably His

Undeniably Hers

Undeniably Theirs

Undeniable Series Boxset

Working Men Series

The Mechanic

The Carpenter

The Bartender

The Welder

The Electrician

The Landscaper

The Firefighter

The Cop

The Paramedic

Working Men Series Bundles

Working Men Series Books One to Three

Working Men Series Books Four to Six

Working Men Series Books Seven to Nine

Other World Series

The Vampire's Kiss (Book One)

The Vampire's Love (Book Two)

The Shifter's Mate (Book Three)

Rescued By The Wolf (Book Four)

Claiming Quinn (Book Five)

Choosing Rose (Book Six)

Elena Unbound (Book Seven)

Other World Series Box Sets

Other World Series Books One to Three

Other World Series Books Four to Six